# QUASI REDUX

BOOK EIGHT OF THE ANGELBOUND ORIGINS SERIES

CHRISTINA BAUER

# COPYRIGHT

Monster House Books
Brighton, MA 02135
ISBN 9781946677068
Second Edition

# DEDICATION

For All Those Who Kick Ass, Take Names
and Read Books

# CONTENTS

# COLLECTED WORKS

**Angelbound Origins**

*About a quasi (part demon and part human) girl who loves kicking butt in Purgatory's Arena*

**Angelbound Offspring**

*The next generation takes on Heaven, Hell, and everything in between*

4. Rhodes

5. Kaps

6. Mack

7. Huntress

## Angelbound Lincoln

*The Angelbound experience as told by Prince Lincoln*

1. Duty Bound

2. Lincoln

3. Trickster

4. Baculum

5. Angelfire

## Fairy Tales of the Magicorum

*Modern fairy tales with sass, action, and romance*

1. Wolves and Roses

2. Moonlight and Midtown

3. Shifters and Glyphs

4. Slippers and Thieves

5. Bandits and Ball Gowns

6. Fairies and Frosting

## Pixieland Diaries

*Sassy pixie Calla loves elf prince Dare. Too bad he hasn't noticed her. Yet.*

1. Pixieland Diaries

2. Calla

3. Dare

4. Winter Prince

5. Ley Queen

## Dimension Drift

*Dystopian adventures with science, snark, and hot aliens*

1. Scythe

2. Umbra

3. Alien Minds

4. ECHO Academy

*This is a completed series.*

## Beholder

*Where a medieval farm girl discovers necromancy and true love*

1. Cursed

2. Concealed

3. Cherished

4. Crowned

5. Cradled

*This is a completed series.*

# QUASI REDUX

## MYLA

*T*he Titan of Chaos needs an ass kicking.

*Color me happy.*

In fact, I'm so pumped for this anti-demonic action that I check my smart watch for the umpteenth time. The little screen reads:

*TODAY'S MISSION - Destroy Bedlam, the Titan of Chaos, a demon who's locked in an underground prison-tomb. If Bedlam gets loose, he'll try to make Queen Myla his wife and use her powers to erase the Almighty.*

Queen Myla... that's me. Needless to say, I can't wait to kill this Bedlam loser.

To that end, I now march across the Sahara along with my *real* husband, Lincoln. Waves of heat roll up from the sand. The sun burns down from an impossibly blue sky. The landscape is empty, except for three Hathor nomads trudging by on camels. As they pass, the trio chat with each other. I can't help but eavesdrop.

Okay, I could help it, but it's a barren desert and marching is boring.

"See that red-haired girl?" asks one.

My interest perks. Technically, my hair is auburn. Still, this human is clearly talking about me.

"She's hard to miss," answers the second. "I think I've seen her in movies. Maybe she plays Black Widow? And the brown-haired man who's with her could be Captain America. I bet they're here for filming."

I adore Marvel movies, so this convo has me cheering inside.

"That can't be," says the third. "There's no crew around. Plus, they're both wearing black body armor. These two are warriors and dangerous ones at that. We must alert the authorities."

*Which can happen.* Hathor know how to find two things in the desert: water and satellite connectivity.

My husband and I exchange a dry look.

"Shall I do the honors?" I ask. There's no need to explain what comes next here. These three must forget they ever saw me and Lincoln.

"I can handle it," replies my guy. He's awesome like that. Whether it's dishes, diapers, or mind-wiping magic, Lincoln steps up like a man.

My husband pulls out what appears to be a penny from the pocket of his body armor. In truth, it's a charm for erasing memories. With his left hand, Lincoln snaps the coin in half. Purple smoke rises from the broken item before wafting over to the unsuspecting humans. They inhale the fumes and—*yes!*—none of them will remember us now.

This is one advantage of *not* being from Earth, by the way. I'm a native of Purgatory, home to quasi demons. Lincoln grew up in Antrum, which is an underground realm for part-angel warriors. Long story short, we have *all* the good toys. It starts with magic coins and gets better from there.

After hiking over two more dunes, Lincoln and I finally reach a large stone disc that rests flush against the desert floor. The rock itself measures about six inches high and five feet across. My heart pitter-pats with all kinds of happy.

*Here it is: the 'door' to Bedlam's underground prison.*

Lincoln kneels beside the stone. With gentle movements, he brushes sand from the rock to reveal markings underneath.

"This is covered in ancient Egyptian hieroglyphs," announces Lincoln. "The first part says, *here rests Bedlam, Titan of Chaos, Lord of the Tumult, and Master of the Curse for Wadget and Ra.*"

I frown. Wadget and Ra is an ancient Egyptian myth like Beauty and the Beast. Only in this version, if the Beast fails to find love, he gets encased alive in glass.

Ancient Egyptians. They knew how to curse.

My guy keeps reading. *"Bedlam shall claim his queen and erase the Almighty."* Lincoln frowns. "I really dislike that part."

"About the Almighty?"

"No, although that certainly is disturbing. Destroying the Almighty would wipe out all creation." Muscles tighten down Lincoln's neck. "What angers me is the part where you become Bedlam's queen."

"Sha. For any marriage spell to work, I must agree and—*news flash!*—that'll never happen."

Lincoln's voice drops an octave. "I. Am. Not. Happy."

*Truth time.* Do I enjoy it when my husband gets possessive? *Hells, yeah.*

"The faster we destroy Bedlam, the better," declares Lincoln. He inspects the stone once more. "It ends by saying, *Chaos controls all. As Bedlam's queen shall discover, there is no true love, only triumphant manipulation.*"

I suck in a shaky breath. That word, *manipulation,* cuts me in unexpected ways. Because I'm more than a quasi demon from Purgatory. I'm also the Great Scala, the only entity who can move souls to Heaven or Hell. It's like being a rock star with extra stalkers and no music. I picture the many billboards lining Purgatory's roads. All say the same thing:

*BEWARE THE ANGELIC CONSPIRACY! Verus, the Oracle Angel, tricked our Great Scala into a false love. A quasi could never care for a thrax demon killer. That's not marriage, it's angelic manipulation!*

And the worst part? It's kinda-sorta true. Verus *totally* used her oracle mojo to bring me and Lincoln together. So far, I've brushed off the haters. It's not easy, though. Everywhere I turn, someone's complaining that I got manipulated into marriage. I'm talking newspapers, talk shows and even random people on the street. And now Bedlam's joined the Angelic Conspiracy Club? *Ugh.*

Before I know it, Lincoln pulls me into a warm embrace. "It's all right, you know," he whispers.

"What is?" I ask.

When my husband next speaks, his voice is low and soothing. "Everything."

Wrapping my arms around Lincoln's waist, I soak in the solidity of the man.

*Screw the Angelic Conspiracy.* Lincoln's my guy. I actively ignore the teeny-tiny voice in the back of my head that says, *of course, Lincoln's yours. But don't you wonder how Verus' manipulation guided your heart and life?*

*No,* I reply to my own annoying self. *I don't. At all.*

Denial. What a valuable life skill.

Suddenly a hundred tiny lightning bolts appear. Lincoln and I step apart, allowing the small forms to swirl through the air between us. These are igni, the little entities that help me move souls as the Great Scala.

A thousand child-like voices call out at once. "Time is running out," warn my igni. "Bedlam sees you as his treasure... his beauty... his Queen of Chaos! Stop him!"

Lincoln winces. "Whoa."

My mouth falls open with surprise. "You can hear them?"

Lincoln nods.

*That's a shocker.* It's rare for my igni to show up at all, let alone speak in complete sentences. And when they do talk, usually only I can hear them. So the fact that Lincoln shares in this Igni Screech-A-Palooza? It means my little buddies are seriously freaking out. For the first time, I wonder if kicking Bedlam's butt is a good plan.

That lasts all of four seconds.

*Meh.* It'll be awesome.

"Calm down, little ones," I declare. "Bedlam is locked up." I gesture toward the stone as evidence. "We're here to break in and take him on."

But my igni aren't listening. "Watch out!" They howling at an even higher volume. "You have mastered more of us than any before! Bedlam must not control you!"

*Meh, part two.* Everyone wants to pull strings on the Great Scala. I get threats. Pleading. Odd lyrics sung to the tune of Kumbaya. Random gifts that cover my front lawn. And now this demon, Bedlam, who insists we get hitched. Whatever.

My igni flare more brightly. "Only you and Lincoln can defeat the Titan of Chaos!"

"Wait a second." My eyes widen. "You guys are acting like he's already free." I look to Lincoln. "Do you have a breeze charm handy?"

"Sure."

This time, Lincoln pulls out what looks like a silver nickel from his pocket. He snaps the coin in half. Once more, the spell begins.

Winds churn around us. Particles fly up from the earth, making it clear that Chez Bedlam isn't all that hides beneath the sand. After the gusts die down, five things are now clear on the ground.

Human skeletons.

A shiver rolls up my spine. As the Great Scala, you'd think I'd get used to death. Hasn't happened yet. My heart sinks. "Poor souls."

Lincoln scans the bones. "These are recent kills. Looks like someone's been a busy titan."

I shake my head. "Bedlam can't be out of jail. The mission brief would've told us." Kneeling beside the stone, I inspect the seam between the desert and the rock itself. A thin line of particles roll deeper into the ground. It's like gazing down onto the top of an hourglass.

*The sand is sinking.*

I glance between the skeletons and the stone. A realization appears. "Crud. These humans just moved the rock and tried to replace it, only they got flayed before finishing up."

"So Bedlam is free." Lincoln shakes his head. "This complicates things. We've lost the element of surprise."

I sniff. "As well as the element of, *where the Hell is this demon?* Bedlam might have ran off."

The words barely leave my mouth when a puff of indigo-colored mist rolls up from the desert. An electric charge fills the air. *Magic.* A realization slams into me.

*Oh, no.* Bedlam's been watching us this whole time. We wanted to sneak up on him, but now the Titan of Chaos got us instead.

My thoughts race through everything we learned in the last few minutes. Beauty and the Beast magic? Flaying humans and covering it up? I've never heard of any evil this powerful, and I collect demonic trivia for fun.

Bedlam is one scary dude.

I turn to Lincoln, ready to talk up a change of plans. Hey, I'm queen enough to admit when it's time for a retreat.

Yet before I can say a word, the sand crumbles beneath me.

And I fall.

# LINCOLN

Fast as a whip, Myla sinks into the sands before me. Shock and alarm battle it out in my nervous system. I lurch forward, trying to prevent her descent.

The ground gives out beneath me as well.

I tumble through darkness. Every nerve ending in my body stays on alert, ready for the inevitable impact.

*Slam!*

I land in a crouch on the floor below. Cool air surrounds me. Rising, I scan my surroundings and exhale with relief. Myla stands by my side.

But for how long?

I inspect our surroundings. We've reached the short side of a massive rectangular room made from pale stone. Hefty statues line the walls. These are massive sculptures of ancient Egyptian men and women in tunics and kilts, their bodies stuff and straight while their hands press against the ceiling, as if they're holding up the chamber itself.

Along one wall, a single hieroglyph comes to life as it glows with golden brightness. Another follows. Then many more. All repeat the same phrase.

I read the glyphs aloud. *"Chaos does not rest. It waits, storing up the energy to strike."*

"Fuuuuuuuuuck," groans Myla. "That means this isn't a tomb at all. It's some kind of charging station."

"Agreed." Turning, I meet Myla's gaze head-on. "We aren't the hunters here."

The implication is unspoken but clear. *Myla and I have been lured into a trap.*

My pulse speeds. For thousands of years, Bedlam's been hiding in this lair, charging up power and waiting for the chance to spring his plans in action.

And according to our mission brief, the Titan of Chaos has only one prey.

Myla.

A low stage lines the opposite wall. Upon it, there stands an Egyptian sarcophagus covered in paintings, jewels and glyphs.

A long creak sounds; the sarcophagus slowly swings open. Alarm shoots through my system. Within the depths of his coffin, Bedlam's eyes glow white in the darkness.

Still he does not attack.

Which is to be expected. Bedlam is a senior class demon who wants Myla's magical agreement to his marriage plans. He'll try charming her before he resorts to violence.

I pull my baculum from their holster. These are two metal rods that I can ignite into any kind of weapon. The motion says, *I'm ready to fight.*

With my baculum in hand, I scan for any exits. There are none. Whatever entrance Bedlam created to bring us here, it has vanished. Patting my pockets, I pull out an escape charm. This one looks like a paper clip and creates exit doors in any situation. I snap it in two.

Nothing happens.

I pulls out another and try the same thing.

Still no magic.

Bedlam is blocking my spells. It's a rare caster that can create a magical null zone. We are in serious trouble.

From his lurking spot in the shadows, Bedlam's voice booms across the chamber. "Greetings, Lincoln Vidar Osric Aquilus, Heir of the Archangel Aquila, and King of the Thrax."

"Not quite," I declare. "You missed my title as Consort to the Great Scala."

In reply, Bedlam chuckles. "And now, for the moment I've long anticipated," he continues. "My heartfelt greetings go out to Myla Lewis, Daughter of the Archangel Xavier, Heir to the power of the Furor dragons, Mistress of Igni, Greatest Scala in History... and my future wife."

Blinding rage overtakes my soul. Every instinct in me screams to protect Myla and kill this demon now. But we thrax don't strike those who aren't attacking. That said, we have no qualms about moving things along with some goading. I ignite my baculum into a long sword and shift into battle stance.

"Come on, Bedlam," I announce. "Make one move. That's all I need."

"As you command," says Bedlam.

I brace for the attack.

## MYLA

*T*hree words seem to blink in front of my eyes, all of them written in huge neon letters.

*As you command.*

Bedlam plans to take down Lincoln.

Things are getting dicey. Even my tail is turning anxious. Being a quasi-demon means I have powers over two deadly sins —lust and wrath—as well as a tail that's covered in dragonscales and has a mind of its own. In this moment, my tail pokes my back in a steady rhythm that says, *is Lincoln all right?*

I call over my shoulder. "He's fine, boy."

"Behold my wrath," announces Bedlam. Indigo-colored smoke rolls off the stage at the far side of the room. I've seen this before. This is the same shade of mist that appeared on the desert before me and Lincoln got yanked down here. *Magic.* Adrenaline courses through me. Lincoln's a warrior, not a sorcerer. And I have just one source of supernatural power. Closing my eyes, I summon my igni.

*Come to me, little ones.*

No response. They really do suck sometimes.

My thoughts flip into battle mode; I sort through scenarios. There are three choices now. First, Lincoln and I can try to vamoose. That's unlikely. There are no doors. I already noticed how Lincoln's escape charms failed.

Second, we can fight. Trouble is, swords don't do well against magic.

Which leads to option number three. Bedlam wants my agreement to a marriage spell. That's why the Titan of Chaos started off with flattery instead of battle. It was only when Lincoln confronted him that Bedlam got aggressive.

All of which means that I have a blabby enemy who's easily upset. It's like my dream situation, right here.

Stepping forward, I move right into the path of the rolling smoke from Bedlam's stage. "Ho, there."

The mist stops. *So far, so good.*

I set my fists on my hips. "Listen, bud."

"Bedlam," snaps the demon.

"Whatever. You want to talk? Step into the light and let's have a conversation like a person. Er, demon."

Little by little, Bedlam moves out of the sarcophagus and into the brightness. He looms over six feet tall with a hefty body, pale skin and long black hair that's tied at the base of his neck with a small scrap of leather. He wears a tunic top over leather pants. Definitely handsome if you like the *I have a lightbulb-shaped chest and no neck* type of look.

Bedlam raises his left hand. A trio of signet rings shine out on his fingers. My skin chills over with awe. I'd know the pattern on those bands anywhere.

These are three of the most powerful magical items in the after-realms. *The signet rings of Eden.* No wonder Bedlam packs so many high-voltage spells.

My thoughts rush through everything I know about these bands. There were three Edens in total: Garden for land, Ark for waters and Ether for sky. Every Eden was led by two stewards, and each of those folks wielded a magical signet ring.

Three Edens. Two stewards, each with a magical band. Six signet rings in all.

Somehow, Bedlam got his hands on three of those six bands. Based on the patterns, Bedlam wields one ring from the Garden, Ark and Ether.

Lincoln and I share a worried gaze. There's no need for a discussion. We've faced archdemons and expert sorcerers. Giants and sprites. The King of Hell and the Queen of the Ice Dragons. Yet none of those enemies comes close to Bedlam in terms of raw magical energy. And he's been building up his power for thousands of years.

All while waiting for me. *Blech.*

Bedlam raises his arms. "I summon the Tumult!"

A pair of rats skitter across the floor, pausing before the stage. Indigo smoke surrounds them before soaking into their small bodies. *Another spell.* When the mist vanishes, the rats expand and change. What began as tiny vermin end up as partly-human creatures with pointed bat ears and compact faces. Their overly-wide mouths are lined with sharp teeth. Long rat tails sway behind them.

I look to Lincoln. "Bedlam wields retrograde magic."

My guy nods. "Right."

Retrograde casters can rewind someone's DNA to an earlier stage of development, then fast forward them along a new path. This power can easily turn a regular person into a humanoid beast. It's the classic spell for all signet rings of Eden, only it's meant to be used for healing.

A fresh veil of mist surrounds Bedlam. When the indigo vapor fades, the Titan of Chaos no longer resembles a handsome human. Instead, he's a hairless creature who's covered in dark scars. It's a tricky spell and shows this guy is truly a master of retrograde magic.

"Have I shown enough power yet?" asks Bedlam. "Are you willing to discuss terms, my beauty?"

There's only one answer to this particular question. "Never."

"Then just state your desire to marry me," explains Bedlam. "My magic will do the rest."

*Huh.* Someone has listening issues. Best to be clear.

I point to my open palm. "Let's pretend I hold your little *birdy of hope* that we'll get married." I toss the imaginary bird into the air, lift a pretend shotgun, and then pull the trigger. "Boom! Tweet! Ack! Is that clear enough for you?"

"How unfortunate," snarls Bedlam. His eyes light up even more brightly. "If you won't go willingly, then you shall change your mind when facing death at my hands."

I crook my finger toward him. "Let's see what you've got."

Before, I was ready to retreat. Now my inner wrath monster is wide awake and pissed as Hell. Sure, Lincoln and I will meet our end one day. But in this moment, I know one thing to the very core of my soul.

*We're not dying at the hands of some nut job who looks like a diseased Mister Potato Head.*

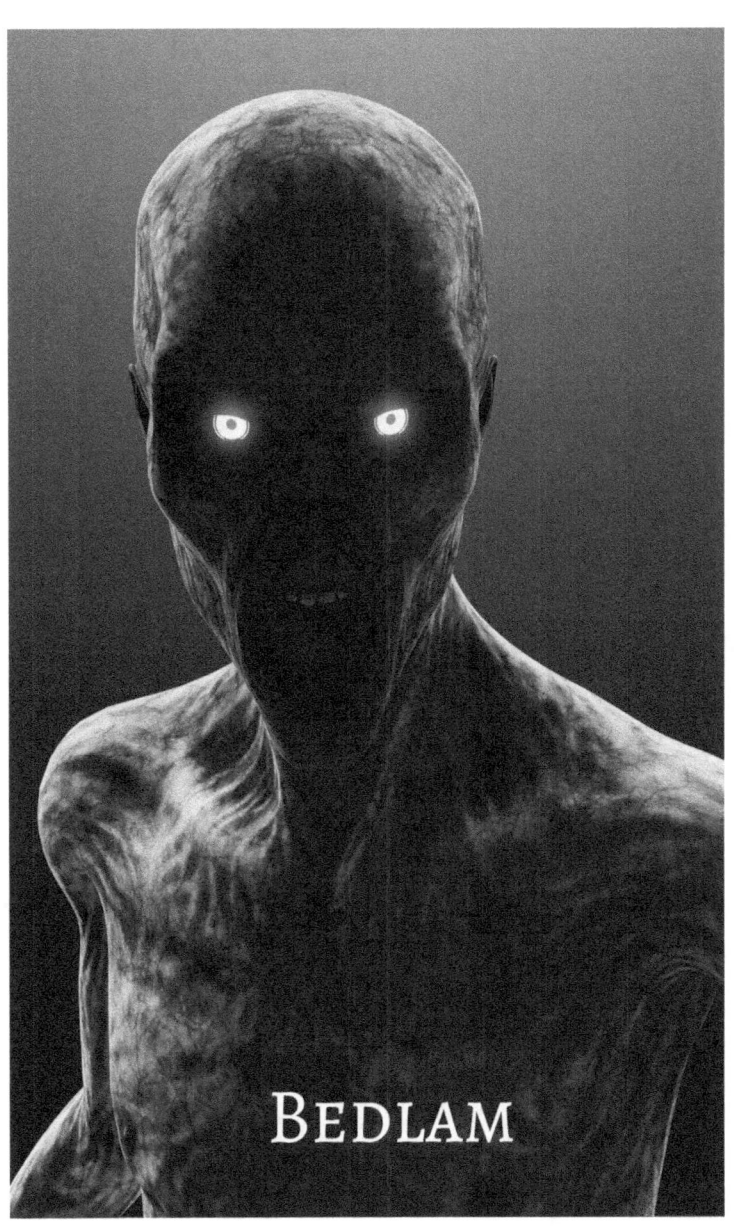

BEDLAM

# LINCOLN

*M*yla and I stand side by side, waiting for the magical assault from Bedlam. Smoke surrounds his figure.

Then he vanishes, along with his Tumult.

I step about in a slow circle, not believing what I'm seeing. The Titan of Chaos just took off? Unlikely. If anything, Bedlam is planning another trap. Chaos doesn't just kill, it creates pandemonium and plays with its prey.

*Boom! Boom! Boom!*

One by one, the pillars that hold up the chamber collapse to the floor. Boulders, rocks and dust careen in all directions. Every nerve ending in my body goes on alert. Long cracks form in the ceiling. Hefty slabs of stone wall buckle, but don't cave in. Yet.

I hold out my hand, waiting for a thin trickle of sand to cascade from above. Instead, water drips onto my palm.

Myla frowns. "Bedlam changed some rats into the Tumult. What's he up to now?" Myla shrugs. "I got nothing."

My thoughts spin through everything I know about retrograde casting. I stare up at the cracked ceiling. "Perhaps Bedlam can rewind and fast-forward *time and place* as well as DNA."

*Snap!*

Another great fissure opens along the ceiling. Heavy rivulets of water cascade down.

Myla nods. "Back in dinosaur times, what was the Sahara?"

"The Thethys Sea." I love history of all kinds. Remarkable how handy it becomes in battle.

"Let's say you wanted to really screw with us," says Myla. "When would you rewind this particular place?"

"No question. The Early Miocene era. That's when the worst predators ruled the Thethys."

Speaking of the ocean, I search my pockets for water-breathing charms, but don't find any. Not that I'd usually pack them. We were heading to a desert, after all. And even if I did have water-breathing charms along, then Bedlam would probably block them from working.

Myla cups my face in her hands. "Whatever happens, we stay together."

Turning my head, I kiss her palm. "Always."

*BOOM!*

The ceiling collapses above us. Ocean water pours through, cold and deadly. A thought occurs to me.

That may have been my last word to Myla.

*Always. It's a good one.*

## MYLA

*A* torrent of water gushes in through the ruined ceiling. Needles of cold jab into every inch of my skin. Dim liquid rolls off in every direction.

One fact becomes clear: You never realize how nice it is to breathe until you're stuck in an ocean from the dinosaur era.

A monster-sized dolphin swims past. It's got an extra long snout and sharp teeth. Still, it doesn't seem to notice me and Lincoln. *Nice.*

Another shape comes into view. At first, I think it's a school of fish swirling before me. Then I realize it's something else entirely. Unlike Lincoln, I'm no expert on dinosaurs. That said, even *I* know what this thing is.

A megalodon, the biggest-ass shark in the history of ever.

Not gonna lie. This thing is scary as fuck. I could stand upright its opened jaws and still have plenty of space around me. Right now, it doesn't seem too interested in either me or Lincoln. Instead, it keeps swimming around in circles.

The shark's movements reminds me how Striga horse breeders make mares trot about in order to impress potential buyers. Only in this case, the horse is a massive shark. And instead of trying to impress me and Lincoln, Bedlam wants to scare the Hell out of us.

It might be working. A little.

Lincoln gestures to the shark. Since he's the hunting part of this relationship, Lincoln always goes in for a closer look when it comes to wildlife. My guy is big on avoiding unnecessary kills for innocent living things. For my part, I enjoy *not paddling around* when my lungs are already burning for air. I shoot him a hearty thumbs-up and Lincoln swims away.

The moment my guy is done, a new version of Bedlam glides into view. This one has green scaly skin along with frilly gils down his neck. He points to his own snake-like face and nods. Then he gestures toward me.

The implication is clear. If I nod now, that will mean I agree with Bedlam... and all this not-breathing will go away.

So I give him a lewd hand gesture instead.

*Take that, dickhead.*

Reaching into the holster at the base of my spine, I pull out my baculum and ignite them as a long sword. The white flame of the weapon's blade is instantly surrounded by bubbles as the nearby water boils.

Jutting my arm forward, I ram my sword straight through Bedlam's heart. The snake version of the Titan of Chaos hunches over, lifeless. One thought echoes through my mind.

That was way too easy.

Not that I can worry any more about Bedlam right now. My lungs ache for air. White dots speckle my vision. I need to reach the surface and fast.

All of which leads to one question.

*Where is Lincoln?*

## LINCOLN

 y body screams to breathe, but I fight back against the urge. Myla and I must reach the surface. And this megalodon?

It's our ticket to oxygen.

Sharks must swim forward to stay alive. I just need to change direction on this particular megalodon. To that end, I ignite my baculum into a pair of short swords, swim around to the shark's side and jam my blades into the edge of the animal's fin. A shiver runs through the megalodon's body. It's regrettable to cause this creature some temporary pain, but it's our only chance at safety.

Thanks to my weapon, the left fin angles down. The megalodon veers upward and to the right.

With my hands busy, I can't signal to Myla. I simply must have faith that she'll figure it out.

She does.

Myla swims over to the megalodon's right fin. Her eyes glow red as she ignites her own baculum into short swords and punctures the fin's edge.

Now the megalodon swims straight upward. As we near the

surface, I spot a shadowy form in the depths below us. It's humanoid, green and has scaly skin.

Bedlam. And he looks dead. I'd be relieved if I weren't internally screaming to breathe.

At last, the megalodon breaks the water's surface. Myla and I gulp in fresh air. As oxygen hits our system, a heavy indigo-colored mist falls over the ocean. A sense of weight returns to my limbs. My feet hit solid ground.

When the magical cloud vanishes, Myla and I are no longer surrounded by water. Instead, we stand back on the Sahara at the exact same place where we started. Once again, the round entrance stone looms nearby.

Any signs of liquid are gone. Even the water on my clothes has vanished. I turn to Myla. She's dry as well. "Are you all right?"

She winks. "Just fine and dandy."

I pull her into a deep embrace. "I saw Bedlam's body in the water. What happened?"

"Oh, Bedlam thought I'd agree to anything before getting chomped by a shark. So I stabbed him."

"What a woman you are." And because I can, I pull her into my arms and kiss her deeply.

My Myla.

## MYLA

*L*incoln's mouth moves over mine. I run my hands over the muscles of his chest. After an adventure, there's often a rush to celebrate life and get out of our clothes. It's a definite bonus of demon patrol.

I nip where Lincoln's neck meets his shoulder—this place makes him crazy. He guides me onto my back and sets his own weight above me. Desire heats my core and awakens my inner lust demon.

Lincoln pauses.

"No one's around," I whisper. "And you're wearing way too much body armor."

Lincoln leans forward and gently kisses my cheek. Then he rises to stand. "Sadly, we're on a time schedule."

I lace my fingers behind my head in a way that says, *this is me, not ready to give up sexy desert time.*

"What time schedule?" I ask slowly.

"Don't you recall?"

"Nuh-uh. Wait." My heart sinks. "We promised our baby sitter to be back already."

"That we did. But there's more to it. Shall we head back to the transfer station?"

"What if I say no?"

Lincoln pulls me onto my feet, stopping the momentum when our bodies are only inches apart. "Then I'd counter that we treat our babysitters with respect. And more importantly—" here he nuzzles just behind my ear "—anticipation makes everything better."

That bastard. This is becoming a competition.

And I do so love to win.

I grin at him for all I'm worth. "I'm all for anticipation," I state. As I stride away, I take care to shake my backside with extra sass.

*I'll get what I want eventually. I always do.*

## MYLA

*L*incoln and I head for the nearest Pulpitum transfer station. It's not too far as the crow flies, but no crow is stupid enough to go winging over the Sahara. After what feels like forever, we reach our destination. Like all Pulpitum, this one's magically charmed to be invisible to humans. In this case, it looks like a regular boulder.

Lincoln and I pause outside the Pulpitum. This is our standard routine. Once we get inside the station, the thrax of transfer central can overhear almost everything we say. Best to share mission secrets out of earshot.

Lincoln gestures in the direction of Bedlam's lair. "We'll need to get a thrax containment crew over there."

"Good idea." The crew in question will identify the human skeletons and make up comforting excuses for their deaths.

"What about Bedlam?" asks Lincoln. "Do you think he's really dead?"

"I don't know." I rub my neck and think through the fight. "Wasn't much of a battle, really. Killing him was super easy. And his magic didn't die out right away afterward. You know the saying, *kill the caster, kill the spell.*"

"Which is true. Although sometimes it takes a little while for the magic to unwind after the mage is dead. You still might have destroyed Bedlam."

Lincoln taps his very yummy lips with his pointer finger. For the record, I'm still adjusting to the idea of *sexy time on the sand* getting cancelled.

*Focus, Myla.*

"We need to ensure Bedlam is dead," says Lincoln.

"Agreed." I dig my boot heels into the sand and think things through. "When it comes to magical power, nothing can touch the rings of Eden. We need to find the remaining three bands. If Bedlam is dead, then those rings will confirm he's gone. And if Bedlam's alive, then the other bands are the only magical weapons strong enough to destroy him."

Lincoln nods, his eyes lost in thought. "Three rings remaining, one for each Eden. The stewards are the best place to start."

"The Garden of Eden burned down ages ago. Adam died and Eve vanished. Do you know anything about the other Edens?"

"The stewards for the Ark of Eden are Noah and his daughter, Norah. There's been no word on them, either. And I'm not even sure what the Ether of Eden looks like, let alone how to access it. All I know are the names of the stewards, Grace and Victoria. There's probably more information if we really dig into it. Finding out about the Edens hasn't ever been a priority before."

"So we need to hit the royal library. All the best books and scrolls are in there."

"Ah, no."

"The ghoul archives, then? Maybe Walker can get us into the Dark Lands." The Dark lands are the realm of ghoul kind, and Walker is my honorary older brother.

"No again."

I make my *ick* face. "You can't mean we visit Earth for information? They suck." I narrow my eyes. "Hey, now. You're toying with me, aren't you?"

My guy winks. "Only a little."

And since two can play at *whatever game this is*, I lean in and kiss Lincoln's face off. As our tongues slide and tease, I wonder how I could ever have questioned my feelings for Lincoln.

Angelic conspiracy? *Bah.*

Bedlam's manipulation claims? *Kiss my quasi ass, you diseased potato head freak.*

Lincoln pulls me closer against him. That's when I make my move. Stepping away, I turn and saunter toward the Pulpitum. To humans, it will look like I walked right into a rock and disappeared.

Although I'm not gone yet.

Before I vanish, I swing around while unzipping my dragon-scale battle suit at the neckline. Once Lincoln's mouth drops open, I know I'm winning.

So I step inside.

It's a mega exit, if I do say so myself.

# LINCOLN

*D*esire heats my blood. Myla just unzipped the front of her dragonscale fighting suit. Now my black body armor pulls in uncomfortable ways.

Once again, Myla proves that two can play at the anticipation game.

*And what a lovely game it is.*

I step into the boulder. One moment, I'm out in the desert. The next, I'm inside a round stone room. The space is rather simple, what with its curved walls and torches. The only unusual decoration is a large metal disc that sits at the center of the floor. That's where the transport magic happens.

Myla leans against a segment of curved wall. "I'm forgetting something, aren't I?"

She's talking about the fact that we aren't having sex on the desert right now. "In a word, *yes.*"

"Why don't you just tell me?"

I shoot her the side eye. "If things were reversed, would you let me off the hook?"

"Sha. Never."

"Then how about we make this a bet?"

"You don't think I'll figure it out, do you?"

"In another word, *no*."

"Then *yes*, let's make it a bet. I wager I'll remember everything without requesting any help."

"Perfect." This is an ongoing game that Myla and I play. When we bet on a topic, the loser must grant one kiss at any time and place of the winner's choosing. Things rarely end with kissing.

Myla steps into the center of the room. "Activating standard station. Queen Myla Lewis."

A grid of white laser beams crosses the Pulpitum floor, performing a body scan on both of us.

A woman's voice echoes through the chamber. "Identity confirmed. Glad you're returning home, your Majesties."

"Thanks, uh…" Myla winces. *Names are not her forte.* "Mary?"

"Leandra."

"Wow, I was way wrong. So." Myla smacks her lips. "We royals have that *big thing* coming up."

I step up beside Myla on the platform. "Fishing for clues?" I whisper.

Myla holds her thumb and forefinger a centimeter apart. "Only a little bit," she retorts. "And as long as I don't outright ask, I still win."

"What did you say?" asks Leandra.

"I was just thinking about our *big day*," states Myla.

"So impressive," sighs Leandra.

"Right," confirms Myla. "And that's because it is…"

"The talk of Antrum!" cries Leandra. We can't see the speaker since this is audio only, but I've no doubt that Leandra is fanning her self with her hands at this point.

For my part, I take to biting my knuckles to keep from laughing. This is really too much. I whisper once more to Myla. "If you ask a direct question, you lose."

"I don't need to ask anything directly. Not me. Nope." Myla

purses her lips in a silent whistle while looking around the Pulpitum chamber. "Fuck it. I'm asking."

I can't help but chuckle.

"Hey, Leandra!" calls Myla.

"Yes, your Majesty?"

"Come on, just tell me what the big deal is all about. It's been a busy day and I forgot."

"Your yard sale," replies Leandra.

Myla buckles her knees slightly while staring up at the ceiling. "Ooooooooooh, the yaaaaaaaaard sale."

My wife receives all sorts of gifts. Some are useful. Most are not. We've been piling them onto the front yard. It's gotten so crowded, there's no room for Maxon to play. Tomorrow morning, we're having an exclusive yard sale for friends, family and select dignitaries. Although the big event begins at dawn, we—and by this I mean Myla—haven't gone through the items yet. There may be things we wish to keep.

All of which is why we must return home tonight. It's a lot of stuff to go through. Not to mention the fact that we're keeping our babysitter waiting.

"There's one good thing about tomorrow," says Myla. "Everyone will be there, from our parents to Walker. We can ask them all about Bedlam and the signet rings of Eden. We're bound to get a tidbit or two of good info—"

"So you know," interrupts Leandra. "Our thrax diplomat to Purgatory is attending the sale tomorrow. I have a request in for any item that you've placed in your mouth. I'll even take old dental floss."

"Okay," says Myla. "Eew."

"Unless you have something you'd like to give me now," adds Leandra hopefully.

*This conversation is going off the rails and fast.*

Best to step in.

"We must return to the main Purgatory station immediately," I declare. "Prepare for transfer."

"Yes, your Majesty." There's a palpable tang of disappointment in Leandra's voice. *She'll live.* If Myla started handing out used dental floss to random fans, then that's all she'd do, 24-7.

"One minute." A static hiss sounds as Leandra goes offline to set up the transfer.

Myla wraps her arms around my waist. "One last thing," she says in her most sultry voice.

I do appreciate the sexy tone, but I also know my wife. She's scheming.

"No need to thank me about Leandra," I state.

"I do appreciate the help," says Myla. "But that's not what I meant. I want to go double or nothing on our bet. I'll pick a trivia question for you this time. We'll see who wins, smartypants."

"Double or nothing?" I lift my brows. "Two kisses, whenever and wherever the winner calls for them? That's what you're betting?"

"Yup" Myla pops the 'p' on yup.

"I'll take it."

A static hiss sounds and Leandra returns. "Transfer confirmed and ready at your signal."

"Excellent," I call out. "Launch transfer on my mark. 3, 2, 1."

With a jolt of movement, the circular platform whips downwards, hurtling through the ground. A minute later, the platform comes to an abrupt halt. We've stopped at another stone temple, only this time in Purgatory.

"What's the wager then?" I ask Myla.

"You'll just have to wait and find out," she replies.

"More anticipation?" I ask.

"Of course, it does make everything better, after all."

*Which is absolutely true.*

## MYLA

*A*fter Lincoln and I leave the transfer station, we hop into a limo and head back home.

*A side note on limousines.* I get that our ride's all tricked out with extra protection, but honestly? I'd rather have my old station wagon, Betsy, back. I don't like the idea of having to call someone every time I want to enter our mega-warded-up compound. But that's the Scala life for you. Whatever I do, having magical security is key.

Soon Lincoln and I stride through our front door. The moment we're across the threshold, Maxon bounds toward us.

"Pop Pops gave me a new sword!" Pop Pops is my father and maxon's babysitter for the evening.

These days, Maxon looks like an oversized cherub, what with his big blue eyes and round face. What offsets his angelic cuteness is a dragonscale tail and the ability to summon lighting. My kid is not your typical four year old.

Dad races over to kiss me on the cheek. "Sorry, I have to run. I promised your mother I'd be at the Drizzle Festival already."

I make my *eek* face. Just like the yard sale, I'd forgotten all about the Drizzle Festival. Technically, it's called the Celebration of Spring, but over the years we locals gave it another name, mostly because this realm is always overcast.

"Sorry, Dad. We got caught up with Bedlam, a super evil and rare Titan of Chaos."

This is a somewhat sneaky move on my part. My father loves fighting unusual baddies as much as I do. In fact, our best bonding moments are over sharing notebooks of unusual demon kills. Normally, dropping something like the *Bedlam bomb* would sidetrack Dad for hours.

Not so this time.

"Must run. Love you!" And with that, Dad rushes outside and is gone.

Once the door is shut, I turn to Lincoln. "What was that all about?"

"Tonight's festival is a joint celebration with thrax and quasis. A warrior tournament is taking place."

"Oh, I forgot about that, too." We're trying to have more of these joint *quasi-n-thrax* thingies lately. "Still doesn't explain why Dad ran off."

"My guess? Xavier has one or two angelic warriors in the fight. Your father trained all their best soldiers."

"So Dad's own fighters are about to take down demons for a crowd." I lift my brows. "No wonder he ran off."

All this time, Maxon has stood beside me and Lincoln while clasping his new wooden sword to his chest. "Can I keep the sword from Pop Pops with me always? Can I? Can I?"

Some kids snooze with a teddy bear. For Maxon, it's a wooden sword. When Lincoln was a kid, I guess he did the same thing. All of which is why I now turn to my husband. He's the *sword sleeping* expert in the family. Not that this weapon is anywhere near sharp, mind you. We're warriors, not idiots.

When Lincoln next speaks, it's with his most kingly voice. "You may keep the sword with you, but only if you put on your pajamas on right now."

In reply, Maxon races off to the bedroom to change. These days, that process usually takes two songs and a story, minimum. Lincoln just found a short cut.

"Well done," I declare.

"Let's just say I understand how things work between a boy and his sword."

Thuds sound from down the hallway as Maxon gets ready. He rushes back into the living room wearing blue PJs and a leather sword belt. Our son pats the new wooden blade which hangs from his side.

"What will you name this one?" I ask.

"I'll call it the Beast," announces my boy.

I shoot him a thumbs up. "Good pick."

Maxon rounds on Lincoln. "Can we watch the nice furry demon, Daddy? Can we? Can we?"

By asking for the *nice furry demon*, Maxon is requesting to watch a true classic of human entertainment, namely the animated version of *Beauty and the Beast.*

"Sure thing," says Lincoln. *Beast-time* is a recent ritual for them.

While Maxon crawls up onto his favorite spot on the couch, Lincoln unlatches the top of his body armor and sets himself beside our boy. The scene is so cute, I'm pretty sure that I spontaneously ovulate.

For a long minute, I just soak in the sight of my son. Was it just a year ago that my baby was taken by Armageddon, the King of Hell? Maxon never talks about it. And other than a few nightmares, you wouldn't know our kid was effected at all.

To figure out if Armageddon still bothers Maxon, Lincoln and I spoke to Verus, the oracle angel. According to her visions, Maxon will need to face his time in Hell one day. But it's not something we can fix for him. As his parents, all Lincoln and I can do is provide him a home filled with love, support and safety.

*Safety.* The word reverberates through my soul.

I'm pretty sure Bedlam will return eventually. And my chance to interrogate my family on the subject of the Titan of Chaos is tomorrow morning. Which means I need to look through all those odd gifts on our front lawn. I want to spend the morning asking questions, not sorting through stuff.

By this point, Maxon leans against Lincoln. My son's eyes are at half mast. Almost zonked.

This is the critical time for Maxon's sleep ritual. If you can get him past this half-doze, there will be about twenty minutes where the kid is so conked out, you can set him into bed without any more of the *water-story-song* ritual. Some nights, all that extra time together can be fun, but not after the day Lincoln and I just had. The faster we're all asleep, the better.

I motion to Lincoln. Since he's seen this movie a ton, I gain his attention easily. My guy tilts his head in a silent question. *What's up?*

I pretend-walk my fingers toward the door. *I'm leaving.*

He mouths two words. *Scala junk?*

I nod. *Yes.*

"Want me to go?" Lincoln whispers.

"No, I've got it."

Lincoln turns toward the front bay window. It provides a nice view of our front lawn. He gestures between his eyes and mine in a motion that means, *I'll be watching.*

I shoot him a thumbs up and saunter out the front door, careful not to make too much noise in the process. Once I'm outside, I carefully inspect the scene. For the first time in a while, I really register what's been dropped off here.

What a ton of crap.

## MYLA

*I* step closer to the junk pile. Surveying the area, I stifle a groan. Boxes and wooden bins are piled everywhere. Large and mysterious things hide under heavy tarps. Massive bags are tied up and stacked into mini-mountains. Everything is heaped so high, I can't even see the far row of tall hedges that mark our property line.

Did I say before that security was key?

Maybe I should remove our trio of magical ward stones. That way, some nice criminals could come in and steal all this stuff off my lawn.

Not a real option, though.

Better get to work.

I sidle up to the closest bin. Inside, I find hundreds of Scala dolls. I hold one up and groan.

*Ugh, not again.* Why do they make my boobs and butt so huge?

*No question what to do here.*

Uncapping my handy marker, I mark the exterior of the bin with a big NK—for Not Keeping—and move on.

Next up is a bunch of mystery blobs that are covered in a tarp.

The stuff is bumpy and waist high. Scrunching up my face, I try to imagine what Hell awaits me here.

I got nothing.

Pulling back the covering, I find about thirty animated lawn ornaments. It's like the human's *It's A Small World* ride, only with yours truly. In one statue, I ride a plastic unicorn.

I must admit, that's pretty cool.

Taking out my marker, I write K for Keeper on the unicorn's butt. How awesome is this thing? I'll find a home for it somewhere. The other ornaments show me blessing people while my arms automatically wave. Once more, these figures show me in my Scala robes. But this time, only my ass is ginormous for some reason. I take that as an insult to my boobs.

NK for the rest of this stuff. The only keeper in this section is the unicorn.

Next I move onto a box of super cool Myla action figures from my Arena days. If you stick your thumb in the middle of my plastic back, my tail whips out to skewer whatever's in front of me.

Total keeper. But I don't need four thousand of them. I pick out a set of figurines and place them beside the unicorn. Everything else gets a big NK.

At this point, I'm feeling pretty good about my bad self. Time to tackle whatever lurks under the biggest tarp of all.

This time, when I pull back the covering, it reveals a massive stone fountain. It's a round structure with a statue of me in the middle. Once the tarp is gone, the thing springs to life. In the center, Statue Me spits water into the circular basin below.

*Why, people? Why?*

Now, I'm not getting any awards from Miss Manners, but I certainly don't go around spitting.

Around the base of the fountain, words are carved in huge letters, announcing *Magical Wishing Well Of The Great Scala Mother.*

I take a moment to soak in this entire creation. *Wow, do I ever hate this thing.*

Without a doubt, I want this fountain out of my sight. My ass looks bigger than ever, my eyes way too goggly, and I definitely do not spit. They got the tail right, though. That said, it's not like I trust someone to take this thing away and make decent use of it somewhere else. Some things just don't belong in public.

From the corner of my vision, I catch a flash of light from behind a stack of plastic bags. We don't have a gate here, mostly because the magical ward stones are so powerful, no one can get near us, anyway.

So how would anyone trespass onto our property?

A chill runs through my veins. Could Bedlam be back already?

The moment the thought hits my consciousness, my igni go berserk. They screech so loudly, all thought vanishes from my mind. All I know is pain and eardrum-shattering noise.

On reflex, I curl into a fetal position and wrap my arms over my head. Not sure how long I stay that way, either. It could be a few seconds or many hours. At some point, I whisper eight words under my breath.

"Sometimes, I wish I weren't the Great Scala."

Blissful silence follows. Little by little, I unwind my arms from over my head and rise to stand once more.

A figure steps out from behind a mini-mountain-o-bags. Every nerve ending in my body goes on alert.

*Bedlam.*

"You wish you weren't the Great Scala?" he asks. "What a coincidence. I want the same thing as well. And you spoke your words at a magical fountain; that gives me just the magical opening I need to move forward."

"Just because I'm not the Great Scala, that doesn't mean I'll marry you."

"Clearly. But don't you know how it works with chaos? Quick spells and easy answers are no joy to me. I like to watch things slowly collapse in pain and anarchy." His glowing eyes narrow. "Your words allow me to change time. And I'll throw in a little curse as well, just for fun of watching your spirit break, little by little."

My heart sinks. Changing actual history is a massive spell; it does require my permission. But I've never heard of a caster twisting someone's words this way.

Then again, he *is* called the Titan of Chaos. Bedlam somehow stole three signet rings of Eden. Who knows what he can do?

Indigo mist rolls out across the lawn. I try to run, only my feet stay rooted to the spot. Bedlam's eyes glow more brightly than ever before.

No matter what I try to do, the dark mist crawls up around me, enveloping my body from head to toe. After that, I only sense myself falling through empty space.

The spell is cast.

## LINCOLN

*M*axon leans into my side as the music begins.

*Little town*
*It's a quiet village*
*Every day*
*Like the one before*

He's watched this film about a hundred times. I figure it's a healthy obsession. When we're in Antrum, Maxon gets fed a lot of anti-demonic talk. That makes sense; our people's purpose is to make Earth safe from demon-kind.

But there are limits. We don't attack demons who don't strike at us first. And there are some demonic folks who are valuable allies. The Beast would definitely qualify in this category.

An image appears in my mind. I see the inscription on the stone covering to Bedlam's lair.

*Here rests Bedlam, Titan of Chaos, Lord of the Tumult, and Master of the Curse for Wadget and Ra.*

In other words, Bedlam casts the same spell as the enchantress who cursed the Beast in this movie. It's an interesting idea—and retrograde casting can certainly turn someone beast-like—but Bedlam hasn't shown any signs of using this particular spell.

I run through the day's adventures in my mind. So far, Bedlam conjured up a megalodon shark and the Tumult. Neither of those activities qualifies as a full Beauty and the Beast curse. Bedlam also make the Tumult, which combines the human and animal. But is that really the same as what I'm watching on screen? I'd say no. The full curse involves roses, castles and other people. It's a far more complex spell.

In any case, it's not a mystery I can solve right now. Perhaps Xavier will have some insights in the morning.

Maxon curls over to rest on his side. I've seen this move before—he's trying to stay awake longer by avoiding a Daddy snuggle.

*Won't work for long, kid.*

My boy's eyes flutter shut despite how he fights to keep them open. Amazing how at his age, falling asleep is something to battle. When you get older, you can't wait for rest.

While the movie's music continues, I switch my focus to the main bay window. Through the glass, I watch Myla pull back the tarp on the largest eyesore on our lawn.

That fountain.

Suddenly, every muscle in my body goes on alert. My hunter's sense awakens.

We're not alone here.

From the darkness beyond the fountain, I catch the gleam of white. Someone peers at my wife through the shadows... And their irises glow with power. That describes only one creature in existence.

*Bedlam.*

Pulling my baculum from their holster, I ignite them into a long sword while rushing for the window. As I leap toward the glass, I swipe at the clear panel with my angelfire blade. The windowpane bursts as I jump through.

I land outside in a waist-high field of indigo smoke.

*Magic.*

Bedlam steps forward. I raise my sword, ready to strike.

"Why attack me?" asks Bedlam. "I'd be more concerned for your son."

Panic zings through my nervous system. Turning around, I spy Maxon still curled up on the couch. A thin layer of indigo mist surrounds him.

*More magic.*

The dark cloud grows heavier, then it disappears. Once the mist is gone, so is Maxon.

"No!"

I rush back toward the house with all my strength. What happens next seems to move in slow motion, no matter how hard I push myself to race at greater speed.

The house itself starts to disassemble.

Walls collapse into dust. Floors melt into muddy bogs. Furniture changes into scraps of animal fur that drift into the air.

I recall what happened back in the tomb. Bedlam's a retrograde caster who returned a section of Sahara into an ocean. Now he's reversing everything in my home.

Grief and rage battle it out inside me. Maxon is gone for now. But we've lost him before; we'll find him again. And there's one way to end evil spells like this one.

*Kill the caster.*

Spinning about, I raise my angelfire longsword and speed back toward Bedlam. He stands in the mist and glares at me. The Titan of Chaos doesn't even try to pull out a weapon in any kind of defense.

Once I'm close enough, I swing my weapon down toward Bedlam's head. But before my angelfire blade can strike the demon's skin, indigo smoke surrounds me as well. I'm instantly engulfed in an endless cloud as the ground beneath me vanishes.

And I'm gone.

## 13

## MYLA

Dark blue smoke surrounds me as I tumble through what seems like one massive cloud.

It isn't, though. This is more of Bedlam's magic.

That creep.

I *will* take him down. All I need are those three remaining rings of Eden.

My thoughts circle back to Lincoln. All my life and heart belongs to that man.

*Please, let him be safe.*

Energy and love envelop my soul. A colored loop appears before me in the mist. For a moment, I'm stumped. Then I recognize it. *A rainbow.* Normally, I only see half of these colored lights. This time, the rainbow is round and whole.

Brightness flares in the loop's center. Thousands of igni come through. I smile my face off as the little lightning bolts dance around me, keeping me company as I tumble. With another flash, the round rainbow disappears.

The colored lights may be gone, but hope sparks in my soul. Somehow, thinking of Lincoln brought both the round rainbow and my igni. That's super encouraging. After all, I never gave

Bedlam true assent for whatever weirdness he's casting right now. Perhaps his spell is incomplete.

In any case, that's my story and I'm sticking to it.

An orb materializes above my palm, its weight is as heavy as a glass ball. A movie from my past plays within the sphere.

The truth hits me.

*This isn't a movie; it's a memory.*

Inside the orb, I see myself at age eighteen, stepping out onto the Arena floor to fight an evil soul in solid form. I remember this battle well. My opponent's named Deacon. I speared that guy through the chest with my tail.

The orb flies away from my palm. My head turns fuzzy, and it's not just because I'm falling through a supernatural cloud.

*One of my memories was stolen, I know it.*

Closing my eyes, I try to recall what I just saw. There was something inside an orb. A battle played out within the sphere, just like a mini movie. And I was fighting. But who was my opponent? I can't recall the name.

I reopen my eyes to see fresh orbs on both my palms. More movies flicker inside. This time, it's all from my life at age eighteen. One sphere shows Mom freaking out because she doesn't want me fighting in the Arena anymore. Another shows me and my best friend, Cissy. We're at Purgatory High, sitting through another interminable class taught by a ghoul named the Old Timer, one of the worst teachers ever.

Those memories fly away. Once more, I try to reach for them. There was something about Mom, maybe? Cissy? I can't recall a thing. A flurry of orbs rise up from my palms and disappear. These are all vanished memories, and I know exactly who's to blame.

*Bedlam.*

My inner wrath demon roars with fury. How dare some nasty-ass freak steal away my history? Well, the Titan of Chaos doesn't know who he's dealing with. The Great Scala doesn't go down without a fight.

All this while, my igni have been looping around me. Now I call out to them.

*Help me, little ones. My memories are being erased. Please make it stop.*

Igni surround my palms, their small forms coating my flesh like a set of gauntlets. Fresh orbs try to bubble up from my skin, but they're held back by my tiny glowing friends. I send another mental message to my igni.

*You're doing great! Keep going!*

Then I notice it. These aren't the same igni that keep my memories in place. Holding back the orbs burns out their little forms. New ones must fly in and replace those that are gone. My little supernatural friends are getting erased.

Alarm rattles through my nervous system. Igni are the power that transfers souls to Heaven or Hell. They're more important than any one Scala. I send a new message now, my intent more frantic than ever before.

*Do not sacrifice yourselves!*

Yet my igni keep up their work. More get deleted by the moment. Panic zooms through me. There are millions of souls in Purgatory. They're my responsibility. If the igni vanish, who will care for them?

*Stop!*

In reply, the childish voices of igni sound in my mind.

*We are not all gone. Many remain and can come to you, but only for one final visit. Choose the moment well.*

Another orb appears on my palm. Inside it, I see a memory from just a few minutes ago. In the sphere, I think of Lincoln. The round rainbow materializes and my igni travel through that loop. Panic zings down my spine. This recollection is important; it's how I fractured Bedlam's spell.

By now, only a handful of igni remain. They try to hold onto this latest sphere of history, but it's no use. The igni burn out and the orb flies away.

The memory vanishes.

Bands of worry tighten across my rib cage. I just lost an important piece of my past. With all my focus, I try to grasp what it might be. It concerned breaking through Bedlam's spell, didn't it? And it had to do with summoning my igni, right? Why can't I remember?

## 14

## THE BEAST

*I* step through another passageway in Arx Hall. Like the rest of the palace, this corridor is made of smooth gray stone. Cobwebs dangle from the vaulted ceilings. A musty scent hangs in the air.

Suddenly, an arc of color and light rises up from the carpet.

It's waist-high rainbow.

*Not again.*

A servant steps toward me. She has long blonde hair, fair skin and freckles. Time was, I'd remember the names of everyone in Arx Hall. Not any more. The girl wears a simple black dress with long open sleeves. Her garb is medieval in style, like everything else here.

I brace myself, hoping she'll pause by the edge of the small rainbow and ask how it got here.

That's not what happens.

The servant freezes in place. "Greetings, Beas—" She clears her throat. A blush colors her face and neck.

"My *name* is Prince Lincoln," I say, my voice rough. It's no secret that everyone calls me the Beast, but my own servants should know to keep such things to themselves.

"I was just looking at your…" She visibly shivers. "I mean, you always wear a…" The girl seems too frightened to finish a coherent sentence.

Even so, I know what she means. I wear a lion's pelt over my shoulders. It's a gift from Rufus, a sentient feline from a realm called the Primeval. This isn't a fashion choice; the thing contains healing properties. And when I set the lion's skull on my head as a helm, I gain extra strength in battle.

Sure, I know it scares the servants. One day, my curse from Bedlam will end and I'll spend eternity encased alive in glass. In the meantime, everyone can handle seeing me in a lion's pelt.

"Leave me," I order. The girl doesn't move. "NOW."

At last, the girl races away. Sadly, she rushes right through the small rainbow and keeps on going.

Like always, the rainbows are something that only I can detect. I'm losing my mind.

Little by little, the rainbow rises off the floor until it's a full circle. In the center of this loop, I see a boy. He's a four-year-old cherub who stomps about in blue pajamas. Like always, I can only see what play out inside the circle, as if I'm watching a human movie without sound. Even so, I know the child's name. *Maxon.*

Colored lights flare within the circle. The scene within it changes. In this vista, I stand facing a stained glass window. Only my back is visible, but my posture says I am relaxed and enjoying the moment. A woman waits at my side; she leans her head on my shoulder. I can't see her face, but I feel certain she is beautiful. We seem connected and happy.

Another flare of color appears within the loop. The final scene ends. The circle whirls down to a single point and then vanishes completely.

It's over.

A weight of sorrow settles in my bones. This is all part of

Bedlam's curse. There is no child in my life. No precious woman at my side. I am alone. A Beast.

Picking up my pace, I navigate through the maze of palace corridors until I spy the royal library. Years ago, the entrance to this place was gilded and gleaming. Now, it's chipped and molded.

Twisting the handle, I open the door to a familiar sight. Two stories of shelves stretch from floor to ceiling. Half the books are missing. Scrolls and maps sit in piles on the floor or atop rickety tables. All the clutter comes from my many years researching how to stop Bedlam and the Tumult.

I haven't figured it out yet.

That said, I *have* discovered certain things. In the beginning, my rainbow illusions gave me useful visions of where to find secrets on Bedlam. These days, they only torture me with nonsense about a family I'll never have.

A knock sounds at the door. "My Prince?"

"Come in."

The door swings open to reveal Nat, my Master at Arms. He's a grizzled man in tattered black body armor. Hefty muscles and a barrel chest mark him as a warrior. He pauses beside me. "You promised that when you got back from your last battle, you'd get some sleep." He scans my outfit and sighs. "You're spattered with blood."

"Now you want me to bathe as well?" Nat means well, but his intrusions are annoying in the extreme.

"And eat."

I stomp toward a nearby table. "I must check the new scrolls that arrived."

"What can be so important?"

"A fresh report from the House of Nephthys."

"That pack of hedge witches and false wizards? Why would you ask them for anything?"

"I haven't given up on finding a supernatural cure for my

curse. Here it is." I pick up a scroll and scan the contents. "Or perhaps they are incompetent, as you say."

"It talks about the tale of Beauty and the Beast, doesn't it?"

"Octavia must have gotten to them." My mother is convinced that if I find true love, my curse will be over. She refuses to understand that this spell is cast by the Titan of Chaos. This is no fairy tale. Bedlam likes to toy with his victims. Any pursuit of true love is only a distraction from what I truly need to do: find the three rings of Eden and destroy the Titan of Chaos.

"What nonsense." I toss the scroll aside.

Suddenly, a blinding spike of pain shoots up my forearm. Hissing in a breath, I pull a dagger from the holster on my thigh. Working past the hurt, I set the blade's tip against my wrist.

"Is it happening again?" asks Nat.

"We'll see."

I slice up my arm, careful to cut through the body armor without slicing my skin. Once done, I toss the blade aside, peel back the rubbery fabric, and inspect my flesh.

At one time, I had a long line of what looked like tattoos winding up my arm. All of them were black roses. They aren't human-made marks, though.

*They're signs of my curse.*

Nat stands over my shoulder. "How many blooms do you have left?"

"One."

"Oh." Nat does a poor job of hiding his sorrow. The last time he asked me this question, I had three full roses remaining. "How many petals on that bloom?"

I scan the final rose on my forearm. "Four."

It's a lovely rose as such images go—all swirling lines. A single petal pulses on my arm, blinking in and out of existence. Fresh pain shoots up my wrist.

"No," whispers Nat. "You can't lose another petal again so soon."

Dark blue mist rolls out across the floor. This isn't something that Nat can see; it's all part of my curse. Indigo vapor surrounds me. *Magic.*

When the haze vanishes, I no longer stand inside the library.

*I step about in a slow circle, trying to determine my location. Around me there stretches what was once a cemetery. Now it's a refugee camp. Tents have been erected around the headstones. Mausoleums house the living as well as the dead. A heavy mist hangs over the ground. Moonlight provides the only illumination.*

*Cries rise up from the distance. "Tumult are coming! Run!" My heart sinks. I've seen what happens when the Tumult attack humans. It isn't pretty. I must stop this.*

*Desperate, I look for any sign of the location. The single yell transforms into a chorus of screams.*

*"Where is this?" I whisper. "Where should I fight?"*

*At last, I see it. A crooked sign hangs from a nearby tree which reads,* Sector Seven, Old Milwaukee.

*I exhale. Now I know the location of the next Tumult attack.*

*The ground mist thickens. Soon I can only see a cloud of blue around me.*

When the mist fades, I find myself back in the library. A very worried Nat stands at my side.

"What happened?" asks Nat. "Was it another vision?"

Nat isn't aware of how I see rainbows. That part of my life stays secret. That said, everyone knows how I get visions of future attacks.

"Yes, I know where the Tumult will strike next." Turning, I march toward the door. Nat steps into my path, blocking me.

"Don't go."

"You know the situation. Whenever a petal falls, I get another vision. Now we're only minutes away from the next attack. To help these humans, I must leave now."

Nat grabs my wrist. "But you said it yourself. The petal falls when you get another new vision. That means you have only three petals left. We can send in other warriors."

"Who will all get slaughtered."

"You don't know that," whispers Nat.

"The Tumult are invisible to anyone else but me. It's another so-called gift of my curse. We've lost too many thrax already. This palace is manned by old women and pubescent boys. I will go."

"You can't," pleads Nat. "The Tumult will stop once they've killed all the humans within a league or so. It's not all on you. You have one final rose. Three little petals. That's a countdown clock to end your life. Once the petals are gone, so are you. Your father, King Connor, is ill and dying. Queen Octavia locks herself in his chambers, nursing her grief. Who will care for the thrax when you're dead?"

Closing my eyes, I picture the refugees. "If you were the only one who could save them, could you stay here?"

"Honestly, I don't know."

"I do." Pressing past Nat, I head out the door.

## 15

## MYLA

*I* tumble through the indigo mist. My mind's a jumble of sensations and memories. There's the fountain on my front yard... the screech of igni... and the nasty form of Bedlam. Some recollections are clear while others stay blurry. What is happening to me?

All of a sudden, I land on solid ground.

Sort of.

My body seems to merge into someone else's. There's no other way to describe it. There are two of me, and then there's only one.

A voice sounds in my head. "At last, you're here." After that, it's pure silence.

*Wow. This is a really fucked-up dream.*

Little by little, the blue mist around me vanishes. I find myself standing in the center of Purgatory's Arena. Big improvement. I dream about this place all the time.

As a teenager, I came here to fight. I try to recall some of my best battles, but can't seem to remember anything good. *Oh, well. That's dreaming for you.* These days, I use the Arena to move souls as the Great Scala. I check my outfit to find I'm wearing my dragonscale fighting suit.

Am I about to have a dream battle? Those are always fun.

I blink hard, trying to clear my head. Doesn't happen. Leaning back on my heels, I soak in the scene instead. All around me, demons fill the stands. The audience is a mixture of creatures with wings, fur, fangs and scales. More heavies guard the entrance and exit arches. Quasis and ghouls are nowhere to be seen.

A memory appears. I was falling through blue clouds. My igni were there. I close my eyes, ready to summon my little supernatural friends. Then I recollect their final words.

*We are not all gone. Many remain and can come to you, but only for one final visit. Choose the moment well.*

What a freaky dream.

Shaking my head, I pinch my own arm, trying to wake myself up.

Doesn't happen.

Another fact bubbles up into my consciousness. Bedlam cast a spell on me that tried to erase all my memories. My igni somehow appeared.

I press my palms against my eyes. How did my igni materialize, exactly? There was a trick to it that was super important. Try as I might, I can't recall.

That said, I do know that some of my igni died protecting my history. Clearly, they weren't able to save the memory about how I got them to show up in the first place, but they did saved a bunch of other stuff. A cold suspicion slowly creeps my spine.

This might not be a dream after all.

*Nah, it's too weird.*

A figure in torn black robes steps out from a nearby archway.

He's gray-skinned with large coal-black eyes, a skull-like hole for a nose, and teeth that have been filed to tiny points.

*Sharkie!*

This guy was the old emcee from my days fighting in the Arena. Before every match, I'd take care to verbally torture him just a little. Good times.

I wave in his direction. "Hey, Sharkie!" My voice comes out really croaky for some reason. I clear my throat, take a deep breath, and start again. No way am I missing out on a chance to give Sharkie some lip, even in a dream.

Sharkie frowns. "My name is SKE-12, *slave.*"

I pat under my eyes in mock-tearfulness. "You haven't changed a bit."

Sharkie pauses before me, his seven-foot-tall frame looming over mine. "I loathe you."

"Back at ya." I snap my fingers, as if remembering something. "Hey, I haven't seen you since Armageddon's invasion. Guess you got crushed by a falling building. What was the name again?" *More snapping.* "That's right. The Lewis Tower. Fate's a bitch, eh? All those good souls you helped send to Hell... and then you're squashed by a tower dedicated to my family."

"I am not destroyed, as you see." Technically, ghouls are already dead, so they use the term *destroyed.*

"Sure, you aren't."

"Today, you shall get what you deserve."

"Sounds like a plan. Where's Walker?" That's my honorary older brother who just so happens to be a ghoul. Walker always joins me in Arena stuff, even in my dreams.

"WKR-7 is back in the Dark Lands, serving the Oligarchy. He is our greatest drone."

A pang of sorrow moves inside me. Sure, this is only a dream, but the very thought of Walker serving the evil Oligarchy makes my eyes prickle with tears. *Which is dumb.* After all, none of this is real. Who cares what dream Walker does?

Sharkie slams his tall staff onto the Arena floor. The demons in the tiered seats fall quiet.

"Hear ye! Hear ye!" announces Sharkie. "All hail Armageddon!"

The crowd roars with delight as a familiar figure steps out onto the nearby balcony—it's a tall demon with an elongated face and skin like polished stone. His squat body is stuffed into a tiny tuxedo. All my blood seems to sink to my toes.

This is Armageddon, the King of Hell and my personal nemesis. My pulse speeds. This demon stole away my son and tortured my father.

*Stay calm, Myla. Armageddon is definitely dead. You watched him get killed.*

Sharkie thuds his staff once again. "Three cheers for the King of Hell and Purgatory!"

The Arena erupts in a series of happy roars as Armageddon raises his arms in triumph.

Numbness creeps across my skin. I knew Armageddon ruled Hell. But Purgatory? Armageddon always ran Purgatory through his puppet leaders, the ghouls.

I inspect Arena seats once more. I still don't see any ghouls or quasis. What happened to them? And why do I care so much, even though this is just a dream?

Someone moves in the shadows of a nearby access archway. I know the spot since it's sealed off from the rest of the Arena. If you want to hide, that's the place to do it. As I focus on the shadows, a familiar face becomes clear.

It's my best friend, Cissy.

Cissy is tall and willowy with a golden retriever's tail as well as a power over the mortal sin of envy. Normally, she wears the purple robes of a Senator for Diplomacy. Only in my dream, she's wearing gray sweats. It's a style I haven't seen on Cissy since Purgatory High.

That chill crawls up my neck again. The facts are becoming more clear. I can't avoid the truth.

This isn't a dream, after all.

More memories appear. My head fully clears. This is all Bedlam's doing. He wants me to become Mrs. Chaos. Since I refused, he cast a spell that sent me through a dark blue cloud.

And this is where I've landed.

My heart sinks. Bedlam rewound all of time, not just for me, but for everyone. When I stood by the fountain, I wished I weren't the Great Scala.

Here's the result.

I'm no longer the Great Scala. Armageddon invaded Purgatory and runs both realms now. Ghouls are gone. I can only hope my fellow quasis are safe.

And what's become of me? I scan my body, looking for clues. My beloved dragonscale fighting suit has tears. I'd have to wear this every day for years in order for it to get it this nasty. And the fact that my voice sounds so rusty? Maybe I haven't been using it.

What happened to me?

Armageddon lowers his bony arms. The Arena turns quiet.

"My demons!" cries Armageddon. "The Tumult are a plague upon both Hell and Purgatory. Even I have been unable to detect them, let alone face them in battle. The question has been asked— how do we fight this new enemy?" Armageddon scans the Arena with a dramatic sweep of his head. "I think I have the answer."

Sharkie reaches into the folds of his cloak and pulls out a chunk of stone. I recognize it immediately. It's part of the seal that once covered the entrance to Bedlam's underground lair. Sharkie raises the rock high.

"We've all seen these rocks before," says Armageddon. "For some reason, pieces of this particular stone always draw forth the Tumult."

Inviting Tumult into the Arena is not a popular idea. The

demon audience loses their minds. Demons move in a mad rush, hoping to scramble or fly away. For his part, Armageddon snaps his fingers. Manus guards pour out from the entrance archways and up the aisles of the stadium. I shiver, remembering these heavies from Armie's invasion. Manus are furry knuckle-draggers with extraordinary strength and bad attitudes.

Manus guards slam into the stands, keeping the demons in place with pain. Wings are torn off. Fists smash into skulls. Blood splatters everywhere. Within minutes, the audience is back on their benches.

This is classic Armageddon. Even with his own kind, the guy is a bloodthirsty sicko.

Armageddon points to Sharkie. "Set down the stone."

The emcee does as told. Since I stand close to Sharkie, I can see how his bony hand shakes as he places the rock onto the sandy floor.

Immediately, a clawed hand breaks through the earth, followed by a second. A moment later, a human with a bat-like face pulls itself free from the ground.

That's one of the Tumult, all right.

The demons aren't so sure. From the stands, I hear their confused chatter.

"I saw the ground break open," says one.

"Nothing came out," adds a second.

"No one sees the Tumult, you idiot!" cries a third.

The Tumult turns to Sharkie. It grips the emcee's chin with its left hand. With it right hand, the Tumult grabs Sharkie's shoulder. All the while, Sharkie screams while his head tilts back from the pressure.

"Where is it?" screeches Sharkie. The emcee bats at the general area where the Tumult grasps him, but misses every time. Lines of black blood stream down the emcee's chin.

Now Sharkie isn't my fave guy in the after-realms, but I can't stand by while he's torn apart.

I seem to be alone in that sentiment. The demons, who were terrified before, now cheer with glee. A general shout of "kill kill kill" rises up from the audience.

I round on the Tumult. "Leave Sharkie alone," I declare.

What happens next takes less than a second, but it seems to last much longer. Instead of listening to me, the Tumult tightens its grip. In one sweeping move, the Tumult pulls Sharkie's head off his shoulders.

The demons cheer as Sharkie's body falls to the Arena floor, lifeless.

Anger heats my veins. Again, Sharkie is no friend to me. Still, no one deserves to die like that.

I glare at Tumult. "I told you to leave him alone."

A fresh chorus of demonic voices sound from the stands.

"Prisoner 412 hears the Tumult!" cries one demon.

"She sees it, too!" yells another.

There are two key revelations at this point. First of all, how did I get to be called prisoner 412? That's a worry. And second, it seems I'm the only one who can see—and so fight—the Tumult. That's a smile.

Fresh calls of "kill, kill, kill" rise up from the stands. In all my years of Arena fighting, this marks the first time demons have actually cheered me on to do anything but die.

The Tumult turns to me, its claws raised and eyes blazing. "My Master has a message for you. He's granted your wish. You never became the Great Scala. My fellow Tumult now terrorize human kind. Armageddon rules both Purgatory and Hell. Your fellow quasis suffer worse than ever before."

The Tumult stalks closer. The crowd screams with glee.

I set my feet shoulder width apart while my tail arcs over my shoulder. *Battle stance.* "Move closer and you're losing a leg."

The Tumult grins. "Say the words and my Master will return everything to what it was before. All this suffering will end. Just say it."

I tilt my head, considering. Life going back to normal would be pretty awesome. "And what does Bedlam want me to say?"

"Speak the words, *I wish to become the Queen of Chaos.*"

"Bedlam can stuff it."

The Tumult clacks his teeth together in what might be laughter. "My Master knows you are strong. You just need time to realize that marrying him is what's best. Or perhaps there's no need to wait. Some agony right now may give you instant clarity."

A minute ago, I was just adjusting to the basic idea that my world had been changed. But this is a battle. *Hello, happy place!*

"You want a lesson in pain?" I ask. "I'm right here."

The Tumult leaps for me. The crowd cheers.

Jumping up, I link my legs around the Tumult's neck. Flipping over, I jam the Tumult head-first onto the ground, while my tail spears it through the chest.

Blood seeps out of the Tumult's broken body. The demons in the stands begin to chatter once more.

"I see it now!" cries one.

"The Tumult is right there!" howls another.

I lift my brows. So a dead Tumult is a visible Tumult. *Learn something new every day.*

Up on the balcony, Armageddon raises his arms. The crowd falls silent once more. "As you can see, prisoner 412 is in league with both the Tumult and Bedlam." Armageddon focuses his beady red gaze on me. "Have you anything to say?"

This is what you call a crossroads. I could give a snarky reply —that's my fave kind of interaction when it comes to Armageddon. But I can't ignore the fact that my life has been served up a huge meal of shit burger. If there's any chance I can get help, I need to try. Even if the assistance is coming from my arch enemy.

Trouble is, doing this will be about as pleasant as an attack from the needle leech brigade. After fighting those demons, I was picking tiny teeth out from my skin for weeks.

Closing my eyes, I picture Lincoln and Maxon. I'm doing this to bring them back.

"Any reply, prisoner 412?" asks Armageddon.

Somehow I force the words past my lips. "Well, I can't believe I'm about to say this, but you do have a point. It's sorta my fault the Tumult are attacking. But—*good news!*—I have a simple solution here. Help me find the three remaining signet rings of Eden. With their magic, I can kill Bedlam and end all this mess."

Armageddon's mouth winds into an impossibly large smile. "What a liar you are." He points right at my nose. "Prisoner 412, I hereby sentence you to death at dawn!" Armageddon turns his focus to the crowd. "How shall we kill her?"

A fresh mix of voices call out ideas. There's being fed to rabid dogs, poisoning and—my favorite—death by manicure, whatever that is.

While the demons yell themselves hoarse, I take the opportunity to scan the exits for a quick escape. There are lots of archways to choose from, but it won't be easy to run with a stadium of demons chasing me. Besides, if they're killing me in the morning, they'll have to put me somewhere overnight. And to do that, the guards must haul my ass through the network of tunnels under the Arena.

Sweet.

I know those passageways better than anyone. And if the aboveground Arena is any indication, Armageddon hasn't made any improvements to this place.

That settles it. Once I'm in the Arena tunnels, I can make my escape. And there's also a hidden Pulpitum nearby that I can use for a quick getaway.

My plan appears with perfect clarity. First, I team up with Lincoln. Second, I get the remaining three signet rings of Eden. And third, my guy and I kill Bedlam.

The cheering dies down as Armageddon raises his bony arms

yet again. "It is decided! We shall have an old-fashioned hanging at dawn!" The audience yells its pleasure once more.

I almost tell them all to suck it, but I decide to keep my yap shut. I can save my snark for the tunnels.

A pair of Manus demons lumber toward me. Both carry shock sticks in their meaty fists. The one on the left swipes the stick toward a nearby archway.

"Go there or get hurt." The Manus has a distinctively gurgle in his voice, like he's speaking through a mouthful of milk.

Gross.

"Yes, Sir." I take care to slump my shoulders and shuffle-walk toward the exit. It's an effort not to smile.

*This next bit will be fun.*

## 16

## THE BEAST

*I* march out onto the cemetery. Everything appears just as I saw in my vision. The place is vast and packed with miserable humans. A yellow moon hangs low in the night sky. The air feels heavy with the electric charge of panic.

"Tumult are coming!" cries a voice. "Run!"

Women rush from their tents, dragging children in tow. All are dirty and thin.

A Tumult steps onto the cemetery ground. It's semi-human form is framed in a far-off gateway.

I pull the lion's skull helm over my face. Energy and power thrum through my muscles. I hold my baculum in my left hand, igniting the weapon into a longbow. When I set my right hand against my left, a fiery arrow appears.

Meanwhile, the Tumult leaps onto an elderly man's back and bites into the poor human's throat. Blood sprays everywhere.

Screams rise from the crowd. A great mass of frightened people run away from the dying human.

I step toward him.

The Tumult tears deeper into the man's neck. A low moans sounds from what's left of his throat. The human falls over, dead.

I release my arrow. The projectile strikes the Tumult in its leg. The demon wheels and screeches, clawing at its injured limb. I change my baculum into a longsword and stalk closer.

Once near enough, I slice off the creature's head.

As it falls to the ground, the Tumult becomes visible to the crowd of terrified humans.

"It's the Beast!" they cry. "He summons the Tumult!"

In truth, I *kill* the Tumult. But all the humans see is a lion-man who stands beside a suddenly-visible demon. It's not worth it to correct their misconception. As long as everyone stays out of my way, things are fine.

More Tumult appear. I hack, slice, aim and shoot. Fresh blood stains my body armor and lion's pelt. Hours pass before all of Bedlam's creatures are destroyed.

When the last Tumult is down, I reset my baculum into their holster and head back to the pulpitum.

A young thrax man stands in my way, blocking me. There's no missing his heritage. Only thrax have one iris that's blue while the other is brown.

"What do you want?" I ask. My voice carries more than a little snarl.

"I am Romil from the House of Kamal. Six months ago, I became separated from my demon patrol. Now I wish to return home… and bring others with me." Romil waves his arm. A young woman steps out from behind a tall tombstone. She carries a plump baby on her hip. Another human man stalks behind her. Based on how the two look alike, they are clearly brother and sister.

"And?" I ask.

"I've heard you will take refugees from other realms. Will they have your protection?"

"No. Antrum only accepts after-realmers. No humans."

The woman's brother steps forward. "I told you. We need to find another way to keep my sister and nephew safe."

"No," says Romil. "They will go to Antrum." He focuses on me. "My prince won't turn them away."

Pulling back my helm, I take a closer look at the boy. His pupils are dilated. A hefty lump marks one side of his head. This child is injured. An image flashes in my mind. The cherub boy in blue pajamas. *Maxon*. What would I do if he were hurt?

I shake my head, trying to dislodge the thought. *Maxon is only a torturous illusion.*

Still, Romil is right.

I focus on the mother. "Your son is injured." I turn to Romil. "Take the boy and his mother directly to the royal infirmary. I'll make sure it's known they're all under my protection."

Romil sighs. "Thank you, Beas—I mean, brother. You're good with children. I never would have expected it."

Those words cut me deeply. *It's like Maxon doesn't exist.*

I pinch the bridge of my nose. It's *like* Maxon doesn't exist? He's a painful vision from Bedlam, nothing more.

"How can I thank you?" asks Romil.

"Stop talking to me and find your own way to the Pulpitum." Without waiting for a reply, I stalk off into the darkness.

# THE TUMULT

## 17

## MYLA

*ack in the Arena tunnels. Yay.*

    I stride through the Arena's hallways. With every step, the Manus guards guide me deeper underground. That suits me fine.

*All the better to ambush you with, my dear.*

I've no desire for there to be witnesses when I kick me some Manus butt. Plus, the extra walk gives me time to scheme. One fact becomes clear. If I'm this prisoner 412, then I've surely used my tail before to try and escape. After all, the Manus are carrying shock sticks.

I glance over my shoulder. *Or not.*

If the guards are worried about my tail, then why follow me so closely? Well, whatever the reason, I'm not looking a gift demon in the mouth.

With each step lower into the Arena's tunnels, my pulse speeds faster. My inner wrath demon lurches to life.

She's getting happy.

At last, we reach the perfect spot. Back when I was fighting here, we used to call this hallway Stank Row. It's where the ghouls stored the Fector demons. I'm talking ooze, goo and all things nasty.

As a result, no one comes around here.

Which makes it the perfect spot for an ambush.

My tail thinks so, too. It reaches out, the arrowhead end looping around a shock stick like a mittened hand. My tail then yanks the shock stick free and starts whaling on both demons. By the time I turn around, the pair of Manus are on the floor, unconscious.

I pat the arrowhead-shaped end. "Nice work, boy."

Sure, it's a little odd for the Manus guards not to see that coming. But whatever. Maybe they're new.

With the guards knocked out, it's time for me to blow this popsicle stand. I'm almost ready to run when I see it: a steel door that's covered in chipped white paint. The writing on the exterior stops me cold.

*Prisoner 412.*

I know I should run. But that's so not happening. Instead, I push the door open to find a small cell whose walls are filled with graffiti. There's a low bench covered in a filthy blanket. One wall reads, *Myla Lewis, Prisoner 412. Stay out.*

I pull on the frayed cuffs of my dragonscale fighting suit. That's why my outfit is such a mess. I've been wearing it as my prison uniform. Turning, I scan another wall. This one marks the days in the cell. I make some quick calculations and gasp. I've been locked up for the past five years.

A third wall is lined with frantic scratches. I pick out a few phrases.

> *Cissy is my friend.*
> *Maxon is my son.*
> *Lincoln is my love.*

My skin prickles over. *I remember now.* My igni protected

some of my memories, but not all. Somehow, they gave some of those recollections to prisoner 412 before she merged into me. I find another phrase.

*Almost time.*

My heart sinks. The other version of me knew how to escape, same as I did. She was waiting for my arrival. I think back to the sensation of merging with someone when I landed on the Arena floor. Words sounded in my mind.

*At last, you're here.*

It was prisoner 412.

Moans sound from the outer hallway. The Manus demons are waking up.

I hustle my way out of Stank Row and into some other access tunnels. These corridors are used to haul trash in and out of the Arena. The fact that I'm using them now to escape is an odd kind of poetic justice. *Myla Lewis, taking out my own trash.*

The garbage tunnels surface in a large metal shed. From here, it's a short trip to the dumpster which hides a Pulpitum station.

So close now.

Suddenly, the shed door swings open. An unexpected visitor rushes inside. I blink hard, not believing what I'm seeing.

Cissy is here.

My bestie looks just as she did in the Arena: blonde ringlets, gray sweats and a fluffy golden tail. So much has happened, I'd completely forgotten that I'd seen her before.

That said, there is one thing about Cissy that's entirely new. She hauls a massive duffel bag on her shoulder. Shuffling into the shed, Cissy kicks the door closed behind her and drops the duffel to the ground with a thump.

My bestie turns to me and beams. "Prisoner 412, you're really here! I mean, I got all your letters but I didn't really think this would happen."

For the first time in my life, my friend Cis has knocked me speechless.

It seems Prisoner 412 has been quite the scheming quasi.

## 18

## MYLA

For a long minute, I can only stare at Cissy. She's here and she thinks me—*I mean, Prisoner 412*—lured her to this spot.

I keep waiting for my mind to catch up.

Total fail.

What can I say? It's been a busy few hours. At this point, I'm amazed I'm upright and speaking in complete sentences. The fact that it's taking me a bit to handle my *Cissy surprise*?

Pretty minor, really.

At some point, my mind starts to function once more. Before, it just looked like Cissy was moving her mouth in nonsense ways. Now her words become actual speech to my ears. Turns out, Cissy's on a roll. She's also bobbing on the balls of her feet as she speaks, which means my bestie is overexcited and-or freaked out.

Probably both.

Cissy forces a smile. "So Prisoner 412—*can I call you Prisoner 412?*—that's how you signed your letters so I guess it's okay. We've never spoken face-to-face before."

"Call me Myla."

"Myla. All right." Cissy frowns. "Where did you come up with that name?"

"My mother. How does anyone get named?"

"But you were birthed in a laboratory. You know that, right?"

I set my fist on my hip in the universal movement for, *you're so full of it*. "And how would you know this?"

Cissy shrugs. "You promised to help me escape Purgatory, but you're also a known criminal. So I made some contacts and asked around." She winces. "That must sound unbelievable."

"Nope. I buy it." Mostly because, in my reality, Cis is amazing at this kind of thing.

"Your birth is pretty cool," says Cis. "You were created from little bits of DNA pulled out of the best Arena fighters."

As the news sinks in, my mouth falls open in shock. Laboratory birth? Best DNA? I shake my head.

*Focus, Myla. It doesn't matter how you started in this reality. What's important is how you get your ass out of here.*

"We're getting off track." I raise my hand, palm forward. "Let's start at the beginning. How did we meet?"

Cissy's eyes widen. "You don't remember?"

"Pretend that I'm actually from another world and I don't know anything."

"That's really weird." Cissy nibbles her lower lip with her teeth. "Then again, I did see photos of your cell in *Purgatory Times*. You're pretty much bat-shit crazy."

"Right. So give it to me from the start."

"It began five years ago. You sent me a letter, saying you could escape at any time."

"I *could* escape at any time."

"Well, I didn't know that, did I? You were just a lab-rat quasi with a number-name who was locked up on Stank Row."

I raise my pointer finger. "You make a good point."

"Of course, I do. Your last letter said how today was the day and if I wanted to escape Purgatory, you could help me."

"You *want* to escape?"

"Armageddon is rounding up *bad quasi souls* for Hell." Cissy makes little quotations marks with her fingers when she says the words *bad quasi souls*.

"Which means that Armie's picking purely good quasis to send to the fiery down under." Some demons like nothing better than torturing the good. The King of Hell is one of them.

Cissy stares at her feet. "My name made the latest list."

"Oh, Cis. I'm so sorry. I'm sure the Great Scala wouldn't really send you to Hell."

"You're way wrong. The Great Scala is an old guy who's related to Armageddon and does whatever he wants. He's named Maxon Bane, did you know that?"

"I did. The igni asked me to name my own son after him. Before Armageddon got his hands on Bane, the guy was a really good Great Scala, if that makes any sense."

"No, that makes zero sense. Your igni? A son? Maxon Bane a *good* Great Scala?" Cissy takes a half-step backward. "Do you need to go write on your wall before we go? You're acting totally unhinged."

"Forget I said anything. Back to your story. So you got my letters saying how I can help you escape... and then your name comes up on the list for Hell. Remind me. Where am I taking you again?"

"You're really looney tunes, Prisoner 412."

"Call me Myla. And hanging with me is better than an eternity in Hell, let's not forget that part."

"True. Over the years, you only wrote me a million times that you'd take me to Antrum. Prince Lincoln is really good about taking in refugees. I've heard some even get roles in diplomacy."

My heart lurches against my rib cage. "Prince Lincoln is alive and well?"

"Sure." Cissy narrows her eyes at me. "You *can* get me into Antrum, can't you?"

"I got my own ass out of prison, didn't I?"

"That you did." Cissy shakes her head, a movement that sets her golden ringlets bouncing. "I can't believe it. You've been able to escape all these years. You were just waiting for the right day."

"I'm cool like that."

"Shouldn't we get going?" asks Cissy. "Armageddon wants you dead."

"At this point, good old Armie is more scared of the Tumult than he is of me. We've got a few minutes. You know why I want to escape, don't you?"

"Yes, you mentioned that a kazillion times in your letters." Cissy makes her *eek face.* "I was hoping you'd forget all about killing Bedlam, though. The Titan of Chaos is bad news."

"Hence why I'm killing him. And I need some information. I have allies here in the after-realms. Like Xavier, the General of the Archangels. He might know some secret stuff about Bedlam. Any idea where he is?"

"You mean, Xavier the diplomat?"

I nod so fast, I might hurt my neck. "That's the one."

"I read some books about him. He died before Armageddon invaded Purgatory."

"Oh." I try to remind myself that this isn't real, but that isn't helping. My heart sinks to my toes. "And Senator Lewis?"

"She broke into Hell with some poison." Cissy lowers her voice to a whisper. "They killed themselves together. Armageddon was torturing Xavier, you see. It was the only way she could free them both."

Waves of sorrow crash over me. *This is all my fault.* I wasn't there to free Xavier. And much as Mom worried herself sick over me growing up, at least she was focused on something positive like keeping me safe. This way, both of my parents wound up dead.

"Prisoner 412—*I mean, Myla*—are you all right?"

I force my spine to straighten. "I can still fix this. They aren't really gone."

"Of course not." Let the record show that Cissy is totally playing along with me at this point. I definitely appreciate it. "Do you need to know anything else?"

"No, I've gotten as much bad news as I can handle for now. The important thing is that the prince is all right. Once I get us into Antrum, I'll find Lincoln and we'll fix everything."

"I want to believe you," says Cissy soothingly. "But like I said, you are a kook."

For some reason, that makes me feel better. It's like Cissy and I are back in high school and she's wondering why I keep insisting on practicing wrestling moves on her in the hallways. In the end, I've always been bat shit crazy. Somehow, it works out for me that way.

I gesture toward the duffle on the floor. "What's in there?"

Cissy kneels by the bag and zips it open. "This is all the stuff you asked me to bring. These are uniforms for Purgatory's sanitation workers, only I picked off all the insignias."

My eyes widen as I realize the brilliant plan from my alter ego, Prisoner 412. "That's because in Antrum, there's something called the Privy Squad. They clean out toilets and wear almost those exact outfits. It will be the perfect disguise when we break in."

"And how will we do that?" Cissy nibbles on her thumbnail. "Break in, I mean?"

"There's a secret transfer platform not far from this spot. It will take us directly into Antrum. Normally, we'd have to go through security. But this secret pulpitum will let us in without anyone in transfer central knowing a thing."

"I hope so. Everyone wants to flee to Antrum, only no one can get inside. It's the only realm where the Tumult haven't been sighted."

"We'll get there soon." I pull out some vinyl overalls and heavy boots. "These look your size." I hand them to Cissy.

She doesn't take them from me. "One more thing," says Cis. She's *really* going to town on nibbling that thumbnail.

"What is it?"

"When we break into Antrum, there will be no fighting. Not to be rude, but you are a genetically engineering battle machine. You were supposed to kill Armageddon's enemies, but you didn't. So I know you also have issues with authority. I need to be sure you won't go around murdering people."

"I won't fight. But I will protect myself if attacked."

Cissy exhales. "I can work with that. Let's go."

After a few minutes, we're both done up in our Privy Squad best. I sneak up to the shed door, open it a crack, and peep through. So far, everything seems fine. No guards, no onlookers. This should work.

I wave Cissy over. "See that dumpster across the parking lot?"

"Sure."

"There's a Pulpitum transfer platform behind it. I say the magic words, and it will take us into Antrum." I risk pushing the door open a little further. This way, I can get a better view of the entire lot. "No one's around." I look to Cissy. "Be ready to run on my signal."

"One last thing." Cissy fishes around inside the duffle and pulls out two tail cuffs. "I got these, too. The cuffs will hide our tails from the thrax. Also, they'll make our eyes look mismatched." She hands me what looks like a simple loop of metal.

I turn the tail cuff over in my palms. "This is pretty impressive."

"I had to work the blackmarket to find them, but I figured they'd be helpful."

I can't help but grin. "You know, I bet if you ever became a diplomat, you'd build up one of the best spy networks in the after-realms."

Cissy blushes. "Thanks."

"We go on the count of five."

"Okay."

"Five... Four..."

A deep voice bellows across the parking lot. "Prisoner 412 is in the supply shed!"

I've heard that particular tone before. This is Gurgly Guard, one of the Manus who tried to take me back to my cell.

"One!" I cry.

Kicking the door open, I race toward the dumpster. Alone. Looking back, I find Cissy staring at me from the doorway, a stunned look in her big blue eyes.

"Move it," I race back over, grab Cissy's wrist, and haul her toward the dumpster. As we rush across the parking lot, shadows move over the gravel.

*Wait. They have Manus guards that can fly?*

I risk a look upward.

*Yes, they sure do.*

"Faster, Cissy!" We scoot behind the dumpster.

"Is this the spot?" asks Cissy.

"Yes. Sure."

In truth, my brain is still a little fuzzy from my trip to this reality. After all, my igni couldn't protect *all* my memories.

"But you aren't certain," says Cissy.

"They're behind the dumpster!" calls Gurgly Guard. Based on the loudness of his voice, the guard is still half-way across the parking lot.

"One way to find out if this is the right place," I declare. "This is the pass phrase: *In thrax sic hunt.*" These words are all-purpose magic. I cross my fingers, hoping they'll do the trick here.

Seconds pass.

Nothing happens.

Gurgly Guard rounds the dumpster. An evil grin stretches across his squished-up face. "There you are." He raises his shock stick high. A single thought echoes through my mind.

*That's gonna hurt.*

Taking in a deep breath, I yell at the top of my lungs. "In thrax sic hunt!"

This time, it works.

A metallic disc appears beneath me and Cissy. Gurgly Guard brings down his shock stick. The weapon whistles harmlessly above our heads as the round platform hurtles into the ground.

I exhale. That was close.

*Next stop? Antrum.*

## 19

## THE BEAST

*T*he Pulpitum drops me off inside Arx Hall. As I step off the platform, every muscle in my body screams for sleep. Which I most definitely need to do.

After I finish one last task.

I speed into the infirmary. Once there, I find that Romil and his two humans have already arrived… and a royal guard is trying to kick them out. I explain the situation and the child is looked after.

With that, I can finally get some rest.

I'm half-way to the door when someone grabs my wrist. Looking down, I see an elderly quasi woman with a rattlesnake tail. Bandages loop around her arm and leg. She tightens her grip on me.

"I'm from a quasi coven, Beast."

"My name is Prince Lincoln. Remember it if you wish to stay here under my protection." As it is, this lady will get sent to our quasi palace once she's done being healed. My people loathe anyone demonic in our realm. I've grouped all the quasis in one place, just to keep them safe.

"My coven had a vision. You must stop Bedlam before he destroys the Almighty. All of creation will end."

I pat her hand. "I'll do my best."

"Good." She releases me and leans back on her cot.

That should mark the end of interruptions. It doesn't. Nat strides through the doorway.

"Glad I found you," exclaims Nat. "Let's get you some rest." He pulls on my sleeve, urging me toward the door. All the while, Nat refuses any eye contact.

Now I've known Nat all my life. This particular combination of actions means one thing.

"You're hiding something," I state.

Nat sighs. "It's like this. You have training session today with the young lords. Since you're about to sleep, you can't attend. Please let me run the session instead."

"That depends," I state. "Will Aldred be there?"

Nat lets out a long sigh. "Yes, my Prince."

I shoot him a sideways look. Aldred is the dreaded Earl of Acca and a scheming pain in my royal backside. If I do not attend today's training, then Aldred will see me as weak and launch some kind of attack. All in all, it's easier to simply attend the event and leave quickly.

"You're going to the practice, aren't you?"

I set my hand on his shoulder. "But I promise to shower and eat beforehand. How does that sound?"

Nat rolls his eyes. "You're a stubborn one, you know that?"

"Yes. Because you're the pigheaded fool who trained me that way."

We share a brief smile before I head off to my private chambers.

Time to get ready to train the young lords.

And face Aldred.

## MYLA

The Pulpitum platform comes to a halt behind Arx Hall. A great cavern now looms around me and Cissy. Rows of oversized wheelbarrows stretch off in every direction.

This is a medieval dumpster farm, thrax style.

I step off the platform. Cissy stays put. "You can't stay on that thing," I warn.

"Oh," Cissy hops off, which isn't an easy thing to do, considering how she's wearing thigh-high industrial boots. "That was my first Pulpitum ride."

For a moment, the statement throws me. My mind automatically throws up images of all the times Cissy and I have ridden to Antrum together. Then I shake my head and remember.

*This isn't my Cissy. Not really.*

Cissy steps around in a slow circle, taking in her surroundings. "Where are we?"

"Trash pick up for Arx Hall. We need to head to the training grounds."

"We do?"

"Do you want to get declared a refugee by Prince Lincoln?"

"Absolutely."

"He'll be at the training grounds right about now. Once we arrive, I'll talk to him."

Cissy's face falls slack with shock. "You?"

"Hey, who got you into Antrum?"

"Sure. You're right. I guess I'm a little nervous someone will find us."

"Not to worry. Thrax guards don't hang out by the trash."

A trio of huge guys in silver armor stomp out from behind one of the taller dumpsters. "Who are you?" calls the biggest one.

"We're on the privy squad," I declare.

I inhale deeply. A stuffy scent fills my lungs... and none of these guys are wearing their helmets. It all adds up to one fact.

"You three are smoking on duty." I point between their faces. "That's not allowed."

Turns out, you can take the queen out of Antrum, but you can't shut her up when guards are goofing around on work time.

"What's it to you?" asks the one I've decided to call Big Guy. Hey, it's been a long day. I'm low on snappy names.

"I'll find your commanding officer on the duty roster," I counter. *There, that told him.*

"You're both privy workers from the House of Stercore," says Big Guy. "A couple of nobodies. Just try to report us."

My skin prickles over in shock. Lincoln has always been huge on equality between the houses, and that was before we ever met. "You can't be serious."

"These days, no one matters but Acca," says Big Guy.

Sadly, that sounds very possible. In my reality, Lincoln and I only barely ended that evil house.

Big Guy struts over to Cissy. He has a square jaw and little beady eyes. "You're pretty."

My bestie shifts her weight from foot to foot. "Leave me alone, please."

Big Guy goes to grab Cissy's arm; I step between them. "No touchy."

"None of your business, Stercore scum." Big Guy grips my shoulder, trying to push me out of the way.

"That would be..." And here I pause for dramatic effect. "Touchy."

And just because my tail is cuffed, that doesn't mean I can't use it in battle. So while I elbow Big Guy in the throat, the end of my tail curls into a fist shape and nails him right in the nuts.

*Ouch. My tail's working some serious rage today.*

Big Guy crumples to the ground. Meanwhile, his two smaller buddies now get into the act. Both break the *no touchy* rule with yours truly. I jump high into the air, kicking in the face of one guard. Using his cheekbones for leverage, then I do an air somersault and land right on the back of the third guard. A little nerve pinch later, and he's down as well.

All three lie on the ground, immobile.

*Meh. They'll live. Plus, it serves them right. No touchy means no touchy.*

Cissy stares at the same scene. "This isn't right. You promised that—and I quote—*when we break into Antrum, there will be no fighting.*"

"True, but that wasn't a real battle. I just tripped those guards by mistake."

Cissy rolls her eyes. "Myla, you punched that guy in the nuts."

I give an eye roll right back. "My tail did the junk punch. Besides, it's the same outcome as tripping. The Big Guy is down, isn't he?"

"Big Guy?"

"I name people. It's a thing. You'll get used to it." I stare at the guards, debating whether to whisper or speak in code. Nah. They're way out of it. Whatever Cissy and I say is basically in a vault. "Let's head for the practice grounds."

Cissy shoots another nervous look at the guards, who remain passed out on the ground. Except for the junk-punch guy. He's awake, just not moving yet.

Cissy narrows her eyes. "And why are we going there again?"

"Because at this time of day, Lincoln will be training the young lords. I can catch up with him, easy peasy."

Cissy goes back to nibbling her thumbnail. "And why will he talk to you?"

*No point sugar-coating this.* "He's my husband in another reality."

For the first time, Cissy seems to accept that statement at face value. Or at the very least, she doesn't give me any speeches about being batshit crazy.

"But the prince won't know you here."

"Correct." My tail arcs over my shoulder. Even though my tail is invisible to others, I can clearly see how the arrowhead end now points right at my face. I've seen this move before. "I know, bud. Cis is acting strangely." I refocus on my friend. "I feel like we've covered most of this before. What's up? These guards won't stay down forever."

Cissy exhales. "Just give me the plan one more time."

"I'll talk to my guy and all our troubles will end." Cissy still looks skeptical, so I continue. "Lincoln is a rock. I haven't changed; he hasn't changed. Sure, there's probably some spell on his memories and—*just like you*—he won't know me right away."

"I don't know you at all, really."

"Doesn't matter. Once I explain things, Lincoln will believe me. Then together, we'll fix this mess."

"So you say." Cissy throws up her hands. "How can I be sure?"

"Here's the deal. When it comes to me, you always have a healthy dose of skepticism, but then I bulldoze you into things anyway. Come on, let's go before the guards get mobile."

And as I suspected, that speech works perfectly. Without another word, Cissy follows me as I go to find Lincoln.

Things are moving along pretty well, if I do say so myself. Because once I see my husband? Those signet rings of Eden are as good as mine.

## THE BEAST

*L*eaving the infirmary behind, I march back to the library. With all the research I do, it's been years since I visited my own chambers for anything. By the time I arrive, the servants have already set up a tub of steaming water and fresh clothes for the training session. There's even a plate of bread and cheese.

Nat sent these servants their orders, clearly. He knows I live in the library and worries that I'd dive into the books if given a free moment.

*He's not wrong.*

Even as I strip down and get into the tub, the walls of books seem to call to me. It's been years since I've had a legitimate vision about Bedlam, but back when I had them, it was always while reading a book or scroll, mostly about the rings of Eden. I'd see that round rainbow and make a useful discovery.

Perhaps if I just open one parchment...

I shake my head. Aldred is too great a foe to risk being late. And he'll definitely be at the practice today, searching for any sign of weakness.

After a quick bath and a few bites of food, I change and head off to the practice ground. Today, the training schedule calls for climbing instruction.

Soon I reach a large cavern made of white stone. All the walls are naturally notched and perfect for climbing. A set of elaborate wooden platforms create a semicircle around one stretch of wall, offering seating for those who want to watch the practice.

An image pops into my head. *Purgatory's Arena.* It, too, has tiered benches around the central battle grounds. In my mind, the image of the Arena is so detailed, it's as if I've been there a thousand times.

Trouble is, I've never set foot in Purgatory.

It's another odd illusion. Why would I see Purgatory's Arena of all places?

I shrug off the thought. I've greater things to worry about now.

Like Aldred.

As I set foot onto the practice ground, the Earl of Acca rises to his feet. As expected, he's taken a seat in the front row. Aldred is a stout man with a shock of red hair and an overhanging paunch. He points to me as I enter.

"Lincoln, my boy! We were wondering when you'd arrive."

Ignoring Aldred, I scan the tiered benches. There are representatives from most of the great thrax houses here, including Striga, Kamal, Horus and Acca. A few from my own house, Rixa, are in attendance as well. A weight settles into my heart. Too many of my fellow Rixa warriors have died trying to help me fight the Tumult.

A small group of young warriors wait by the climbing wall. All are in their early teens. On average, I'm less than a decade their senior. Still, I feel like a wizened old man beside their wide-eyed innocence.

They can't wait to fight the Tumult.

None of them would last an hour.

"What?" asks Aldred. "No greeting for me? Don't tell me you'll to hide your infamous marks from us all?"

I reach the climbing wall and strip off my Henley top. I hold up my forearm and show off my marks to the assembled crowd. Gasps sound. Silence falls over the bleachers.

For the first time, I stare at Aldred head-on. "Sit down, you bastard."

Aldred plunks down so quickly, he might have injured his tailbone. Fine with me.

Turning, I focus on the half-dozen young lords nearby. "Let's begin."

Little by little, I haul myself up the wall. At some point, I feel the heat of someone's gaze on my body. A woman. Something deep within me awakens. I pause during my climb, holding on with one hand. Angling my body, I scan the chamber, spying only the same nobility in the stands, as well as a few privy workers lurking beyond the wooden bleachers.

No one of importance is close by.

I get back to my lesson.

## MYLA

*I*'ve found Lincoln. At last.

This is my chance. Sure, Bedlam cast some kind of spell to erase my true self from history, but this is Lincoln. *My Lincoln.* I'll explain things to him. My guy may not remember me, but he will listen. And afterward? We'll fix this together. That's what we've always done before.

Across the cavern, Lincoln scales up a climbing wall. A small group of younger guys in tunics and leather pants watch him move. It's a training session, just as I thought.

After that, all rational functioning of my brain screeches to a halt.

Lincoln clutches onto the wall with his right hand. There's strain in his face and body, but voice stays calm and low as he explains climbing technique and safety. It's hard to pay attention to the specifics of his speech, though. Mostly because Lincoln is buck naked except for a pair of camouflage pants.

All of which leads to a problem.

As a quasi-demon, I've powers over the deadly sins of lust and wrath. Before Bedlam rewrote history, I also had an angelic side. All my life, I figured that Angel Me didn't do much besides give unwanted advice once in a while. Oh, and help me manipulate igni.

But now, one thing becomes clear. My angelic side is gone. I'm all quasi lust and wrath, all the time.

This is a problem.

Turns out, the Angel Me was keeping Lust Demon Me in check.

Case in point. At this moment, I should be plotting how to approach Lincoln. Instead, I can't help but notice that a single bead of sweat runs down my guy's abs… only to disappear into the waistline of his cargo pants.

Long story short, I must force myself to focus on Lincoln's face. If I keep ogling Lincoln's very yummy body, I'll end up tackling him in front of all the nobility.

Which is a thought at that.

I shake my head. *Focus, Myla.*

Lincoln appears a little paler than usual. Definitely more frowny. That isn't a big shocker. His life seriously sucked before I came along. Nothing but ceremonies and running the kingdom without getting any credit. And through it all, the prince always stays picture-perfect at every event. Never yawns or snort-laughs, that kind of thing.

Lincoln flexes his arm while doing a tummy curl to regain his footing. I might be drooling a little.

Cissy whispers. "Myla, you're staring."

"Huh?"

"We're supposed to be palace servants. Not seen or heard."

"What? Oh, right. No staring." I try to look away. Not sure it works.

"You're still doing it," hisses Cissy. "What's the plan?"

"At my signal, you run onto the central practice ground while yelling that the privy charm backfired. That means there will be a poop volcano in about thirty seconds, tops. Everyone will run.

Then I tackle Lincoln and pin his mostly-naked body to the ground."

"Myla," Cissy's voice takes on a warning tone.

"Right, right. I have powers over lust and wrath. At this point, I'm having some serious issues controlling them."

"How serious?"

"Not too bad." *It's terrible.*

Cissy stares into the central yard. "So I run out there and say that the pirate is about to explode."

"Privy."

"Right, privy." She twists her fingers together at her waistline. "I'm just so nervous."

"You'll pull it off, no problem. Just channel your anxiety into worry about a big geyser of liquid crap pouring down on everyone's heads."

Cissy narrows her eyes. "That helps a lot, actually."

"Any time. Now go and scare everyone!"

Cissy races into the courtyard, waving her arms wildly. "Everyone! The privy charm backfired!"

All the nobles gasp, turn pale and run for the exits. Lincoln stops mid climb with his right leg cranked up onto a foothold, which gives a really good view of his butt. All I need to do is go up and start talking. Some small part of me screams that I need a better plan here. In truth, I have no idea what to say, and Lincoln looks grouchy in the extreme.

But.

Glutes.

More raised voices surround me, but I ignore them. Scooping up a towel from a nearby bench, I decide my approach. I'll simply offer to dry the sweat off Lincoln's bare chest. Sure, he doesn't remember me, but that's still a perfect conversation starter. I rush over to wait at the base of the wall.

While everyone else runs away, Lincoln maintains his grip on the wall. Releasing his hold, my guy drops to land right before me. I can't help it; I smile my face off.

"Hello, Lincoln."

In reply, I get the iciest stare in the history of ever. "Fix the privy," snarls Lincoln. "Get out of my way."

"But—" I open my mouth, hoping for some brilliant comeback to appear on my lips.

For once in my life, I've got nothing.

*Who is this beast?*

# THE BEAST

# THE BEAST

*U* *nbelievable.*

A random servant from the privy squad stands before me. How is this person taking up my time? At this point, I need to sleep and review my scrolls on the Rings of Eden... in that order.

A new sensation creeps back into my soul. It's the same one I felt while climbing. This servant is the same one who was staring at me. Awakening me.

How is that possible?

I sigh. Time was, I would have looked into this issue. Who is this woman, exactly? How did she get the strength to approach me when all other servants run and hide from the Beast? And worst of all, how can her very presence effect me so deeply?

The servant opens her luscious mouth and begins to speak. "I can help you fight Bedlam. If we team up, we *will* find the three signet rings of Eden and destroy Titan of Chaos."

I pinch the bridge of my nose.

*Not again.*

At least once a week, some stranger offers supposedly critical information about ending my curse from Bedlam. Secrets about the signet rings of Eden are a particular favorite.

"I'll say this one last time," I growl. "Do. Your. Job." Turning, I take a step away and pause. "And never approach me again." I stomp off back toward the main palace. She does not follow.

Which is all for the good.

Until something bad happens.

I recall that image from inside the rainbow loop: a woman who leans her head on my shoulder. I pause. Not sure why that memory makes me question things, but I wonder if I should return and talk to that servant once more.

Yet the moment the thought hits me, I dismiss it. *Totally useless.* There's no point worrying about a random girl from the privy squad when there are far larger issues to contend with.

Such as the end of the Almighty, the never-ending threat of the Tumult, and my own evil fate.

## MYLA

*a*s the Beast marches away, my lust demon fades. As a matter of fact, I barely notice how the muscles move on my guy's back as he stalks off.

I did say *fade*, not *vanish*.

Meanwhile, my inner wrath demon awakens with a vengeance. Rage pulses through my nervous system. The conversation with Lincoln repeats in my mind.

> *Get out of my way.*
> *Do. Your. Job.*
> *Never approach me again.*

I suppose I should feel weepy and hurt. After all, the Beast looks like my husband and the way he acted was hella mean. And no doubt, that will probably happen at some point. Not now, though. In this moment, I feel nothing but white-hot fury.

Cissy skip-walks to my side. It should be a silly move, but on Cissy, it somehow works. "I scared everyone away, just like you said. It was amazing!" Cissy lowers her voice to a whisper. "How did it go with Prince Lincoln?"

"I get that he's having a hard time," I tell Cissy. "I mean, that's a scary level of pasty skin he's working there. And those red eyes? The guy hasn't slept in days. But the way he acted toward me? We *never* treats servants that way. At least, *my* version of Lincoln doesn't. And I only get saucy when the staff are being sneaky. Case in point. I caught a chambermaid stealing my underwear to sell it on the blackmarket and yeah, I lost it on her. But who wouldn't?"

"Sorry, Myla. I don't understand what you're saying."

"Just stand by for a minute and let me get this out." Without waiting for another comment from Cissy, I continue. "And now, my whole plan is off schedule." I count off the steps to said scheme on my fingertips. "One, team up with Lincoln. Two, get the signet rings of Eden. Three, kill Bedlam. I'm stuck on step one! The guy is an asshat, and that's why I'm calling him the Beast."

"Wait, you're doing *what* to Bedlam? I thought we moved past that." Cissy rests her hands onto her neck. It's her *holy Hell, this isn't happening* pose.

"I'm destroying him. We talked about this." I wave my hand dismissively. "Trust me, the Titan of Chaos has been on my to-kill list for a while now." I let out a long breath along with a *hoo* noise. "Okay, I'm better now."

Cissy scrunches up her mouth onto one side of her face. "Should I just ignore… whatever you just said?"

"Probably." I tap my cheek and contemplate my next move. Where can I next ambush the Beast? Thrax royal life is one long list of mandatory boringness. Without me around to shut Octavia down, there's probably a ball every evening. "Ah, I've got it." I refocus on Cissy. "What day is it?"

"April 23rd."

"Perfect. Octavia will be holding her annual Festival of Reflections tonight."

"Is that a formal ball?"

"With Octavia, it's always a formal ball." I tap my cheek at a quicker pace. *Octavia.* She'll be in Arx Hall right now. It might be worthwhile to chat her up. Since the Beast is an unreasonable grouchasaurus, his mother may be much easier to convince. I flash Cissy my best smile. "Want to meet Queen Octavia?"

"She's not receiving visitors. King Connor is sick; Queen Octavia is nursing him. They're locked into their chambers."

"What's wrong with Connor?" Lincoln's father isn't my favorite person in the world, but I hate to think of him as ill or hurting.

"Rumor is, the Earl of Acca is poisoning him."

This changes things. Octavia is the most reasonable person in the after-realms, except when it comes to Connor. Right now, she's probably a wreck. Having a random quasi show up and claim to be her daughter-in-law won't help much.

What Octavia needs is for Connor to recover. And that leads me back to where I started, namely that the best way to aid everyone is to kill Bedlam.

"Change of plans," I announce. "We're off to the royal gown warehouse."

Cissy gives me the side-eye. "And you can get us there dressed like this?"

"Just watch me."

We step around to a dusty access hallway. The place is all grimy rock and dangling cobwebs. Once we're well out of sight, I run my hands along the rough stone wall. Eventually, I find what I'm looking for.

*Helloooooo, loose rock.*

I press against the spot; a hidden door swings open.

Cissy eyes widen more than ever before. I'm starting to worry she'll go permanently goggle-eyed. "That's a secret passageway."

"Yup, they're woven all through Arx Hall. My Lincoln taught me where to find most of them." I step into the darkened passage. Cissy follows. Once we're inside, the stone door auto-*magically* swings shut behind us. On reflex, I pat the base of my spine, which is where I holster my baculum. I can ignite them into a torch, no problem.

Trouble is, there's nothing there.

Which makes sense. I never met my Lincoln in this reality, so he never could have given me his own baculum. And even if I still had them for some reason, I'm not Xavier's daughter anymore. You need archangel blood to wield baculum.

*Nope.* In this world, I'm some kind of lab rat. Literally.

"It's really dark in here," whispers Cissy.

"Stay close. I can still find our way to the warehouse. It'll just take longer without a torch."

About an hour and three attempted exits later, I finally find the secret door to the royal wardrobe warehouse. This place stores dresses, tunics and warrior gear for every house in Antrum.

And it's a total shit show.

Normally, lines of tall metal racks line the floor. The gleaming walls are painted with the crest of each house. The racks are then carefully placed before their correct image. Finding what you need is easy peasy.

Or it used to be.

Now the perfect walls are eyesores that mix splintered wood, chipped paint and alarming splotches of mold. The racks are all over the place. Many have toppled over, leaving the formal gowns to rot in puddles of icky-smelling goop.

And of the racks that remain upright? Few of the garments are mended and ready to wear. Those that are intact are in either super-small or crazy-large sizes.

The only positive point about no one maintaining things is that Cissy and I are alone here. There are no awkward stories to tell about why we're dressed up as privy workers.

Cissy and I get right to work. I soon find a super-skinny gown for the House of Acca which fits Cissy perfectly (she doesn't have the mega boob-n-butt issues like me). Also, with Cissy's blonde hair, she'll fit in well with Acca.

It's trickier finding something suitable for me. Eventually, we uncover a simple red gown that will work. Back in my Antrum, red symbolized that someone is unmarried and not affiliated with a house. The shade is reserved for when we bring in an outsider who needs an introduction to court. This particular shade is a little different, but I'm sure it means the same thing.

A small voice in the back of my head says that there can be a darker meaning to a red dress. I get flashes of another ball and underwear with the word CUNNUS written across my butt cheeks. The memory is incomplete, though. No matter how hard I try to access more of that evening, I come up blank.

*Oh, well.* My igni did a great job salvaging the recollections I have. No need to get greedy.

Cissy and I get gussied up as best we can. Then comes the big decision. What do I do with my dragonscale fighting suit? It doesn't really fit under the gown. This sucks up an hour at least. I'm starting to get desperate.

I wrap the thing about my neck. "Do you think I can wear it as a scarf?"

"No. It smells, it's full of holes, and it's clearly battle gear."

"I can't leave it here. I'll need to wear it again soon."

"Myla, can I be honest with you?"

"Sure."

"Your butt cheeks totally hang out of that thing."

I gasp so hard, I almost pop a lung. "No way." I pull the suit from my neck and check it over carefully.

Cissy is right. My butt cheeks were totally hanging out this whole time. "Why didn't you tell me?"

"I just did."

As much as I love my dragonscale fighting suit, I am not running around with an uncovered ass. So I hide the thing in the safest spot I can find, reminding myself that once Bedlam is dead, my suit will be auto-*magically* repaired. Plus, I can come back here later when I find some repair stuff. There are amazing things you an do with duct tape.

I'll fix that fighting suit yet.

With that decided, Cissy and I are ready. I lead us through more hidden tunnels, this time into Acca territory. Along the way, I give Cissy a rundown on how to act in order to make nice with the House of Acca. I encourage Cis to find Lady Avery. She's sweet and has a ton of ladies in waiting. In terms of warnings, I suggest Cissy steer clear of Aldred, the Earl of Acca, as well as his oldest daughter Adair, who is—in my opinion— the megalodon of mean girls.

I might go on too long about Adair but what can I say? Adair and I have history. For Cissy's part, I'm pretty sure she tunes me out when I launch into my lengthy list of anti-Adair trivia. Normally, my bestie is a chatterbox. But while I go on about Adair, all Cissy does is make 'uh' or 'oh' noises every so often.

Once Cissy is safely off in Acca, I turn my attention toward tonight's ball.

I've had all day to plan my next speech to the prince. Tonight, I'll get past step one and secure the Beast's help.

Definitely-maybe.

## 25

# THE BEAST

*H*eavy knocks sound at the library door. Staying slumped in my chair, I keep examining the page I've scanned a hundred times in the last hour alone. Nothing seems to stick.

The heavy knocks continue. A familiar voice follows.

"Lincoln, it's Nat."

"I'm busy."

"You're due at the Festival of Reflections in ten minutes."

"Will Aldred be there?"

"Would I bother you if otherwise?"

Hauling myself up, I cross the library and open the door. Nat eyes me carefully from the hallway beyond.

"Did you sleep?" he asks.

"I tried." *Which is true.* I kept picturing that privy worker, though, and couldn't get any rest. "Earlier today, you weren't too keen on disturbing my possible rest. What's changed?"

"Queen Octavia sent me a message. Aldred will be there tonight; she wants you to attend as well."

"Anything else?"

Years ago, I agreed to a compulsion spell where I cannot

approach my parents on any subject, yet they can reach out to me. At the time, it seemed a kind gesture to ensure Octavia had quiet time with an ailing Connor. It never occurred to me that I would no longer be able to confront Mother for meddling in my life.

Nat rubs his grizzled chin. "Meaning?"

"Do you think Mother is scheming something extra for this evening?"

"Octavia? Always."

"Right."

Not that I mind Octavia letting me know about Aldred and tonight's ball. It's more all the other things she's done over the years. Everything is planned in the spirit of supposedly ending my curse. Sadly, it's all awkward with a capital A.

In any case, it doesn't change what happens next.

"I'll be there as quickly as possible," I tell Nat.

And I close the door.

## 26

## MYLA

*T*hrax are all about their rituals. They have super-specific ways to walk, dance, greet royalty, eat cheese, you name it. As their queen, I've learned to tune most of it out. Every once in a while, their obsession with doing things *the exact same way* works out in my favor.

Like now, for instance.

The Festival of Reflections is always held in the Versailles Ballroom. I enter the chamber through a mirrored panel that opens behind a row of heavy square columns. No one notices me as I sneak in. *Yes!*

I step around the periphery of the room. An intricate pattern of mirrors covers the walls; each one is encased by a different gilded frame. Normally, everything is gleaming and bright.

Not so any more.

These mirrors are so grimy, they only reflect vague shapes. Long cobwebs dangle from the dingy frames. That settles it. Octavia is totally locked into her rooms with Connor. She'd lose her mind if she saw this room.

Along with me, about a hundred thrax nobles circulate the floor. I recognize the colors and insignias of the various houses.

A handful of men and women wear my same shade of red. It's a good sign. I blend.

A tall man steps into my path. It's Lucas, the Earl of Striga. He's a towering figure with olive-colored skin and long gray dreads. He pauses, trying not to step on my foot. The quick stop makes his long purple robes sway.

Lucas is the most powerful wizard in Antrum and—in my reality, anyway—he's also a great friend. I can't count the number of times Lucas has cast a spell to help my Lincoln and I save the after-realms. I've come to rely on his wise, lopsided smile as he states, *I can cast a spell for that.*

And now? Lucas stares at me as if I'm transparent. He pauses all of one second, steps to the side, and keeps on marching right for the dessert table. Normally, he and I hang out by the chocolate section at events like these. It's strange for him not to know me at all.

As I watch Lucas move away, a chill crawls up my arms. A single thought ricochets through my soul:

*I'm open and exposed in a place where no one knows me.*

The realization weighs in my bones, heavy as lead. In this reality, my parents are gone. Connor and Octavia are out of it. Walker is some kind of an Oligarchy-loving douchebag. Cissy is sweet, but she's not exactly a warrior. So in terms of additional help in the *killing stuff category*, it really is the Beast Show.

Across the room, the herald steps into the archway that marks the main entrance. Strange. He's not a face I've ever seen before, and I've gone to a ton of these events in my reality. *Oh, well.* Maybe there have been changes over at the Herald's Guild. Wouldn't be the biggest difference around here.

The herald in question looks in my direction and does a double take.

*That's right, guy. You didn't announce me.* It takes everything in me not to rub my palms together and call out, *heh heh heh.*

Eventually, the herald shakes his head and lifts up his trumpet once more. After playing a quick tune, the herald lowers his instrument. "Announcing our future king, Prince Lincoln!"

That gets my attention. The Beast strides under the archway and into the room. Once again, I'm struck by the pallid color of his skin. The Beast could use some sunshine. His eyes look sunken and red. Although he wears the traditional royal outfit—tunic, chain mail and leather pants—a lion's pelt hangs over his shoulders. He prowls around the room, barely looking into anyone's face.

It's way odd.

Normally, the nobles all clamor to greet my Lincoln and ask for something. Here the crowd parts for the Beast as if he'll spontaneously explode. He truly does look like something wild and hungry. It makes my heart crack with sorrow.

What are the five stages of grief? I'm pretty sure it goes anger, denial, and... something, something and something. Seeing the Beast this tormented, I quickly move on from the angry phase I felt earlier today. Maybe I'm hitting denial, but perhaps all this guy needs is for someone to be half-way nice to him.

The more I think about it, the further I convince myself. No doubt about it. There's just a misunderstanding between me and the Beast. Earlier today, he could have been sick to his stomach or something. The way this palace is so filthy, food poisoning must be rampant.

No matter what happens, I'm not giving up.

Within reason.

In all honesty, at some point I may have to move on with my Kill Bedlam Plan, even if I have to do it solo.

Even so, that's probably not enough. *Truth time.* I underestimated Bedlam. I'd have taped my mouth shut if I knew he'd twist my words and cause this kind of disaster. I need serious help from someone who knows how to work real missions. Bottom line? It's best if I convince the Beast to join the Myla Plan.

Fortunately, the perfect idea appears.

## THE BEAST

*I* stride to my regular spot for these events. In other words, I lurk in the farthest corner of the ballroom. The mirrors here are especially grimy, so I don't have to check out my own reflection.

Then I notice her.

The privy servant.

My heart sinks. She wears the colors for the newly-founded House of Amour. These are companions in the geisha tradition, and their goal is to provide emotional support in these terrible times. Even so, some Amours certainly cross the line from friend to lover.

If she approaches me, this will mark the twenty-second Amour who's come my way.

All of them have been sent by Mother.

If I had time for therapy, this situation would take years to untangle.

It's all because Octavia is convinced that when I fall in love with my Beauty, that will end my cursed life as the Beast. So Mother sends an endless stream of Amours my way. No wonder I could sense this woman staring at me while I climbed.

I tilt my head as I examine this newest Amour more closely. Her jerky movements have a purpose. It's as if she's protecting something from slamming into table legs or unsuspecting guests. What is she concealing, exactly? My eyes widen as I realize the truth.

A tail.

Whoever this woman is, she's actually a quasi demon. Which makes sense. Quasi Amours must stay in the safely of their palace with the rest of Purgatory's natives. By pretending to be thrax, this Amour will have more access to my person.

This situation has Octavia written all over it.

Aldred, the Earl of Acca, lurches over toward the Amour. "Hey girlie." As he speaks, Aldred shoots spittle across the floor. The man is beyond drunk. "You're a pretty one. Come give us a kiss."

A jolt of protective anger runs down my spine. How dare the earl approach anyone in this manner? I may be surly, but that's very different from assault.

The Amour doesn't seem to do anything, but her tail clearly gets active. For a moment, Aldred's torso turns concave as an *invisible something* wallops him in the stomach.

I must admit, it's a rather beautiful sight. Aldred needs to be gut-punched more often.

"Guards! Help!" cries Aldred. "I was attacked!"

I step forward. "I'll take care of it."

If I allowed the guards to jail everyone that Aldred accused of attacking him, our dungeons would be overflowing. Turning, I focus on the Amour. "Excuse me."

"I was hoping we could talk again." The Amour lowers her voice. "I'm here about Bedlam. I can help you destroy him."

I eye her carefully. "I remember you from the practice ground. I found your words hard to believe then. They're even less likely now."

"It's the dress, isn't it?"

"Possibly." *And how you're scheming with Mother.*

"I couldn't decide between two opening lines. Let me try my other one."

I resist the urge to smile. "Go on."

"I'm your secret wife from another reality."

It's an effort not to burst out laughing, which is a strange sensation to me. I'm more accustomed to growling my way through the day. "You were doing better with Bedlam."

"Okay, I can work with that."

I gesture toward the exit. "You need to leave. I can hold off the guards, but Aldred is rather peevish when drunk and bruised."

The Amour snaps her fingers. "I have it. This is the best line of all." After looking from side to side, she holds up two fingers. "Give me two minutes and I'll rock your world with Bedlam intel."

"I'm interested."

And when I say *I'm interested*, my real concern here isn't Bedlam. This Amour is more persistent than the others. My true interest lies in getting her out of my life.

"Good." The Amour winks. "Take me to the Versailles storage room. We can chat there."

"Take you?"

"Yes, you lead me away and I'll put up a fuss and all that."

"And why would you do such a thing?"

She looks at me like I'm unhinged. "Because it'll be fun. Thrax still don't have television, right?"

"No."

"Then we'll give the nobility something to talk about for weeks."

I scan the room. All eyes are locked on me and the Amour. Everyone has the look of an audience at a polo match. They're waiting to see *who wallops what* next. Perhaps they really are enjoying this display. It had never occurred to me before, but this could actually be a bit of fun for all involved.

"Fine." I move to touch her, but it's hard to pick. Waist... arms... something else? I end up shifting my hands about without making actual contact with her person.

The Amour leans in. "When is the last time you actually touched a girl?"

"None of your business."

"So, a long time." She grabs my wrist and sets my palm on her shoulder. "Good?"

It's beyond good. Heat moves through my veins.

"Move." I shove her toward the exit.

"Perfect," she whispers. And then, in a louder voice, she calls out. "Oh, my! You are such a mean, mean, meanie!"

All the thrax nobility were already staring. Now they add a synchronized gasp into the mix.

"Mean meanie?" I ask. "Is that even a phrase? I would've thought you could do better."

"You asked for it, buddy," whispers the Amour. Next she shouts at an eardrum-slitting volume. "YOU ARE A HUGE DICK!"

Now *that* was unexpected.

Yet somehow, not unwelcome.

MYLA

## MYLA

 *wah hah fucking hah hah.*
The words still seem to echo around the room

*YOU ARE A HUGE DICK!*

Chalk one up for Team Myla.

The room turns perfectly silent. It's like bands of electric interest zing everywhere. *SUH-weet.* They'll be talking about this for months. The royal minstrel might even write a song about me.

Lincoln pauses while gripping my shoulder. "That's rather personal."

The comment stumps me for bit before I realize the truth. My Lincoln was never up on human slang. Maybe this Beast version is even farther behind.

He thinks I'm talking about his actual junk.

"Look," I whisper. "That's just a saying on Earth. It means you're an ass, not that you have a huge dick. Which you actually do, obviously."

The moment those words leave my mouth, I wish I could take them back.

All the while, every set of thrax eyes are locked on me and the Beast. I'm pretty sure they heard my last dick comment.

In this moment, I should stay silent. Or better yet, I could just march out of the room. But that doesn't happen. For some reason, I just keep talking. "It's more that you act like a dick… not that you don't have a massive…"

*Stop talking, Myla.*

And in act of kindness from the universe, I'm able to keep my big mouth shut. At last.

## THE BEAST

*A*nother round of gasps echo about the room. Someone from the House of Acca faints. Even Aldred forgets to whine for five whole seconds in a row.

It's a glorious thing.

I suck in a shocked breath. *Am I actually... enjoying this?*

How very odd, not to mention dangerous. I simply cannot be distracted by such nonsense. Too many lives are in the line, including mine.

Without meaning to, I press the Amour toward the exit archway with more force.

*Why did I think this was a good idea again?*

Oh, right. I need to send this Amour back to Octavia with a message: stop meddling in my love life. Plus, the woman did say that if I have her two minutes, she would rock my world with Bedlam intel.

At this point, I've nothing to lose.

## MYLA

*L*incoln and I sneak into a large room that's crammed with dusty furniture. My thoughts keep circling back to what happened back in the ballroom.

There are some things in life that don't change no matter what reality you happen to visit. For instance, Aldred, the Earl of Acca, is an asshat. And watching him stop mid-whine? Priceless.

"Did you see Aldred?" I lift my hand, ready for a high five. The Beast does nothing but glower at me. "Don't leave me hanging."

Let the record show that the Beast *totally* leaves me hanging… and scowls while doing it.

I roll my eyes. "Or not." Crossing the room, I hoist myself to sit on a nearby table. It's the least dusty sitting option in the room.

"That's an expensive piece of furniture."

"It's a fake. Lord Ashton broke the real one years ago."

The Beast gets even more frowny, if that's possible. "How do you know that?"

"I already told you, but you got all freaky-deaky." *Translation: I explained how I'm your wife in another reality. It didn't land well.*

"I get it." The Beast nods slowly. "Mother told you about the table."

"What? No! I actually saw it with my own two eyes. Three years ago at a birthday party for the Lord Ashton of Horus. The guy drank too much mead and tried to stage dive. He landed on the table instead. The thing was trashed."

"Wrong. Octavia told you this story in order to convince me that we're soul mates."

"What? No."

"But you *do* know Octavia, don't you?"

I worry my lower lip with my teeth. Here comes a big decision. Of course, I know Octavia in another reality. Which leaves me with two choices. Option number one is to lie my ass off. But that's a crap idea, mostly because I'm a horrible liar. Also, the real Lincoln can always tell a fib from a mile away, so this Beast version probably has the same skill. Which leads me to option number two.

*The truth.*

"Yes, I know Octavia."

"And she fed you what to say about Bedlam."

"No, I really know about him."

"All right." But the way the Beast says those two words, it's obvious that everything's all wrong. "Let's clear things up once and for all."

"Clearing up. Great. Awesome."

My mind races. There's so much to explain here and I don't know where to begin. I could talk about Maxon. Or I might explain how we first encountered the Titan of Chaos. I nod once to myself, the decision made. The original Bedlam story is definitely the way to go.

"It's like this," I begin. "In this other reality, you and I are married and have a son. When we're lucky, the two of us get to kill demons together. Our last mission was to the Sahara where—"

"Enough," snaps the Beast. "I don't need a Lady of Enchantment."

"Lady of en-whattie? Is that someone from the House of Striga?"

"No, I mean a woman who shares companionship. An Amour. Or in the case of someone sent by my mother, a woman who exchanges sexual favors for money. You're the twenty-second one she's tried to send my way. None have been successful. This really needs to stop."

"A whore?"

"I said Lady of Enchantment."

"You're calling me a whore." My world tilts on its axis. Fresh waves of rage spike through my nervous system. Hopping down from the tabletop, I wag my finger in his face. "Screw you, and not in the fun way. I can find the rings of Eden on my own."

"Don't play games," growls the Beast. "You already admitted knowing Mother. Now go tell Octavia to stay out of my business."

"Talk to your Mother on your own time."

"You know that's not possible. Octavia made me take a magical vow to leave her and Father alone while he's ill. In truth, the spell only allows Mother to meddle in my life without fear of repercussion. Which brings me back to my first point. Tell Octavia to end this. Now."

"And I'm back to *my* original reply. Figure out how to tell her on your own, douchebag."

The Beast's voice gets deadly low. "What did you call me?"

"Doesn't feel so nice, now does it? Or should I say, Gentleman of the Douche? Using fancy language doesn't really change the main idea, now does it?"

"You're impossible."

Aaaaaaaand somehow we ended up with the Beast's hand on my wrist and our bodies a few inches apart.

It's not easy, but I force my arm and eventually my whole body away from his.

"It's like this," I state. "I'm from another reality where we're married and have a kid. I need you to fall back in love with me so we can return things to normal. Then, in that other dimension where everything is so much better, we can both kill Bedlam. But the trouble is, you're an ass in this reality, and it looks like you won't be any use to me. So right now, I'll have to do all this myself. And *that* is the truth."

"If you wish for me to trust you—let alone have warm feelings for you—then that *douchebag* comment didn't help."

"Neither did calling me a whore."

I realize we've been inching closer again. Now the Beast and I stand a breath apart. His mouth hovers right above mine. I remember how it feels and tastes to kiss him. And even though the Beast is a roaring shit heel, it would feel good to kiss someone that's like my husband.

Sighing, I step back. "You're not my Lincoln, though."

The Beast tilts his head. "Is this some kind of game?"

I shrug. "I don't play games. Not that you'd know that. I'll have to figure out another way to destroy Bedlam."

"So if I fall in love with you, Bedlam will die?"

"We're a team. In my world, we face crap like this all the time. But if we're stuck here fighting and almost-kissing every two seconds, then we'll never take down Bedlam. That was my plan. Get you back. Then destroy Bedlam."

"Get me back?" The Beast shakes his head. "If only things were that easy. My heart burned out a long time ago."

Without saying another word, the Beast stalks back toward the Versailles Ballroom.

I watch him go, my mind a blank of shock. This guy is a bitter and angry ass. What could have happened to my Lincoln to make him change?

After moping around for a few minutes, I straighten my spine and steel my resolve. Whatever happened to the Beast, hiding inside a deserted storage room won't get me closer to having my old life back.

Maybe I will have to go this alone. But I was never someone who gives up easily.

So I follow the Beast and resolve to give it one final try.

## THE BEAST

*A*h, Mother.

Octavia means well, but as Father grows sicker, she becomes more radical. I should never have agreed to that compulsion spell to leave her alone while she's nursing Connor. It's meant nothing but one failed Amour after another.

Until this most recent encounter.

Much as I hate to admit it, some part of me wishes to return to the supply room. The idea of falling in love is ridiculous. But I could go off and kill Bedlam with an untrained Amour at my side.

Or not. The Tumult kill trained warriors with easy. An Amour won't last a full minute. I'd be signing her death warrant.

Picking up my pace, I enter the Versailles Ballroom. In one of the mirrors, I catch my reflection. What strikes me is my deep frown, hunched shoulders, and hefty Lion's pelt. The chamber falls silent. Clearly, they're waiting for the next volley in my game with the Amour.

Was it only a minute ago that I almost laughed at how my nobles reacted to this adventure? If the Amour were at my side, we might even share a sly grin about it all. And for some reason, that fact enrages me.

"Enough!" I bellow.

A moment later, everyone goes back to talking, drinking and eating. Or at least, they pretend to. I skulk around the periphery, counting down the minutes before I can depart while retaining the illusion of strength.

If nothing else, Aldred won't have the satisfaction of seeing me flee my own royal ball.

## MYLA

*B*ecause I'm a sneaky little bitch, I slip into the ballroom using yet another hidden passageway. Once more, no one notices me. All eyes seem glued on the entrance, waiting for someone else to arrive.

Some nights, you just get lucky.

As I walk around the outskirts of the crowd, my thoughts circle back to the big question. How do I convince the Beast to help me… and himself?

Looking back, it was naive to think I could simply talk to the Beast and get his agreement. Just look at the guy. Obviously, he doesn't play well with others.

I recall the five stages of grief. I'm pretty sure that one of them involved bargaining.

*That's what I need to do—make a trade.*

The Beast must want something. Clearly, it's not female company. But I know where other goodies are hidden. After all, Lucifer left a ton of supernatural crap across the after-realms. There are magical gauntlets and a coin-portal, and that's just off the top of my head.

The herald plays another tune on his trumpet. "Announcing Sir Gastonne, Counsellor to the House of Acca."

A man steps into the chamber. He's a bolshy guy in a tunic and leather pants. A loop of black hair hangs down his forehead.

Alarm rattles down my spine. I've seen this man before. Bedlam has many forms, three of which he showed back in his lair. First, there's the diseased Mister Potato Head look. Second, who can forget the snake dude? And third, we have the overly ripped no-neck guy... And he just entered the ballroom.

*Hells bells.*

Plus, it's irony overload here. This third version of Bedlam is running around Antrum under the name of Gastonne! If it were me, I'd have gone for something like Wagette or Rah, but I'm edgy that way.

To make matters worse, this fakey-fake Gastonne has hooked himself up with my personal pack-o-nemeses, the House of Acca.

It's a major turn of events, and all the scheming functions in my brain have stalled. What to do about Bedlam being here? I got nothing.

For his part, the so-called Gastonne looks at me and winks.

*What a turd.*

The herald plays another tune before raising his voice once more. "Accompanying Sir Gastonne is Lady Cissy Frederickson, his Personal Retainer. "

My best friend sashays through the entrance archway, looking all things sunny in her yellow gown. She spies me, smiles and waves.

For his part, Gastonne wears what can only be called a shit-eating grin. Total predator. I may not know how to deal with this Gastonne in general, but I know what to do about his Personal Retainer in particular. I simply must warn Cissy about this guy.

I scan the room, looking for the best route to approach Cis. Along the way, my gaze lands on the Beast. His grumpy self leans against a nearby stretch of wall. Alone.

*Oh, well. I'll deal with him later.*

Turns out, there's no need to seek out Cissy. She and Gastonne head right in my direction. Nice.

The herald plays yet another tune. "Hear ye! Hear ye! Announcing the most important arrival of the evening!"

His next words shatter my world.

"Let us all bow low to the most worshipful Princess Adair, beloved wife of Prince Lincoln, and Future Queen of Antrum!"

If seeing Bedlam as Gastonne surprised me, that's nothing compared to the all-out shock that slams into me right now.

Wife?

Beloved?

What the ever loving HELL?

Adair tiptoes across the chamber to pause at the Beast's side. "Sorry I'm late, my lovey dovey love," she coos.

I can't believe what I'm hearing. *Lovey dovey love?*

The idea of the two of them married is still short-circuiting my brain when something worse happens. Adair goes up on tiptoe and kisses the Beast.

On the mouth.

With tongue.

My inner wrath and lust demons go berserk. Both see no difference between the Beast and Lincoln. The anger side believes that the Beast is ours, damn it, and no one else is allowed to touch him without experiencing serious pain. Meanwhile, my lust demon wants to knock Adair off the Beast and show everyone what a real kiss looks like. Both want to attack.

It's my inner wrath demon who wins out.

I race across the ballroom floor. Jumping high, I land with my knees squarely on Adair's torso. Gravity does the rest of the work as I tackle the princess. No sooner has the Adair's back hit the floor than some guards try grabbing me from behind. My tail goes to work, punching and jabbing. Somewhere along the line, I end up with a chunk of blonde extensions in my hand. Then my tail cuff, which has been hiding my quasi identity, gets shattered in the fight. The thing falls in two neat halves on the floor.

"Look at the tail!" cries one noble.

"She's a demon girl!" screams anther.

A good amount of the party races for the exits. That's fine with me. Now I've only got six guards to deal with.

But as Adair writhes under me, I realize that I really need to rethink my approach here. I can't fight off every guard in Antrum and, no doubt, that's who's on the way. Instead, I should wait for a situation like I had in the Arena tunnels, namely a few guards and an easy exit.

So I allow myself to get hauled off my ultra-nemesis. As a side bonus, being restrained gives me the perfect angle to watch Adair freak out.

The princess is all pinched features and haughty air as she wags her finger in my face. "You're going to the dungeons."

"That's extreme," I state.

In my reality, we never send people to the dungeons. And there are no secret passages out of those cells for obvious reasons. It won't *stop* my escape, mind you. That said, it will slow things down. And I'm not a patient quasi, even under the best of circumstances.

I look to the Beast. "You don't really want do that."

"Go rot," he growls.

*Thanks for nothing, not-a-husband.*

I glance over my shoulder at the closest guard. "What do you think?"

Unfortunately, the guard behind me is none other than Big Guy, AKA the man who got junk-punched by my tail earlier today.

Big Guy grins.

Fine.

I am so going to the dungeons.

# THE BEAST

*W*hile Adair keeps shrieking something about *lost hair extensions*, I watch the woman in red leave the ballroom. A pang of longing and regret moves through my soul.

If this Amour stays in the dungeons under Adair's tender mercy, who knows what will happen?

But how can I risk getting involved with anything other than destroying Bedlam?

*In the end, there is only one choice here.*

Without acknowledging Adair, I leave the ballroom and head back to my library.

The sooner I kill the Titan of Chaos, the better for us all.

## MYLA

So these dungeons are really nasty. The place is all rough stone walls, drippy ceilings, strange smells and old bones in the corners. The only bright spot is that I'm the sole prisoner on this floor, so long as you don't count the growing rat population. It's good to have some quiet.

Hours pass as I rest on a small cot and stare at the condensation on the ceiling. An image pops into my mind. It's the highway billboard back in my version of Purgatory.

*Beware the Angelic Conspiracy*

*Verus, the Oracle Angel, tricked our own Great Scala into a false love. Quasis never care for thrax demon killers! That's not marriage, it's angelic manipulation!*

Bedlam also talked about manipulation. I hate it when this happens. Someone says an off-hand insult and it sticks in your brain like a splinter.

Is everyone else right? Was Verus manipulating me and Lincoln into thinking we'd found our true love?

I've never seriously questioned this stuff before, but I can't deny how crappy things have gone with the Beast. Although, it's not really my husband.

But he's close enough.

This sucks.

A heavy tread of footsteps sounds in the stone passage outside my cell. An unwelcome figure stands before the tall iron bars that mark one wall of my new little world.

"Hello."

I lift my head an inch to check out my new guest. Yup, that's the neckless beefcake show, right there.

"Buzz off, Bedlam."

"How interesting. By calling me Bedlam, it proves that you can remember your past reality. How much do you recall?"

Now, Queenly Me might not blab here. But my regal self is not in the house right now. I am officially unsettled and *in a mood.*

"You twisted what I said at a fountain to change my world. I remember *that* perfectly."

"I am chaos. There's no keeping me away, really. Sooner or later, you'd say something that would allow me in."

"Was I done? Did I say I was done?"

"No."

"So shut the Hell up. After you erased my life, then you cursed Lincoln and turned him into a Beast."

Gastonne waits patiently. As a matter of fact, his stare is more than a little unnerving. I forget the rest of what would surely have been a kick-ass speech.

"Fine," I announce. "I'm done now."

"Have you thought more about my offer?"

"Oh, you mean the one where I willingly give you my hand in marriage as well as my igni so you can destroy the Almighty and end all creation?" I pause for dramatic effect. "Answer's still no."

"You misunderstand. I'm not ending creation; I'm empowering myself to repair it. I shall cover the Earth in a nation of Tumult that I rule." He gestures toward me. "Along with you, obviously."

"Sounds awful. If I refused you again, would you believe it?"

"No."

I lace my fingers behind my head in a move that hopefully says, *I'm in prison and don't care.* "So what are you doing here?"

"Waiting for you. Everyone has a breaking point. It will be interesting to find yours. Might be when your Beast is encased alive in glass as my ushebti." Even though he's talking about a nasty subject, Gastonne flashes me one of those grins where his teeth actually twinkle. "Or perhaps Cissy will snap your resolve?"

I raise my hand. "Hate you."

"Considering how the opposite of love is actually indifference, I consider that progress. Haven't you enjoyed the nice treats I set up for you? You're one of the few who can see and kill my lovely Tumult. Isn't it a fine gift?"

I lift my hand higher. "Still hate you. And it's not progress."

"Just say the words—*I wish to marry Bedlam*—and you can easily regain to your old life. As my wife, I'll even allow you to keep Lincoln and Maxon close. It's only a matter of time. No one refuses me, Little Scala."

I tap my chest. "This is me, refusing you. Now buzz off."

At last, Gastonne slinks away.

I really need to kill that asshat.

## THE BEAST

*F*or hours, I've been staring at the same page in my book. I've read it a hundred times, yet not processed a single word.

This is becoming a habit.

Once again, I keep thinking about that Amour. Every word of our conversation runs through my mind on repeat. Suddenly, a forgotten phrase captures my attention.

*In this other reality, you and I are married and have a son.*

The book drops from my hands as shock moves through my limbs. I've never told anyone that my illusions exist, let alone that they feature a four-year-old boy.

That settles it.

I must speak to her one more time.

## MYLA

Soon after Gastonne leaves, I get another visitor.

*The Beast.*

The prince grips the bars of my cell so firmly, his knuckles turn white. "I'm here to talk."

I've had way too much time to marinade in my insecurities. At this point, nothing good can come out of a discussion with the Beast. I roll over on to my side where I face a beautiful view of the slimy rock wall.

"I'm not in the mood," I declare. "I'm adjusting."

"To what? The fact that I married Adair?"

I sit upright and glare at the Beast for all I'm worth. "You say things like that, and it makes me want to throw up on your face."

"Why?"

"Seriously? I'm from an alternate reality where I know that girl." I shiver. "She's the worst." Reaching over, I grab a ratty comforter from the dungeon floor. Only it's not a blanket, it's an old jacket with a skeleton arm in it. So I toss it back down again and return to glaring at the Beast.

"You're still here," I state.

"What's the name of our son?"

"What?"

"In this reality where you say you're from... in it, what's the name of our child?" The way he asks the question, it's almost tender.

"Maxon. His name's Maxon."

The Beast lets out a shuddering breath. "And what are you called?"

"Here? Prisoner 412."

"And back in your home realm?"

"Myla."

Lincoln turns away. I can't see his face anymore, but when he speaks, there's no mistaking the emotion in his voice. The guy is overwhelmed.

"Years ago, I would receive visions," says the Beast. "They always led me a step closer to defeating Bedlam. Since then I've had what I call illusions. Useless tricks of the senses. Sometimes in those mind games, I'd hear the names Myla and Maxon."

That has me interested. Rising, I step closer to the wall-o-bars. "And?"

"Maybe you *are* meant to help me defeat Bedlam."

"I know I am."

The Beast pulls out his baculum from their holster at the base of his spine. Even when dressed formally, no thrax warrior goes anywhere without a weapon. The Beast ignites the baculum as a dagger. He sets the dagger at his elbow. Then with one swift movement, the Beast cuts open his tunic and mail to his wrist.

"I've something to show you," says the Beast in a rough voice.

I grin. *Ah, progress.*

## THE BEAST

*I*f Myla is surprised that I just cut up my wardrobe, she doesn't show it. For me, I've been doing this for years. The fastest way to reveal my marks is with a quick slice.

I angle my forearm to show off the marking. "Do you see this?"

She nods. "A rose tattoo."

"It's the sign of my curse. Roses, just as in the story of Beauty and the Beast. When this spell began, the roses wound up my arm and across my chest. As each petal fell, I received a vision of where the Tumult would next attack humans on Earth. And I would go to fight." I pause, waiting for the inevitable question.

Myla doesn't say a word.

I tilt my head, confused. "Aren't you going to ask me why I always go battle the Tumult?"

"Nah." She shrugs. "Let me guess. For years, you've been the only guy in the after-realms who can see and slay them."

"Correct. Yet most would say it's not my responsibility to fight every time."

"Then they aren't true thrax warriors." She holds up her hands, palms forward. "Don't get me wrong. You are a total grumpasaurus. Still, you deserve a break every so often. But if you decided to go, I would never question *why* you went."

I scan the woman. It's as if I'm seeing her for the first time. Nat doesn't understand why I fight the Tumult. Even my parents are stumped. But Myla comprehends effortlessly.

"Once these last petals are gone, the Titan of Chaos will imprison me alive in glass. I'll become an ushebti statue."

Myla narrows her eyes. "What aren't you telling me?"

"I believe that Bedlam's version of Beauty and the Beast differs magically from the fairy tale. You see, the Titan of Chaos doesn't believe in true love, only in finding someone's breaking point."

Myla nods. "I can believe that."

"He's placed us on a colliding path as a distraction."

She smirks. "You're distracted by me?"

I step closer. Energy zings through the air between us. "We're distracted by each other."

She stares at my mouth for a long time before answering. "True."

"The only way to end this curse is to kill Bedlam. There is no true love's kiss. This is the Titan of Chaos, not the Brother's Grimm. And you're an Amour, not a warrior."

"Totally false. I am a fighter." To accent this point, she arcs her tail over her shoulder.

"For the sake of argument, let's say you *were* an Arena warrior."

"It's not an argument, I am *still* the best Arena warrior."

"Yet you've spent years inside a jail cell. I find it hard to believe you still can hold your own. If you accompany me on this fight, you'll need to be kept on a tether for your own safety." I step over to the guard's station. A long leather strap hangs from the near wall. I pull it down and offer it to Myla. "This goes around your ankle."

"You're out of your mind." Her eyes light up red. Clearly, this is setting off her inner demons. *Tough.* I'm keeping her safe, even if it's from herself. I rattle the strap in my hand. "What we're about to embark on is dangerous stuff. This tether has an enchantment on it."

"I know what it is." She points at the tether like it's covered in poison. "That's a leash for prisoners."

"It's a safety measure. Using this, you can't get too far away from me. And if you do somehow move out of a safe range, then I can speak the magic words that will send you back to the safety of your cell."

"So you really think I'm weak?"

"I'm concerned with your safety."

"Go concern yourself with someone else. That settles it. I'll escape this dungeon and kill Bedlam on my own, thank you very much." She points down the hallway. "There's the exit archway. Take off before I flatten you."

"So you no longer wish to team up?"

"Ding ding ding! We have a winner!"

I shake my head. *If this woman thinks she's getting away from me, she is sorely mistaken.*

"You don't understand," I explain. "It's been years since I've seen a glimmer of hope for defeating Bedlam. At last, my visions have brought me to you. I won't leave you in this cell. And I certainly won't drag you out into danger without protection."

In reply, Myla raises her finger in a lewd gesture. "I'm leaving. You can't stop me."

I've already seen how Myla has an uncanny knowledge of the palace. No doubt, she could escape this dungeon if given a chance. She must be convinced to leave with me.

Which means I must resort to less savory means of persuasion.

"If you leave, I'll put someone else in this cell in your place. How about that girl who smiled and waved at you during the ball?"

Myla gasps. "Cissy? You noticed her grinning because, of course, you notice everything. But you wouldn't lock her up."

"Try me."

"You really are a beast, you know that?"

"Yes. And I've earned every inch of evil inside me."

Myla paces around the cell for a full minute. The good news is that one thing is now clear: this discussion has become a negotiation. Soon Myla will come back with a counter offer.

"Believe me," begins Myla. "I want to keep my friend out of prison. But I'll never become a pet on a tether. It's simply not in me. If we have to tell the thrax *something*, then let's say your guard."

*And the negotiation begins.*

"You can act as my chambermaid," I counter.

"Guard."

"Personal servant."

Her eyes flare a brighter shade of red. "Guard!"

"I can't help but notice that only one of us here is willing to change their position."

"I'm flexible. I can act as your guard, guard or guard."

"Myla, we just covered this. You're in no shape to be a warrior."

"You still think I'm an Amour, don't you?"

"There is no way you encountered my mother without her sending you toward me as a Lady of Enchantment. Although, don't be too downhearted. I do believe you're a convicted criminal as well."

"Hells Bells!" Myla throws up her hands. "You are so stubborn. I should have taken my chances with the guards back in the ball room."

"And you would have brought every warrior in Antrum down on your head. My people barely accept quasis as refugees, let alone as criminals who attack their beloved princess."

"Princess! PRINCESS!" Myla grips the bars and yanks with

suck force, I'm surprised she doesn't pull the iron out of their stone frame.

"I'm waiting."

Myla rounds on me, her eyes blazing crimson. "Here's my change in position. If I take you down in sixty seconds or less, then you and I will team up against Bedlam as equals. Officially I'll be your guard and we'll never discuss that ankle tether or Adair again. Agreed?"

"I'll consider it."

"That's a crap answer."

"It's the best I'll give you."

"I really hate you, Beast."

"Good." I pull out the cell key, place it in the lock. "Hating me will make this easier." I turn the key; the lock opens with a gentle snick. I take a pointed step backward and speak two final words.

"Sixty seconds."

## 38

## MYLA

The cell door swings open with a slow creak. As the moments tick by, my inner wrath demon awakens. Rage and power churn through my soul. The Beasts' words reverberate through me.

*You're an Amour, not a warrior*

*You'll need to be kept on a tether for your own safety*

*If you leave, I'll put someone else in this cell in your place*

From here, my thoughts slip into a lovely little phase I like to call *battle mode*. Everything around me seems to slow. Attack vectors and approaches flit through my mind. The fact that I'm still sporting a ball gown isn't great. I'll also need to adjust for the fact that I'm not wearing my fave dragonscale fighting suit.

My inner demon scans my body for weakness. The Beast is right that my reflexes aren't what they normally are. When I arrived here and merged with Prisoner 412, I must have taken on some of her limitations.

No matter.

There are things more important than having perfect reflexes. I know my opponent and Lincoln has three battle quirks I can use to my advantage.

*One.* He's right handed, which would help me with a sword fight.

*Two.* When Lincoln summons his angelic power, it always takes a few seconds to kick in.

*Three.* Lincoln's always liked my tail.

I decide to go with weakness number three. Lincoln's never taken my tail seriously in a fight. Mostly because in my reality, my husband and my tail are besties. Long story.

But here? My tail is arced over my shoulder and positively ready to skewer.

My inner wrath demon roars with rage. Energy churns through my muscles. My eyes glow red with power. Leaping forward, I grip the top frame of the opened doorway. Curling my body into a crouch, I prepare to kick the Beast in his face.

He sees the move coming and ducks.

Big mistake.

I swing my body over the Beast, sail through the air and then land behind the Beast's back. After my heels hit solid ground, my tail reaches behind me to loop around the Beast's ankles.

I grin. *So close now.*

Once my tail has a strong grip on the Beast's ankle, it yanks forward. The Beast slams flat onto his stomach. I stroll slowly around the prince until pausing by his face.

*And do I enjoy this moment?*

*You bet your ass I do.* But not as much as saying the next two words.

"Thirty-three seconds." And because I can't help myself, I add seven more words as well.

"And I did it all in heels."

## 39

## THE BEAST

*M*y forehead smarts from where my face slammed against the dungeon floor. Yet that isn't what's truly painful here.

An Amour just flattened me in thirty-three seconds. Which makes no sense unless...

Myla truly is a warrior.

Sitting up, I contemplate this turn of events. Octavia must have looked long and hard for a fighter, knowing that someone with these skills would be irresistible to me. Plus, Myla is witty, strong and intelligent.

*Ah, Mother.*

Again, I wish I'd never agreed to the compulsion to leave my parents in their chambers until Connor is recovered or gone.

Even now, I know I won't approach Lucas to cast a spell and break the compulsion. If it makes my parents happy to interfere with my love life while they deal with Father's passing, so be it.

Besides, it isn't only my Mother at work here.

Bedlam also placed Myla in my path. While I'm staring at Myla's curves or chuckling at her jokes, I could be missing important clues about how to destroy the Titan of Chaos.

Myla sets her fist on her hip. "Well, what do you say?"

"I agree that if any thrax asks, you are now officially my new quasi guard."

"And?"

I rise. "What else?"

"How about apologizing for wanting to put me on a leash like a dog?"

Now, I could explain here that it was't a leash but a magical tether. And that I didn't want to do this because I saw her as my pet, but in order to preserve her safety. However I anticipate that will only cause more delays. Instead, I go for the easy reply.

"No," I state.

"No?"

"I'll now return to the royal library. I assume you know the way."

I march past her and through the exit archway to the main palace. Some small part of me says that it would be the noble thing to apologize for underestimating her. And that, yes, a magical tether looks a Hell of a lot like a leash.

Yet I don't.

Myla already consumes far too much of my time and thought, and I've barely met the woman. Between my new feelings for Myla and the way petals keep disappearing from my arm, one thing is certain.

I'm in total chaos.

Which is just where Bedlam wants me.

## MYLA

*he Beast marches off. I take a different route to the royal library because, *fuck him.*

By the time I reach the library door, the Beast is already inside. He stands before a wall of books, his back facing to me as he sifts through different titles.

The Beast doesn't greet me; I say nothing to his royal douchbagness. We have a very healthy relationship.

As I walk inside, my teeth start chattering. "Is it me or is it cold in here?"

The Beast doesn't even turn around to reply. "It's you."

*What an ass.*

Not that I'll cave in and ask the Beast for different clothes. Or a jacket. I'll sneak off when he isn't looking and get some things on my own, thank you very much.

"We need to get together and share information," I declare.

"No. The things I've learned would take years to impart. What's best is for you to stay quiet until called for."

My eyes almost bug out of my head. *Stay quiet until called for?* Maybe I can knock the Beast onto his face again. That was fun.

Faces appear in my mind: my Lincoln and Maxon. The Beast

may look like my husband, but he's just a bag of dicks in a lion's pelt. I refuse to allow his rudeness to place my plans at risk.

I force my voice into a semblance of calm. "I'll pretend you didn't say that. Maybe you don't want to share your super-complex stuff, but I'll be a reasonable person and tell you something that could be useful. Guess who visited me in the dungeon right before you stopped by? Gastonne. And here's another tidbit. Gastonne is actually Bedlam."

"I'm aware."

"You knew about Gastonne?" I march over to the Beast's side. It's really hard to have serious conversations with someone's back. "Why don't you tell me these things? Aren't we a team?"

"Not really."

"Liar, liar, lion pelt on fire. Back in the dungeons, you promised to treat me as an equal. That means answering reasonable questions."

"If you insist, I shall explain the situation. Bedlam plays at being Gastonne in order to torture me. I can't tell you the years I wasted trying to poison, explode or otherwise kill Gastonne. Not to mention trying to steal or copy his signet rings. He's simply too powerful to kill to deceive via direct means." Turning, the Beast stalks off into mini maze of tall bookshelves.

*Guess the conversation is over.*

Surprise prickles across my skin. I'm just so used to my Lincoln; we talk about everything. With the Beast, it's like it doesn't even occur to him to share with someone who isn't his own growly self inside his own thick skull.

*Oh, well. Enough worrying about the Beast.*

Leaning back, I really soak in the space around me. The royal library is one of my fave spots in Arx Hall. In my reality, Lincoln and I spend hours reading by the fireplace.

And doing other things.

My lust demon awakens, sending me mental images of all the times Lincoln and I have had sex in the *real* version of this room.

I step around a small maze of bookshelves to reach the fireplace itself, which is one of our favorite places to get naked.

What I see instantly cools all my desire.

Bedlam's sarcophagus stands before my once-favorite hearth. I frown. Who puts an ancient Egyptian coffin by a fireplace? And what else has changed around here?

I scan the library with new eyes. Half the books are missing. The carpet is threadbare. All the furniture looks as if it's held together with popsicle sticks and glue. The only improvement are the new ward stones. They're all over the floor, the shelves, you name it. Back home, we had three stones for our whole property. Here, I count twenty-seven by the fireplace alone. Guess this place is super secure. So there's that.

Still, this isn't the library that my Lincoln and I cherished. It certainly isn't the same fireplace.

I hear the measured tread of the Beast as he stalks up behind me. "What do you think of the new decoration?"

I sniff. "Is this where I'm supposed to go *eek-eek-eek there was a dead body in this thing*?"

"It's the standard response."

"Well, I think it's cool. Where did you find it?"

"Right after I became cursed, I received all sorts of visions. I saw an underground prison and some coordinates on Earth, so I sent a team to investigate. This was the result."

"Was anyone inside the sarcophagus?"

"By *anyone*, do you mean Bedlam?"

"I do. In my reality, Bedlam hung out in this thing for two thousand years."

"I see. To answer your question, no one was within."

I step closer to the sarcophagus. "This used to be decorated. There were glyphs and jewels, that kind of thing."

The Beast's eyes widen. "Do you remember any of them?"

"Not the glyphs," I state. A memory appears. "There was a decoration, though."

The Beast steps closer. He's wearing that heavy lion's pelt, so maybe that's why he radiates heat. And I'm sporting a thin ball gown, which pretty much explains why I want to rub myself all over him.

*Focus, Myla.*

"It was two plates hanging from a stick," I state.

The Beast steps closer and grips my upper arms. "A scale?"

"Yes, that's it."

"Perfect!" The Beast pulls me into a deep hug. He's so warm and covered in muscle, I can't help but lean into the embrace.

Okay, I could easily knee him in the groin but it's been a crappy day. Besides, what's so wrong about a hug?

The Beast releases me to check through his piles of books. "This could be the breakthrough I've been looking for."

I saunter over to stand by his shoulder. It's not that I want to just bug him because I hate being ignored.

But yeah, I hate being ignored.

"I have three goals," I declare. "First is for the two of us to team up, which is happening. Sorta. Second is to get the remaining signet rings of Eden. And third is for us to use those bands in order to destroy Bedlam. Unless, after you've looked at all these books, you found another way to kill the King of Chaos?" I brush my fingers across a nearby volume.

"Do not mess with my organization system."

I gasp in mock-shock. "This place is organized?"

"In its own way. Right now, my job is to finish my research. Yours is to rest up. Although you have shown some prowess in battle, you're not at full form."

"I can read, you know."

"It would take years of research for you to become useful to me. Sleep."

I could walk away. But I won't.

"And since you know so much, why not answer my previous question? Is there any other way to destroy the Titan of Chaos?"

The Beast waves his hand dismissively. "No, the remaining three rings are the only way to end Bedlam."

"So where do we start? The Garden of Eden is burned down to the ground. Adam is dead. Eve's missing. The other two Edens aren't much better."

The Beast flips through more pages. "At one time, I suspected that Eve survived and perhaps kept part of the garden alive with her as well. The documents I received were disappointing to say the least."

"Where are they?" The Beast glares at me. "I don't need years of training to read some reports. Just point me in the direction."

The Beast gestures to a pile of scrolls. "Over there."

I saunter over to the table in question and scan the parchments. "I think you've missed something."

"I never miss anything."

"This information on Eve comes from the House of Cuthbert. They're a spin-off from Acca."

The Beast tosses another book aside. "So?"

"I wouldn't believe a word of this stuff. Don't get me wrong; Cuthbert are great at kissing ass. They're just complete liars. It's not even a choice with these people. They lie about nonsense. These scrolls are worthless."

"I requested this information on Eve. Cuthbert reported what they knew immediately. There are hundreds of minor houses in some kind of alliance with Aldred. If I went and double-checked what each one did, then I'd do nothing else. And the detection spells from Lucas have come up with nothing as well. Finding Eve through the House of Cuthbert is dead."

"What about Octavia's spy network?"

"She's out of it these days. Connor is sick. As I said, I've taken a binding oath to leave them both alone."

I chuckle. "I get it."

The Beast snaps his book closed. "I fail to see what's humorous."

"Octavia totally got you to agree to a magically binding oath that you can't bug her… but she can do whatever she wants to you. And you agreed to that? You must have been having a bad day."

"I was."

My heart cracks. This guy is cursed and alone. He's also facing a *worse than death* situation with being encased alive in glass for eternity.

I can be patient.

Or at least, I can try.

"So you really won't look into this lead with the House of Cuthbert?"

"We have better places to find the first ring. Thanks to your remembrance about the sarcophagus, I know how to enter the Ether of Eden. I knew you'd be useful to me."

That word rattles around my mind. *Useful.* It's like I'm a kitchen appliance instead of a person. My wrath demon stirs inside me. She doesn't like being treated as less than anything.

Still, I force in a slow breath. Fighting this guy does nothing. The sooner I get through this, the faster I'm back to my real life and husband.

"So what do we do next?" I ask.

"We must reach a mountaintop on Earth. Only problem is, we can't be seen leaving by any official Pulpitum. Mother will get word and shut us down. She's overly concerned about my safety."

"Not a problem. I know a secret platform."

The Beast sniffs. "Really?"

"*Really*-really. How do you think I got into Antrum in the first place?"

"All right. You may show me before we depart."

"How big of you." I roll my eyes. "Then let's do this."

The Beast goes back to sorting through a nearby shelf of books. "We leave in the morning."

I raise my pointer finger as if an idea were just appearing to me. "Hey, here's a concept. You're not getting any less dead. Let's go now."

"No."

It would be so easy to take off my shoe and chuck it at his face. I could probably aim the stiletto heel to poke him right in the middle of his forehead.

But that won't get me back to my reality.

*Calm down, Myla.*

I take a ton of deep breaths and go at it again. "It would help if you'd explain these decisions versus being such a dick."

*There, that was much better than using shoe-chucking to express my feelings.*

"As you wish. Tomorrow we shall visit the Ether of Eden. They'll be angry enough when we summon them in the morning. Right now, it's their nighttime. No one likes to navigate through the air in the dark."

"Well, that makes sense," I declare. "Thank you for sharing. Morning it is." I force a grin.

*Don't say it. Don't say it. Don't say it.*

*Screw it, I'm saying it.*

"Now, was that so hard? You explain things. If things make sense, then I agree. Easy peasy."

"Sarcasm is the last refuge of the weak-minded."

I ball my hands into fists, because otherwise they might tear that smirk off his face. "Can I tackle you again?"

Evidently, the Beast is done answering my questions. He marches over to a corner of the room and gestures to floor. "I have much more research to do between now and dawn. While I work, you may sleep here."

I blink hard, not believing what I'm seeing. "That—" I point at the corner in question "—is filled with a pile of blankets."

"Clearly."

"So you want me to sleep there? Like a pet?"

The Beast shrugs. "Unless you prefer the bare floor."

My wrath demon rises yet again. All thoughts of pity or understanding melt from my soul. A cool sense of rage churns through me while I go into battle mode. Thoughts fly. Plans converge.

A moment later, I've plotted my revenge.

And it will be spectacular.

## THE BEAST

*T*his conversation about nighttime accommodations is over. I have larger things to worry about.

Such as destroying Bedlam.

Besides, I work and sleep in this chamber. If it's good enough for me, it will suit her as well.

All of a sudden, Myla stops glaring at me as if ready to skewer my person with her tail. Instead she smiles. It's a lovely grin, but I suspect it's *not* a sign that she's thrilled with the situation.

"Why so happy?" I ask.

"Come on, who wouldn't be thrilled? This mound of dog blankets makes a great bed."

"I don't believe you."

"Boo. Hoo."

And in another sign of Bedlam's diabolical plan, I am working hard to fight a smile. Everyone in my palace runs away from me, pities my fate, or both. None challenge me. If you'd asked me a week ago whether I would enjoy some verbal sparring, I would have bellowed at you to leave the room. Yet there is something about playful about Myla. Magnetic. Light, energy and enjoyment simply radiate from her.

Which makes Myla a more dangerous distraction than ever.

Forcing down my joy, I level Myla with my most serious look. "You're scheming."

Myla steps closer. "That would require complex reasoning skills which we Amours don't have." She moves even nearer, stopping when our bodies are inches apart. "Our abilities lie elsewhere."

That settles it. She is not only scheming, she's creating a plan of epic proportions. Plus, she's trying to distract me with all this desirous talk.

And it's working.

My arms ache to pull her in closer. I want to feel the silk of her hair and press my mouth to hers. I shake my head, trying to regain some semblance of control. If I keep standing here, I'll do something I regret.

I take a pointed step backward. "I'm watching you."

"Thanks, Stalker Beast." She steps over to the corner and plunks down onto the blankets. "I'll be right here."

"Fine." At this point, my feet should be walking away from this situation. I can't seem to motivate myself to move.

"Good." She winks.

At last, I summon the strength to turn around and march over to a nearby table. It has an excellent view of Myla in the corner. I'm a thrax hunter, trained since birth to detect the slightest sign of trouble. Whatever this woman is planning, it won't succeed.

And I still have research to do. There isn't much information on the ether of Eden, but magical scales are another matter entirely. I must be prepared so we have the best chance to get a signet ring of Eden.

Settling onto my chair, I alternate between reading and watching Myla. She's curled up into the corner. A lock of hair hangs over her nose. Her breathing falls into a steady rhythm.

Before, I could hardly hold back my laughter. Now I'm over-whelmed with a sense of peace. Having Myla nearby feels right in ways I never would have expected. The need to doze presses down on me, heavy as stones.

How long has it been since I rested?

Perhaps I can just lean my head on the tabletop for just a moment. No matter what, I cannot allow myself to fall asleep.

## MYLA

*Ha! The Beast is totally conked out.*

Time to kick my revenge plan into high gear. I am so going after Eve and the ring of the Garden of Eden. I just need Cissy's help to wring information out of the House of Cuthbert.

There are no less than six secret passageways out of this library. Fortunately, the one which delivers the fastest path is Cissy is also closest to my not-a-bed. Using maximum stealth, I tiptoe across the room and slip off through a panel in the wall.

As I sneak through the secret passages, I calculate where I'll find Cissy. As a rule, I complain my head off about how the thrax have a tradition for every occasion. But now, I find the iron-clad rituals to be nothing less than awesome. Why? Because based on Cissy's title at the ball—Personal Retainer—she'll be placed into a particular chamber inside Fortes Pointe, which is the very box-like castle of Acca.

Easy peasy.

It's a little drama to get to Acca because I must reach Cissy and get back, lickety-split. To that end, I'll enter the secret passage that leads to the royal storage room for demon patrol stuff. Once there, I can grab a transport charm.

I soon reach the storage room. Normally, this place is brimming with all sorts of cool charms, all of them organized in neat little bins.

Like everything else, it's in sorry shape.

The bins are empty and tossed to the ground. The only charms I can find are ones that fell under a shelving unit or got stuck behind a box.

The Beast said how the Tumult had been thinning the thrax ranks. The situation has certainly done a number on magical supplies. In my reality, the Earl of Striga would blow a magical gasket if he saw this mess.

It takes me an hour, but eventually I find some old transport charms. Not too powerful, but I'm only going a short distance across Antrum. In this case, the charms look like train tickets. While ripping the magical paper in half, I picture my destination. Within seconds, I'm surrounded by purple mist. Once the vapor clears, I find myself inside a certain room in Fortes Pointe.

I grin. Sure enough, Cissy is here.

She sits on a puffy bed. The walls are bare stone, same as the floor. Cissy's painting her toe nails. If she's shocked to see me materialize in her bedroom, she doesn't show it.

"Hi, Myla."

"Hello, Cissy." I plunk myself at the other end of the mattress. "Aren't you going to ask how I got here?"

"Nah. My chambermaid's cousin's friend told me all about transport charms within Antrum. I figured you'd show up, sooner or later." She eyes my tail and gasps. "Oh, no! Your tail is showing! What happened to your cuff?"

Now this is more of the reaction I was looking for. "Oh, that. I fought Adair and it broke."

"You fought?" Cissy stares at me like I'm crazy.

"Yes, then I got chucked into the dungeons and battled the Beast. Took him down in thirty-three seconds, too."

"Oh." The *you're nuts* look does not cease. "And the prince is okay that you're both a quasi-demon and fighting him in dungeons?"

"We're teaming up to kill Bedlam. If anyone asks, I'm officially his quasi guard now. But enough about me. How are you?"

"So happy to be in Antrum. What a life saver! I owe you, big time." She goes back to painting her toes. "What do you want?"

"Who says I want anything?"

Cissy rolls her eyes. "Please."

"Okay, I need some records from the House of Cuthbert."

Cissy purses her lips. "They're a vassal of Acca. Bunch of liars, too."

*Leave it to Cissy.* She's been here less than a day and already she knows all the vassal houses and what they're like.

"Well, you know how I want to kill Bedlam. To get the job done, I need a signet ring from the Garden of Eden."

"That place burned down."

"Yes, but I think Eve is still running around… and Cuthbert knows where she is."

Cissy purses her lips. "What makes you think I can find the secret documents when the prince can't?"

"Because in my reality, you run one of the best spy networks in the after-realms. And you already know more about Cuthbert than most of Acca."

Cissy exhales a long breath. "I'll try."

"That's what I'm talking about. Find me these documents." I hand her a sheet of paper.

Cissy scans the list. "Princess Adair might know more about this stuff than I do. I could ask her if—"

"No."

"But she's—"

"No! I'm having enough trouble pretending she doesn't exist

without discussing her with anyone." That leads to picturing that kiss in the ballroom. The mere thought of them married starts my wrath demon roaring inside my soul.

Cissy rolls her eyes. "Come on. Don't you want to know—"

In a move of extreme maturity, I stick my fingers in my ears. "La la la, I can't hear you."

Just like back in my reality, that particular sequence works like a charm. Cissy drops the subject of she-who-must-not-be-named.

"Thanks, Cis." I hop off the bed. For the first time, I spot a single decoration in the room. It's an ushebti statue. The thing is a seven foot tall pillar of mottled blue glass. The shape is roughly human, but only if you look at it for a while.

Or you know a living person is trapped inside the thing.

I gasp. "How did this get in here?"

"Gastonne asked me to keep it. Don't worry. It's just an old statue."

"No, it's a human being who's been eternally trapped alive in glass." I tiptoe closer. The glass itself is so mottled, it's hard to see what's—*or to be specific, who*—is stuck inside. "You have got to get rid of this."

"Gastonne is my boss. No one's sending me to Hell. The Ush-whatever is fine."

"I guess if it doesn't bug you—"

"It doesn't."

"Just promise me one more thing. I know he's your boss but… Don't get too close to Gastonne."

"Really?"

I shake my head. "So really. He's actually a demon called Bedlam, AKA the Titan of Chaos."

"No need to be dramatic." Cissy rolls her eyes. "I don't like it, but I'll keep my distance. It's what's best anyway. Don't get too friendly with management."

I sneak another look at the ushebti. There's a person inside that thing, I know it. And Gastonne-Bedlam is trying to torture me by putting it in my bestie's bedroom. But what can I do? Cissy has agreed to keep her distance.

And I don't have a ton of time to waste here.

Better return to the library.

Pulling out my second magical ticket, I wave the item in the air. "And now, prepare to witness some magic." My bestie was always a big fan of the supernatural.

As Cissy leans forward, her face becomes the definition of rapt attention. Her golden retriever's tail wags up a storm.

While holding the ticket between my hands, I picture the supply room once more. These ticket thingies are super-useful. I'm loading up. With that image in mind, I call over my shoulder. "You can do the honors, boy."

My tail swoops up to slice the ticket in two. From there, I'm surrounded once again by a purple cloud of magic. Once the haze is gone, I've returned to the supply room where I grab the rest of the tickets from their hiding spot under a shelf. I even find some repair charms that may work for my dragonscale fighting suit. *Yay, me!*

At this point, I can picture my triumph so clearly. I'll get that signet ring from the Garden of Eden and use it to find the other rings. From there, destroying Bedlam will be simple. The Beast can skulk in his library for all I care.

As I head back through the secret passageways, it's tempting to hum *We Are The Champions*. I don't, though. This is me, on a mission of revenge.

After a short walk, I reach the panel that leads to the library, press it open and...

Come face-to-face with a very awake Beast.

He does not look happy.

## 43

# THE BEAST

*here the Hell is Myla?*

I just awoke to find her gone. Is she roaming around Arx Hall? I haven't made any official announcement that she's my guard. My people could do anything to a lone quasi. There's a reason we keep Purgatory refugees in their own palace complex.

A mixture of rage and worry battle it out inside me. Is Myla hurt somewhere? And why do I care so much about the well being of someone I only just met?

Taking in a deep breath, I force my thoughts to calm. Closing my eyes, I reach out with my hunter's senses. A gentle drumming sounds from inside the walls.

I pop my eyes open. *That's no drum. It's Myla's footsteps.* She snuck off through secret passages again.

Instantly, jolts of angry energy move through my limbs. That was far too much unnecessary worry. This situation is irritating in the extreme.

A panel on the library story swings open. Myla steps out. Somehow, she still looks gorgeous in her red ball gown.

Myla kicks the panel closed behind her. "Hey, Beast. How was your nap?"

I grip my hands behind my back. The motion stops me from grabbing her. What I'll do if I catch her is another story. Not sure I even want to contemplate that. "I've an idea. You can sleep *when* you're told and *where* you're told."

Myla steps closer. "Do I need to kick your ass again?" She pauses when we're a breath apart. "I'll even take off my heels this time."

*Oh, Hell.*

Best to step away before I kiss her. Because I very much want to.

Instead, I cross the library and grab one of the tables. With one hand, I clasp the heavy wooden furniture and drag it over to the corner which holds Myla's sleeping space. I point to the pile of blankets. "Sleep. I will watch over you far more closely this time."

Myla juts out her hip. "I'm not tired."

"You're done scheming and it's been a long day. That means you'll pass out in less than ten minutes."

Myla tilts her head. "How do you know that?"

I shrug. "Logic."

"Huh. Sounds like you know me pretty well. Or should I say, part of you knows me." Sashaying across the floor, she plunks down onto the pile of blankets. Turning onto her stomach, Myla rests her chin on her folded arms. She says nine simple words that raise a complex host of questions.

"Tell me about your visions of me and Maxon."

For a fraction of a second, my eyes widen with surprise. I'm able to school my features before my shock is too obvious, though. "Your names merely appeared in my mind, that's all."

"And then what happened?"

I try to tap into some of my Beast-style rage. For some reason, I only feel a sense of wellbeing and humor. It's all rather odd.

"I'm a very busy prince." I pull a random book from the a nearby shelf and open it, careful to hold the volume so it blocks my face. "If you'll excuse me."

Myla rolls onto her back. "Don't think I've forgotten about your visions. I'll get the truth out of you eventually."

I peer at her over the top of my book. There's no stopping the smirk that rounds my mouth. "You can try."

Myla curls into the blankets. As I know from personal experience, it really is a rather comfortable corner. She falls asleep after eight minutes and twenty-three seconds.

Once I hear her gentle snores, a strange mix of emotions move through me.

There's joy because, like Myla said, I did somehow know this would happen.

Yet I'm also burning with fury for the same reason. I'm connected to this woman in ways that are dangerous.

*Damn you, Bedlam.*

Rising from my desk, I stalk around and collect all the scrolls I'll need to review before tomorrow. In just a matter of hours, I'll have my first real chance for a signet ring of Eden.

I can't allow anything to ruin it.

## 44

## MYLA

For sleeping in a corner of blankets, I actually rest pretty well. For most of the night, I dream about my Lincoln and all the fun we had in the real version of this library.

Good times.

When my eyes flutter open, I spy the Beast sitting at his new table by my corner. For a while, I soak in the sight of him. He's so like my Lincoln, and yet not. It's super confusing.

The Beast doesn't look up from his latest scroll. "Don't waste time staring at me. We leave in thirty minutes."

*How charming.* I'm about to sass something about that fact when I notice it.

The Beast hisses in pain while grasping his wrist. It must be his marks. He's changing again. One step closer to a cursed eternity. My heart cracks with grief. The Beast is as alone in the after-realms as I am.

What I do next is more of a reflex than anything else. I rise and step to his side. "Let me take a look."

"No." He accents that word with another agonized wince. "I'm busy."

"Correction. You're a total grouch." I reach forward slowly, the way someone would with a cornered animal. The Beast doesn't back away. His tunic and mail are still slashed open from last night in the dungeon. With gentle motions, I turn over his arm. All the while, the Beast keeps his eyes tightly closed in pain.

"You said you had three petals," I state.

The Beast speaks through teeth that are gritted in agony. "I do."

"One of them is hardly there any more. It's fading. Soon you'll be down to two."

Opening his eyes, the Beast inspects the mark himself. "You're right; it *is* vanishing." He shakes his head. "That's not what they do. They pulse in and out. And when that happens, I get a vision of where the Tumult will strike next."

The last outlines of the sixth petal vanish from the Beast's skin. An electric charge fills the air. *Fresh magic.* The Beast's eyes fill will a dark blue haze. No question what's at work here. This is Bedlam's spell.

When the Beast next speaks, his voice carries a dreamy tone. "I see Purgatory's Arena. Quasi bodies piled high. All dead. The last Tumult vanishes into the ground."

The Beast blinks hard; his vision clears. "What I saw in Purgatory was horrible. It can't be true."

Our gazes lock. Every cell in my body seems to weigh down with worry. "There's one way to know."

Palace messengers send urgent information in red envelopes. I march over to the library's main entrance. Sure enough, a red envelope sits on the carpet by the closed door.

Picking up the message, I tear it open. It's an effort to make myself read the news.

The Beast marches over to stand at my side. In this moment, the man seems just like my Lincoln. We'd always face tragedies like this together.

"The Arena is filled with thousands of corpses," I announce.

The Beast scans over my shoulder. "According to this, the attack finished hours ago."

"There's a list of names here." I set my hand on my throat. "So many people."

Turning, I wrap my arms about his waist. There's no desire in this touch, only sorrow. I weep against his chest. His tears drop onto my face and hair. This loss is beyond words. Sometimes all you can do is cry.

Not sure how long we stand that way, but it feels too good to move apart.

"Bedlam is changing the game," I whisper.

"What do you mean?"

"I'm here now. If you got a message to fight the Tumult, I'd go with you. We'd win and have fun doing it."

The Beast tilts his head. "I can imagine that."

"I told you how Bedlam visited me as Gastonne. He said that he wants to break my spirit. Watching you lose those petals one by one—and knowing innocents will die along the way—that'll be rough for us both."

A long pause follows. Did I just admit that I like this guy a little? *I think I did.*

The Beast twists a lock of my hair about his finger. "Am I so very different from your Lincoln?"

"You've had years of extra weight on your shoulders. And I wasn't here to share the load."

The Beast sets his knuckle beneath my chin. Little by little, he guides me until our gazes meet. Fresh waves of energy and attraction zing around us.

"The humans call me the Beast, too," he says in a low voice. "I'm the only one who can fight the Tumult. When I'm done, all they see is a lion-man and a dead demon."

"So why fight each time?"

The Beast runs his fingertip over my lower lip. "I thought you knew."

"I do, but I want to hear you say it."

The Beast takes in a long breath. "Because every soul has worth."

"Now *that* sounds like the Lincoln I know." I brush a gentle kiss onto his cheek. "I'm sorry I wasn't here."

The Beast sighs and steps away. "Enough sentimentality. We must depart now."

I wave my hand between us. "What was that all about? We were having a moment there."

"You don't want to know," snarls the Beast.

"Try me."

"I happen to know that Mother paid the other Amours a bonus for every kiss they placed on my person."

I throw up my hands. "Are we back to that again?"

"Yes."

"Why?"

"You want a list?"

"It would be helpful."

"You're a part demon girl who snuck into my realm. You've admitted being in league with my mother and interacting with Bedlam. You also admit to being an escaped criminal. And you snuck around secret passages in the halls of my own castle when you promised not to leave the library."

"Well, when you put it like that, it doesn't sound *too* great." I step away.

The Beast said it before, and now I'm starting to see his point. All this emotion between us is distracting from what we should be doing... and that's finding a signet ring of Eden. The sooner this nightmare is over, the quicker I get my life back.

Time to gear up.

## 45

## THE BEAST

*A*n hour later, Myla and I stand on a mountaintop on Earth. Wind howls in my ears. Snow settles on my skin, yet it doesn't cause a chill. Why? Both Myla and I wear black body armor as well as warming charms—in this case, thumb rings—that keep us comfortable.

Myla kicks at the snow with her boots. "Did you bring the duplication putty?"

"Maybe."

"That's not a yes."

"Fine. I'll say yes."

Back at the library, Myla and I had an extensive and rather animated discussion about what charms to bring on the mission. I refuse to shlep along duplication putty. That stuff causes more trouble than it's worth.

"That's not a real confirmation," says Myla. "I told you, I'd carry it. Now did you bring it or—"

"Do you mind? I need to summon the steward of Ether."

Myla mimes my words, *I need to summon the steward of Ether.* Although she doesn't make a sound, her face contorts into a rather convincing impression of my frown.

I'd say we need to work on our relationship, but we really don't have one. Besides, my main focus must remain on Bedlam.

Raising my voice, I call out a spell that I'd found years ago. Summoning a guide for the Ether of Eden was never the problem. The issue was convincing them to lead.

A tiny form appears in the sky.

It might be a bird, but it's not.

What flies toward us is a winged woman.

Minutes later, she lands on the mountaintop beside us. The lady is tall and lean with long black hair and red robes. Great wings arch behind her—they're unlike anything I've seen before. They are a lovely mixture of feathers, ribbons and armor.

"I am Victoria, Steward of the Ether of Eden."

That is certainly a surprise. I've never met a steward before. I scan her hands, looking for any sign of what I so desperately need.

Yet Victoria wears no signet rings.

A different version of me might be more tactful. I'm beyond that concern. "Where is your signet ring?"

"Not on my finger," states Victoria. Her eyes flare with irritation. She clearly doesn't like being summoned to Earth and asked to reveal her magic.

Which is not surprising.

That said, what happens next is rather unexpected.

Victoria's wings hop off her back. They are actually some kind of bird that clings to her shoulders and helps her take flight.

"That is so cool," says Myla. "Does that creature have a name?"

"It's a featherling," replies Victoria. "I wield retrograde magic and I created that one myself." A flash of pain and longing appears in Victoria's eyes, but is gone too quickly to be sure if it was ever there.

"I am Prince Lincoln and this is Myla Lewis. We request safe passage to the Ether."

So far, Victoria hasn't exactly radiated warmth and welcome.

Now her demeanor turns downright icy. "You after-realmers think you've mastered the lore of the Edens. You know nothing and we've worked hard to keep it that way. Why should I bring you to the Ether?"

"That does not matter," I reply. "I request the *test of journeys* for myself and Myla. It must be provided. And if we pass, we will be taken to the Ether of Eden."

"Then you shall have your souls weighed," declares Victoria.

Beside me, Myla raises her hand. "Souls weighed?"

"Correct," states Victoria. "That is the *test of journeys*, after all."

Myla glares at me. "Souls weighed. When were you going to share this little piece of information?"

"You were the one who saw the scale image," I state.

"I didn't know someone was going to yank out my soul and slap it somewhere." She taps her chest. "I'm the Great Scala."

"No," I state. "You're not."

"Maybe not in this reality," says Myla. "But in my own world, I am. Taking out souls is a tricky business. About a kajillion things can go wrong."

Victoria frowns at Myla. "You have your own world?"

"Long story," retorts Myla. "But yes, I do."

Victoria focuses on me. "Sir, this one is bat shit crazy."

"I'm aware," I reply.

Myla raises her hand. "Hate you both right now."

Victoria smiles indulgently at Myla. "Do not worry, silly demon. The scales will never wish to test one such as you in the first place. Magic has no interest in filth from Hell."

"Filth from Hell?" repeats Myla. "That does it." She curls her fingers toward Victoria in a way that says, come here. "Bring on the scales."

Victoria looks to me. "Is this what you wish? For the scales to test you both?"

"Obviously," I snarl.

"I'll try the thrax first," declares Victoria.

"One more thing." Myla raises her pointer finger. "I am not a demon. I'm mostly human with a little bit of demonic DNA. Big difference."

Victoria lifts her chin. "So you say. The scales will tell all." She pulls up a necklace from under her robes. It's a small round disc on a chain.

"You aren't going to use your signet ring?" asks Myla.

"Not for this," states Victoria. "Weighing souls is not retrograde magic."

Victoria whispers over the small metal pendant. A sphere of bronze-colored power rises from the item. The orb zooms across through the air and hits me square in the chest.

Pain radiates through my body as, little by little, a gray form rises from my ribs. Soon a full version of me floats above the snow—it's transparent and powerful.

This is my soul and damn, do I ever look solemn.

A sense of hollowness and despair fills every corner of my being. In some ways, it hurts even more than the pain of having my spirit torn out.

Meanwhile, Victoria presses the pendant onto her free palm. Another bronze-colored orb appears on her hand, a shape that soon morphs into a small copper scale that dangles from her fingertips.

Victoria focuses on my soul. "Come," she orders.

My soul shrinks down to a small size while floating toward Victoria. Once it gets close enough, my soul curls up to sit upon the small plate. The moment my soul takes this spot, a misty form appears on the opposite plate. There, the vapor congeals into a small feather.

"Let the weighing begin," declares Victoria. "For you to pass the *test of journeys*, your soul cannot be heavy with anger or hate. It must weigh as much as a feather."

The scales wobble. Immediately, one thing becomes clear. *This is not going well.* My soul is far heavier than it should be.

In this moment, I've never been closer to acquiring a signet ring of Eden, and yet, I've never been farther away as well. A sense of despair weighs into my bones. This adventure with Victoria is sure to fail.

And I've only two petals left.

# VICTORIA

## 46

## MYLA

*ipes.* The scale test is not going well.

Here is where all my years of being the Great Scala come in handy. When I first got the soul moving gig, I was totally awkward around spirits. Ages passed before I felt comfortable enough to actually touch one with my bare hands.

All of which is why I have no problem with what I must do now.

"Oh, no! I tripped!" Lurching forward, I knock the Beast's soul right off the scale.

Victoria and the Beast gasp. I don't.

I've seen this happen before. Without a Scala around to make a spirit stay in place, souls fly back to their owners. Which is cool if the person in question is alive; it causes nasty hauntings when they're dead.

Sure enough, that's just what happens with the Beast's soul. The grey transparent version of my not-a-Lincoln soars around before flying dead center into the Beast's torso.

"Are you all right?" asks Victoria.

The Beast pats his chest. "I think so."

"He's fine," I state. "Souls always fly back."

"How would you know?" Victoria frowns. "Are you really the Great Scala?" Her mouth pulls right with anger.

Clearly, being the Great Scala will be an issue here.

*Oops.*

"Ooooooooh," I say slowly, trying to buy time. "You want to know how I know about soooooooooouls?"

"Oh, no," says Victoria. "You *are* the Great Scala. I don't want that kind of power on the Ether. It could throw off our balance."

"She's not the Great Scala," says the Beast cooly. "She's studying to be the food musher for the real one."

My brows lift. *That was a good lie.*

"Do you know the current Scala?" I ask Victoria. "Super old dude. Bad teeth. If I'm lucky, I'll get to mush-mush-mush his food for him. But I really need to ace this paper on the Ether in order to graduate from Purgatory Mush Training and—"

At this point, I notice the Beast making a slashing motion across his throat. Guess I'm getting carried away.

"And that's it," I state.

"We are done here." Victoria snaps at her wings, which are still flopping about the snow like a fish out of water. It's more than a little odd.

"What?" I ask. "Don't I get a turn?"

"No," states Victoria. "And his test—" here she points to the Beast "—is a complete failure."

"Hey, now. The two little plate things hadn't quite finished bobbing up and down," I state. "It only *looked* like it was going to go super-badly. And like I said, I'm up next."

The Beast nods sagely. The way he acts, it's like he gets his soul weighed every day. "The ancient laws must be obeyed. All must be tested."

*Is that ever a load of crap.* But I'll give it to the Beast. He lies like a champ. In this moment, he reminds me of my Lincoln. No one fibs like my husband.

Victoria's brows pull together. It isn't a refusal, but it's not exactly ringing agreement, either.

I haven't known Victoria more than a few minutes, but I can already tell two things about her. First, she's a rule lover. When I was growing up, Purgatory was run by ghouls. No one lives for check-lists and instructions more than those undeadlies. As a result, I can smell a rule-loving nature like some piggies sniff out truffles. Victoria's in the I Love Rules Club. Definitely.

Second, Victoria is curious. Maybe even a little bored. After all, she could have sent a minion to chat us up, but she came here herself. I'm guessing that spending all eternity on a cloud taking care of *freaking air* must get tedious. So she's into stuff that's new and different.

*Have I got an idea for her.*

I shoot Victoria one of my very best smiles. It's the grin I saved for super big-bads back when I was fighting in the Arena.

"Guess what?" I ask. "I am actually bred in a laboratory from the DNA of the best quasi fighters. Who knows? Maybe I don't have a soul. Aren't you curious?"

Now, I did just say that it's super dangerous to yank out someone's soul. But I'm chucking that fear aside, considering how the Beast survived just fine.

Victoria narrows her eyes. A long moment passes before she speaks again. "I shall weigh the demon."

"Cool," I state. "Now suck out my soul already."

Victoria points another bronze bubble-o-magic at my chest. Once again, she does the soul-sucking thing. My soul looks a little more sparkly than Lincoln's.

I step closer and take a better look. No question about it. The sparkles are my igni. Warmth and love spread through my heart. A memory appears. I recall tumbling through space and how my igni sacrificed themselves to protect my memories. Their last words appear in my mind.

*We are not all gone. Many remain and can come to you, but only for one final visit. Choose the moment well.*

It's beyond comforting to know my igni are still close. Plus, I've seen the pain of having your soul stripped away. Somehow, my igni are keeping me safe from that misery as well.

*Ah, my little ones are the best.*

Victoria squints as she looks at my soul. "How unusual. Your soul includes bright bits."

*Yipes.* I need a cover story here. Victoria wasn't happy about my Scala-ness.

"Yeah," I agree. "It must be the other people in my system. I wonder what will happen when you weigh it?"

Victoria nods. "Let us discover together." She gestures to my soul. "Come."

My soul shrinks down to take its place on the metal plate. Once again, a feather appears on the opposite side. The scales instantly balance.

Not that it's a competition between me and the Beast, but I totally won here. My soul weighs as much as a feather.

Victoria's brows pull together. "You're a demon and yet pure of heart. That's never happened before. I rarely get surprised."

"What can I say? I'm awesome." I rub my palms together. "Now when do we leave?"

"*You* may go." Victoria points to the Beast. "*He* may not."

"That won't work," I state. "The Rules of Creation clearly state that I get a supernatural plus-one for any visits the Ether."

In truth, there's no such thing as a supernatural plus-one. But I spent years manipulating ghouls. In situations like this, I can get shit done.

"All right," states Victoria slowly.

The way she says those words, I have a feeling something strange is coming.

Or rather, strange-ER.

## 47

# THE BEAST

*M*yla and Victoria chat away. I try to focus on their words. It isn't easy. Every inch of me still feels numb with shock.

Myla's soul.

It was beyond beautiful.

Her transparent form is just like the physical version in how it radiates with light and life.

At some point, I'm vaguely aware that a pair of small dark shapes have appeared in the clouds. When this happened before, Victoria landed beside us. Now, I can only assume one thing.

Two more people are on their way.

I sift through everything I know about the Ether of Eden. Victoria and Grace serve as its two stewards. Beyond that, little is known about either the stewards or the place under their care.

By rights, only one more person should arrive. Since Victoria is here, that would mean Grace is on her way. But two? That's not expected.

Soon the forms become larger. Turns out, these aren't people at all. They're a pair of featherlings. One has red plumage, the other is green. The red featherling swoops down and latches its claws onto my shoulders. Its green counterpart attaches to Myla.

Within seconds, we're both airborne.

Being flown about by a featherling is a surprisingly smooth experience. Bulbous eyes pop up from the wings' peak, allowing the creature to choose the right path. The claws keep a firm hold on my shoulders, yet do not break the skin. The great wings beat in a regular and soothing rhythm.

All three of us fly toward the same spot. To human eyes, this cloud would look the same as the rest of the morning sky. But if you're from the after-realms, you can detect a shimmery spot on the gray gaze.

It's a portal.

The featherlings fly us through the glittering vapors. One moment, we soar above a snow-covered Earth. The next second, we fly toward a shining city of skyscrapers that's built upon a great floating rock.

The Ether of Eden.

As we move in closer, it's clear that the buildings are actually hollow shells. Inside, the structures are mostly roosts for eagles, hawks and every type of bird.

Myla, Victoria and I fly above the city. My heart soars almost as high as the featherlings. One thought reverberates through my soul.

*It's here below me. The Ether of Eden.*

Although I'd no idea what the Ether would be, the fact that it's a floating city makes sense. And somewhere below, there's the signet ring of Eden... the first of three that are needed to defeat Bedlam.

Looking down, I soak in every aspect of the landscape. Birds wheel in and out of every building and across each avenue. The city itself is set up like a wagon wheel with spoke-streets moving out from a central courtyard. A great statue marks the exact midpoint of everything.

My featherling changes direction. Along with Myla and Victoria, I fly toward the city center in long and slow circles.

Moments later, I land on solid ground once more. Around me, the courtyard seems deserted. Even the birds have returned to their roosts. Yet my hunter's sense tells me that we are far from alone here.

Victoria rounds on me and Myla. "Welcome to the Ether of Eden," she announces. "Now you shall meet the Edenians."

"Wait, what?" asks Myla.

I couldn't agree more. In all my research, I've never run across the very word Edenians. They could be any number of creations, just like the featherlings.

Guess we'll find out soon enough.

# THE ETHER OF EDEN

## 48

## MYLA

*V*ictoria raises her arms. "Move forward, Edenians."

*Huh. Guess we're not getting an explanation about what's an Edenian.*

The answer appears soon enough. Adults in black robes march out from the nearest buildings. Children in white onesies lurk behind their parents. Other folks leap from the rooftops to soar through the skies with the help of their featherlings. Soon the courtyard becomes downright crowded.

The Beast frowns. "I thought the Edens were only inhabited by a pair of stewards."

Victoria sniffs. "It's as I told you before. We work hard to protect our true nature. The Garden, Ark and Ether were all founded by both stewards and Edenians." She fixes me with an unreadable look. "You're the first to pass the *test of journeys*. We've had no other visitors in the Ether."

*Not sure what to say here.* "Um, thanks?"

Victoria does not reply. Instead, she gestures to a gray-haired man and woman. "Come."

The elderly couple step forward. The man holds a white box; the woman carries a wounded falcon. At least, I think it's hurt. If not, its wing just naturally hangs at an odd angle. The bird lets out a sad chirp. Okay, it's totally in need of help. *Poor falcon.*

Victoria opens the box. A glimmer of gold shines within. Every nerve in my body seems to scream, *Can it be a signet ring at last?*

I look over to the Beast, wondering if he's thinking the same thing. For his part, the prince keeps fiddling with his pockets. Dollars to donuts, the guy is trying out some charms to get at that signet ring.

*Oh, he's thinking the same thing, all right.*

Now, I know Victoria isn't stuck in slow motion. It sure feels that way, though. Little by little, she pulls the glittering object from the white container and sets it on her finger.

And there it is. The signet ring for the Ether of Eden.

The steward raises her left hand. The signet band gleams on her ring finger.

For a moment, it's all I can do to simply stare at the magical object. This is the key to unlocking my old life.

Closing her eyes, Victoria clenches her fist. She then blows a single breath across her curled fingers. When Victoria opens her hand, the signet ring glows with dark blue light and power. Indigo-colored mist rolls off her opened palm and over to envelop the injured falcon.

The spell has begun.

This is the same magic Bedlam has been wielding for ages. Only the Titan of Chaos sends out his dark clouds-o-trouble from hidden corners. I've never seen him actually use these rings before.

The mist rolls back from the falcon to return onto Victoria's open palm. When the steward closes her hand again, the blue cloud of power is completely gone. The signet ring no longer glows. The spell is done.

Best of all, the hawk is healed. With a happy caw, it soars up to the skies.

Victoria lowers her head. "Let us all take a moment to honor the greatest healer of us all, the Steward Grace of the Ether."

The crowd turns to look behind me. Following their gaze, I discover that a massive statue looms over the entire square.

*Funny, I didn't notice that before.*

*Oh, right.* I was having serious vertigo thanks to the fact that I was being dragged around by a featherling. This statue shows a tall woman with long straight hair, massive wings, and the kind of wide-eyed gaze that says, *come here and I'll fix you right up.*

It's Grace.

My thoughts circle back to when the Beast and I last stood on Earth and asked about the featherlings. At the time, Victoria seemed ready to burst into tears.

Did her reaction have something to do with Grace?

I scan the statue's inscription. It reads, *beloved wife and first featherling.*

Questions zing through my mind. Does *beloved wife* mean that Grace is dead? There are no dates on here like you'd see with a human tombstone. And why does it say *first featherling*?

Back on the mountain, Victoria stated that she *created* her featherling. So why doesn't this statue say Grace is the first *creator* of featherlings?

I shake my head. *You're overthinking this, Myla.* Whoever carved the inscription probably wanted to save on space, that's all.

Victoria raises her head. "Our time of remembrance for my dear wife is over. Our guests shall now introduce themselves."

A jolt of electric interest moves through the crowd. Victoria gestures toward me and the Beast. "Which of you will speak?"

The Beast steps forward. "Allow me."

I let out a series of coughs that sound a lot like *partner* and *equals.*

The Beast glares at me. "Hush."

I flip him an unsavory hand gesture with a glare that says, *is that quiet enough for you?*

The Beast shoots me a dry look. "I am Prince Lincoln," he announces. "This is Myla Lewis. We're here to borrow your steward's signet ring."

All the color drains from Victoria's face. "Borrow? BORROW?"

"That's right," I say. "It's when you take something, use it for a little while, and then bring it back." *Victoria must not get out much.*

The steward marches over to the Beast. "Show me your arm." Without waiting for any reply, Victoria grabs the Beast's wrist and tears up his body armor to the elbow. "You're cursed with two petals remaining." She steps back. "You never said that before."

I raise my pointer finger. I've been doing that a lot since I began hanging out with the Beast. "You never asked."

Victoria rounds on me. "I was concerned that you might bring Scala magic into our city." He points at the Beast. "But this one overflows with the power of chaos."

"I dunno." I shrug. "Everything here seems fine to me."

Suddenly, the city lurches at an odd angle. People scream. Birds caw. Children weep against their parents. Victoria glares at me like she'd love to rip out my heart with her teeth.

"Or maybe everything's going to Hell," I state. "That could be happening, too."

The steward loses her mind. She races though the crowd, screaming, "We're doomed!"

*Victoria. Great at healing falcons. Crap in a crisis.*

While the steward goes berserk, I step over to the Beast. "Where's that duplicator charm?"

"Not here."

"What? I asked you to bring it."

"Those are unreliable at best. Instead, I brought charisma boosters so Victoria would be inspired to share the ring."

"Really. And how's that working out?"

"While Victoria was speaking, I used every charm in my collection. So the answer is, *not well*. As a matter of fact, I doubt that ring will even come off her finger, barring a massive spell. And you and I are warriors, not enchanters."

"In that case, I have good news for you. I figured you might end up being a lying sack of crap, so I brought along some stuff to MacGyver us a duplication charm."

"Mac what?"

"Just shut up and be amazed." Reaching into the pockets of my borrowed body armor, I pull out various items and narrate as I go because *nyah*. "This is a compact mirror charm. It reflects a supernatural object. And here's a lip balm thingy that takes magical impressions. Finally, I brought what looks like eyedrops, but it's actually witchy superglue that will hold both charms together."

While the Beast looks on, I smear the mirror's surface with lip balm before adding a few drops of witchy superglue. "Voila! We now have a magical duplicator." I hold the souped-up mirror high.

"How do you know this will work?"

I point to my own face. "Queen of Antrum in another reality, my friend."

The ground tilts even more dramatically. Victoria screams louder. Everything becomes pandemonium of bodies rushing, birds flying and mad mojo.

Time to make our move.

# GRACE

## MYLA

y mind goes into battle mode. Thousands of contingencies fly through my brain at once. Seconds later, the perfect solution appears.

I round on the Beast. "Here's what we'll do." I raise the mirror charm. "I'll use this to make a duplicate of Victoria's ring. You get some featherlings for the both of us."

The Beast folds his arms over his chest. "Hold on, now. Is a duplicator charm really the best idea here?"

I roll my eyes. "The city is toppling and it's the only charm we have left, so yes."

"Duplication magic is very basic. The chances that it will actually work and create a functioning signet ring are rather low."

"And the better plan is?"

As I ask this question, the street lurches further. This time, it flips to a twenty-degree angle. Buildings wobble. More birds fly out from the windows and squawk their heads off. I narrowly avoid getting pooped on.

It's the near-miss of bird crap that really sets me off.

"Seriously?" I throw my hands up. "You're honestly going to second guess me here?"

"What else would I do?"

"We both know that *I* am the one who's great with last-minute planning. You're really good at listening, acknowledging my plan is awesome, and figuring out a way to make it better."

At this point, the birds are getting downright rowdy. Some kind of eagle thing with two heads flies at me. My tail bats it away.

The Beast purses his lips. At this moment, it really ticks me off that his mouth matches that of my beloved and totally reasonable husband. The Beast pats down his body armor. "I may still have a charm somewhere that could help."

"We went through this before! You tried every charm you brought. Nothing worked."

The ground lurches again, this time to a full forty degrees. The taller buildings sway with more force. Edenians race out into the streets, screaming for Victoria to save them with her signet ring. Other Edenians take to the skies. More race about the ground in a panic, their featherlings left to flop about.

The Beast taps his chin. Did I mention I want to punch him? *I do.*

"We tried *every* charm?" asks the Beast. It's doubly annoying how calm he is through all this. "I wasn't aware of that. You might be carrying a few more on your person."

"Well, I don't." *Total lie.*

"And I'm just supposed to trust you?" A bloodthirsty dinosaur bird flies toward the back of the Beast's head. At the last possible second, he leans to one side and lifts his fist, a motion which punches the dino-flyer in the nose.

"No, you're supposed to watch me. Discussion time is over."

Turning, I take off at a run for Victoria who is screaming at the same old couple that brought her the injured bird. "Flee!" cries the steward.

The couple does not react one way or another. I get the

distinct impression that Victoria may lose her cool on a regular basis.

I race straight for the steward. At the last second, I crouch down low, leap into the air and somersault over Victoria's head. While I'm upside-down, I catch a reflection of the signet ring on my mirror. Then I land on the other side of the steward in one of those hero-kneels where I'm on one knee with my fist to the ground.

Again, the old couple do not seem impressed. "Why didn't you just walk up behind her and shine your mirror on her hand that way?" asks the woman.

I rise. "Because what's the fun in that?"

"Good point," says the man.

"Panic!" screams Victoria.

The city lurches to sixty degrees. Some Edenians slide across the street, but are able to stop themselves before falling off the city proper. For my part, I grab onto a nearby tree, my feet dangling above the ground.

My heart leaps into my throat. Have I mentioned how much I hate heights? *I do.*

The Beast flies overhead. In one swift movement, he scoops me into his arms. I squirm under his grip.

"Where are my wings?" I ask.

The Beast's voice sounds all low and smug in my ear. "As a wise woman recently said, *discussion time is over.*"

Once we're fully airborne, the city snaps back to being level again. A cheer rises up from the Edenians while the birds circle above the buildings in a great loop.

At this point, I'm aware of two things. One, I still hate heights. And two, I do like being called a wise woman.

## THE BEAST

*I* carry Myla in my arms.

This should be an awkward experience. After all, she's a known criminal… a questionable ally of my busybody mother… someone who dressed up as an Amour under odd circumstances… and a person who's broken away from the library after specifically promising *not* to do so.

Yet she feels absolutely perfect in my embrace. It's as if every curve of her body were meant for me.

Our featherling descends through the cloud portal which connects the Ether and Earth. It isn't long before the creature resets us onto the same mountaintop where we began our morning's journey.

I wish the featherling would stay a while. As a hunter, I find this creation fascinating. But the featherling merely places us on the ground before taking off into the sky. Which is probably for the best. Myla and I must return to the library and see what, if anything, can be done with that copied signet ring.

Myla pulls on her ear. "What did you say again?"

I pretend to be confused. In truth, I know exactly what Myla refers to here. I should never have complemented her a few minutes ago.

"Me?" I ask. "I said nothing." Lowering my arms, I set her back on her feet. It's best to gain some distance between us.

"Oh, it was something, your nothing."

"Don't gloat."

Myla grins. "This is me, totally gloating. You called me a wise woman. Admit it. I'm getting to you."

"You're delusional."

"Correction." Myla holds up her hand, showing how the mirror charm already created a copy of the ring. The new band glistens on her finger. "I'm delusional *and effective*."

"Prepare to transport," I announce.

That's what I say aloud, but what I'm thinking is far more dangerous.

There's no denying it. Myla *is* getting to me.

## 51

## MYLA

*S*o this is awesome.

Teasing the Beast is quickly becoming the best part of my day.

I flash my ring some more. "Look how pretty it is. And it's mine. My own. My precious."

The muscles along the Beast's jawline pull tight. He's getting annoyed, all right. I open my mouth, ready to unleash more Gollum humor.

"In thrax sic hunt!" cries the Beast.

*Oops.*

Totally forgot we were standing on a Pulpitum platform.

The round disc lurches into the earth. And since everything in Antrum is now janky as Hell, this isn't a regular transfer jolt. The impact throws me, big time. As in, I'm standing on tiptoe with my arms pinwheeling.

Alarm rattles down my spine. It's not like Pulpitum have safety bars around the edges. Dirt, rock and magma go flying past as we hurtle deep underground. If I reach out to touch the view as we speed by, that's the end of my hand.

I'm about to tumble into handlessness—and that's at a

minimum—when a heavy set of arms wrap around me, setting me upright.

It's the Beast.

He keeps me close against him as the Pulpitum zooms lower. Every so often, the platform jerks from one direction to another. I barely sense the change.

This is so like my Lincoln. I want to relish the moment and all the memories. My husband would do anything to keep me safe.

My thoughts circle back to the Angelic Conspiracy and its *blah blah blah* about people getting manipulated into love. Maybe they're wrong. True love and rainbows might be real, after all.

The platform comes to a jarring halt. We've returned to the same storage room as before.

And we're still holding each other.

With every passing second, my soul soars higher. What we share together must be real.

All of a sudden, the Beast presses me away. "Take your hands off my person," he snaps.

Then again, maybe angelic manipulation really is a thing.

I hate to admit this, but every time I convince myself it's impossible, the Angelic Conspiracy simply becomes more likely. Perhaps if Verus hadn't aligned our lives *just so*, then Lincoln and I would never have fallen in love. Instead, we'd be stuck in this constant loop where we aren't sure whether to kiss or kill each other.

Like we are right now.

## 52

## THE BEAST

*M*yla steps off in a huff.

Clearly, she's not happy that I didn't want her pawing me. She'll adjust. And she'll also find her own way back to the library. I don't follow after her.

Instead, I choose my own return path. There are no servants along the way, but that doesn't mean they aren't lurking in the shadows, ready to share gossip for a price.

No doubt, all of Antrum knows the story by now. They believe Prince Lincoln has taken up with a quasi Amour.

My people can think what they like.

I've two petals left. I do what I must to survive.

As I step through the passageways to the library, it happens again.

A waist-high rainbow appears before me. The colored arc rises until a full loop hangs in the air nearby. And inside that circle, I see him again.

The boy. Maxon.

The child runs about while wielding a wooden sword. A woman steps into the boy's line of vision. Maxon drops the weapon and runs into her arms.

It is Myla. For the first time, I can see her face clearly.

My heart cracks with longing and regret. Is it true that this is my life in another reality? Can I grasp even a sliver of that joy here?

Sadly, I already know the answer to that question. If I'm able to stop Bedlam, then that's the most I can expect in this life. Anything else is a distraction designed to lure me closer to my own oblivion.

The round rainbow vanishes and with it goes hope.

I press open the library door. Inside there stands the same woman who grinned at Myla in the Versailles Ballroom.

Cissy Frederickson.

She wears a yellow dress, which is the color of the House of Acca. Unlike Myla, Cissy's tail is still concealed. She bounces on the balls of her feet while smiling from ear to ear. It's like being greeted by a puppy.

Cissy grips some papers agains her chest. "I have something for Myla. Where is she?"

A panel opens in a nearby wall. Myla steps out. "Hello, Cissy." She glares at me. "Beast."

Cissy's mouth falls open. "Wow. You really know your way around these secret passages."

"She does," I state. "Even when promising *not* to use them."

Some small part of me knows it's unfair to be angry at Myla right now. I can't help it, though.

"Bite me, Beast," snaps Myla. "I never promised not to break promises."

Ignoring Myla for the moment, I round on Cissy. "What is in those documents?"

"You'll never believe it." Cissy clutches the sheets more tightly. "These are the exact details on where Eve is hiding." She turns to Myla. "You were right. The House of Cuthbert was hoarding the info for no reason. They are so weird."

Myla scoops the documents from Cissy's hands. "You're the best."

"You HAVE to come see me after you visit Eve." Cissy clasps her hands beneath her chin. "I want details."

Myla winks at her friend. "You got it."

Stepping up to the pair, I stretch my arm forward in a clear gesture for *give that to me now*. "Hand it over."

Myla mock-weeps. "See how sweet he is, Cissy?" She pats under her eyes while sniffling. "He didn't believe that Eve could be found by the House of Cuthbert and—" *sniffle, sniffle* "—we totally proved him wrong. Now he's acting like a total gentleman, so thankful and kind." Myla shoots me an angry look. "Back off, Grabby."

A long pause follows. Fresh energy zings between me and Myla. I can't decide if I want to send her into exile or marry her. And the fact that I'm even wondering about this is worrying in the extreme.

For her part, Cissy smacks her lips. "So. Seems like you two are getting along." She inches toward the exit. "Oh, my! Look at the time. I have to run."

"Wait," I command. Cissy freezes mid-step. "You've quickly set up good contacts within Antrum."

"She's the best," offers Myla. "That's how she got the info on Eve so quickly. Which is what I *tried* to say before, only you were too stubborn and grouchy to listen." Myla looks to her friend. "In case you were wondering."

Cissy shakes her head so fast, a ringlet smacks her in the eye. "Nope. Not wondering."

I stalk closer to Cissy. "I have one question for you before you depart."

Cissy exhales. "A single question. I can handle that."

"What's the latest gossip from my mother?"

"Oh." Cissy shrugs. "That's easy. She thinks you're trapped in a Beauty and the Beast curse. All this Bedlam stuff is nonsense."

Cissy looks to Myla. "Beauty and the Beast... is that how your story really goes?"

"Nah," replies Myla. "Our tale is more like, girl loves boy... girl loses boy... girl wants to punch boy in the throat because his memory has been wiped. Your standard romance."

"Well," continues Cissy. "Octavia is super-happy that her son may have found a woman who's crazy enough to tolerate him." Cissy turns to me once more. "Oh, and she's shocked that a Beast like you found your own Beauty. Octavia was certain one of her Amours would do the trick. Buh-bye."

Cissy rushes out the door. I'm too surprised to ask her to stay. I keep turning her last words over in my mind, but there's no avoiding the truth.

*Octavia did not send Myla to me as an Amour.* Once again, Myla was correct all along. And I was perhaps acting in a slightly beastly manner.

In the world's most predictable turn of events, Myla begins to gloat anew. This time, she runs about in a circle while pumping her arms in the air and singing a tune from the human movie called *Rocky.*

"Duh duh DUUUUH... duh duh DUUUUH... duh duh DUUUUH... duh duh DUUUUH! Da du da du da daaaat... da da da da dat du da DAT DAAAAAAAAAH!"

"That's quite enough," I deadpan. For some reason, it's impossible not to smile.

"I *told* you that Octavia didn't send me."

"My error."

Myla bobs her brows. "Good. Now you owe me."

"Not sure how that logic follows."

"That was a grouchy statement and I'm going to ignore it. Here's what we'll do. Tomorrow morning, we'll go see Eve at 8:34 AM. You will wait outside. I'll have girl-talk with Eve. That's it. Our planning session is now over."

"Wait," I snap. "Why 8:34 AM? And what's the logic of only you speaking with Eve first?"

Myla opens her mouth in mock shock. "Oh, my goodness. Is it annoying not to get full details? Wow. That's so incredibly rude of me. And selfish and grouchy—"

"Point made." When I next speak, it's an effort to use something resembling a kind tone. "Please explain the specifics. I look forward to following your plan."

After another round of Rocky-inspired running and singing, Myla gets back on topic. "Eve lives in Antrum. Her place is warded to the hilt. We could break in, but that would take up time and magic that we don't have. But she does leave her cottage every day at 8:34 AM."

"Makes sense." I'm forcing a grin at this point, and I'm not sure it's very convincing. "And why would you be the one to approach her?"

"Gut call. I dunno. Give us ten minutes and then knock on the door."

"I agree to this plan, but on some conditions."

Myla rolls her eyes. "Here we go."

*Indeed.*

## MYLA

*This ought to be good.*

"You have conditions," I repeat.

"Obviously. Do you agree to them?" asks the Beast.

"Explain them first."

"Today has already been a rather long adventure. You need food, a bath, and then some sleep. Those are my requirements."

"Hold on." I frown. "Are you being nice to me?"

"No, you're useful and I'm protecting the lives of both myself and my people."

"And *that* is why you're a lonely Beast."

"Do you wish my charity toward your person or don't you?"

"Charity? Nope."

At this point, there is no way in Hell that I'm taking anything from the Beast. I reach into a pocket of my battle armor and pull out my horde of charms. I hold up two enchanted items, namely a breath mint and stick of gum. "I have these for cleaning and food. I don't need help from a grouch. All I need is a decent bed."

The Beast gestures toward the corner. "Then sleep."

I roll my eyes. "So we're back to this."

"The pile of blankets are comfortable."

"As I said before, I'm not a pet."

"Why not? That's where I sleep."

*Side note.* Back in my reality, I sometimes take Lincoln's shirts and cuddle with them in bed when he's away. And the fact that I'm destined for a pile of his scent right now? That just makes me a mixture of lusty and pissed off.

Mostly the second thing.

"Come on," I continue. "Don't we—*I mean, you*—have a million rooms in this place?"

"You're not staying somewhere you can escape again. I can track you far better in here."

Rage heats my veins. "The Lincoln I knew would have ensured I had the best room in the palace, not shoved me on a pile."

The Beast gets closer. When he speaks, his voice rasps with menace. "Only *he's* not here and *I am*. What does that tell you about the fate of good men?"

My tail arcs over my shoulder. The arrowhead-shaped end points at my nose before wagging from side to side. "I agree, boy." I focus on the Beast. "Good men get the great girls, that's what I know."

A knock sounds on the library door. I'm happy for the diversion, mostly because my inner wrath demon is heading straight for berserker mode.

"Come in," calls the Beast.

A small troop of servants enter the library while carrying fresh blankets and linens for my corner. They also haul in a brass bathtub, along with towels and soap. Once done, the group scurries from the room at double speed.

No one wants to be near the Beast. Go figure.

Once the servants are gone, I refocus on the Beast. "What's this? In my version of Arx hall, we have running water."

The Beast fixes his mismatched gaze on me. "The Tumult killed off the house that manages those supply lines. My people risk their lives to bring me hot water for my bath. I intend to enjoy it."

I nod. Now that sounds a *little* like my Lincoln—the Beast actually cares that people are taking risks for his comfort.

The Beast pulls at the neckline of his body armor. "Would you like to go first?"

"No." I raise the mint. "Cleaning charm."

"Suit yourself."

The Beast unlatches the top of his body armor. A line of bare chest appears between the open halves of his top.

Suddenly, the blanket-bed doesn't seem so shitty. It comes complete with a mighty fine view, as a matter of fact. I get very busy with my pile of stuff in the corner. The Beast then slips off his bottoms.

*Truth time.* Am I perving on some random guy just because he looks exactly like my husband and maybe shares some of the same memories?

*Hells, yeah.*

It's been a crap week. I'm taking my happy where I can find it.

I notice some new things by my blanket pile. The servants dropped off a nightgown for me as well as some demon bars, which are my favorite snack food ever. I gingerly pick up one of the treats and cradle it between my hands as the cherished object it is.

"What's all this?" I ask.

"I left a few instructions for the servants."

*And it happens again.* Just when I think this guy is an asshat, he goes and does something nice.

*Who is this man? My prince or a beast?*

## THE BEAST

*I* finish my bath. Although I keep my back toward Myla, I sense her eyes on me the entire time. Her attention is warmth that spreads though my veins.

It's good to have her near.

A realization appears. I always could have placed Myla in another room. To keep her from escaping, I might have lined the walls and outer hallways with guards. Yet that was never an option.

The very idea of our separation makes me want to howl with rage.

I get out of the tub, dry myself off, and slip on a pair of flannel pajama bottoms. For the first time in days, I shall sleep while lying down and not with my head on a tabletop. Can't wait.

Myla eyes the PJs. "Since when did that start?"

"Meaning?" I actually know what she refers to, but I wish to hear her explain.

"Normally, you sleep nude."

A fact appears in my mind's eye. "As do you."

Myla sits up, and it's clear she's wearing the sleeping gown I requested from the servants. "How did you know that?" she asks.

"I guessed." *Not true.*

"You're a good liar," counters Myla. "But not that good. You remember things about me." She gestures between us. "About our marriage."

I sift through the fresh pile of blankets and create my own nest not far from hers. "We should both rest."

"I thought you wanted to sit nearby and watch that I didn't escape."

"Changed my mind." I relax upon my own pile of blankets.

"Don't you think everyone will find it odd that you're still sleeping in here when there are a kazillion bed chambers in this palace?"

"They'd think it far more strange if I actually slept anywhere else."

"Then you're hiding me here?"

I shrug. "I should have thought that was obvious."

*It's also not the full truth. Again.*

Myla rolls onto her side and perches her head against her hand. "Now you'll just snooze."

"Your powers of reasoning are truly amazing."

"Suck it." Myla narrows her eyes. "Is this you trusting me?"

"Only this much." I hold thumb and forefinger apart.

"But—"

"No more talking. More sleeping. See you in the morning."

I wave my hand, which makes all the angelfire lamps in the library die out. It's a neat trick, which is why I save it for special occasions.

And as I'd hoped, all discussion ends.

Time to rest.

## MYLA

When I fall asleep, I basically cuddle against the wall. I decide that once this is nightmare over, I may take up camping. It's kind of fun to rest in something that's not a bed, assuming it's comfy enough.

And all these blankets smell like my Lincoln, so there's that.

So the falling asleep part of the evening is fine. It's waking up in the morning that's a total shock. Why? Because when I open my eyes, I'm lying in the middle of the floor.

The Beast is next to me.

Aaaaaaaaaand we're holding hands.

It's sweet.

And terrifying.

Mostly the second thing.

I hop up to stand. My first thought is that the Beast must have rolled across the floor to commit a nocturnal hand assault.

But that's not the case.

We both rolled half-way across the threadbare rug to meet in the exact middle between our blanket piles.

Somehow, that's way worse.

The Beast stretches. I can't help but notice how he has fewer scars than my Lincoln. The muscle definition is the same, though. My lust demon wakes up, sending me all sorts of mental images of how that chest has looked while we're both naked.

*Uh, oh.*

I force myself to turn around, rush to the door, and ask a messenger to fetch me a bath. Anything but standing around and staring at a half-naked doppelgänger of my husband. The servant warns they won't have time to heat the water, so the bath will be cold.

I say that will be just fine and dandy. Because now it's time to get ready.

*And pretend that I never held hands with a Beast.*

## MYLA

*W*atch out, Eve. It's almost 8:34 AM.

I pace in Eve's courtyard, careful not to trip on the hem of my long velvet gown. Behind me stands the steward's so-called cottage. In reality, the place is a cross between a cathedral and a palace. I'm talking a big and imposing structure with lots of arches and stone angels.

While I keep up my march, my tail does its *up periscope* move by my shoulder, which means it's looking for Eve to appear through the trees.

*Yes, actual trees.*

Few places in Antrum even try to have forests. It's a consequence of life underground. For the few spots that do, the arbors are usually carved from stone. It's attractive and low maintenance at the same time.

But outside Eve's cottage? There are actual green things that need sunlight and whatnot. Growing up in Purgatory, I had one fern that I tried to keep alive. I killed it in a week. But that's me. Eve must have all sorts of mad plant skills, considering her years in the Garden of Eden.

My tail stops to wave at a particular spot in the forest. No question why, either. That must be where the Beast is lurking. The prince has promised to knock on the cottage door after I've chatted up Eve for precisely ten minutes.

I tap on my tail's arrowhead-shaped end. "That's enough, boy. I'm sure the Beast saw you already."

My tail does not stop waving.

Which is a total bummer.

Honestly, I was counting on my tail continuing to be anti-Beast. It makes my life easier. After all, I still may need to ditch the prince and go off on my own here. I can't afford for my tail to get attached.

Who am I kidding? I'm the one who's feelings are really confused here. The Beast totally looks like my Lincoln. More and more, he acts like him too.

My tail pokes my shoulder before pointing in a new direction. Eve must be on her way.

"Down, boy," I whisper. "You'll scare her." My tail dutifully droops to hang by the ankle of my gown.

Eve steps out from the line of trees. She's tall and lithe with an aristocratic air and a traditional thrax gown. She leads her white mare with her left hand while holding a long sword in her right.

There's no sign of any signet ring on her hand. Boo.

Eve eyes me from head to toe. "You're a quasi demon."

"I know." My tail waves to her over my shoulder. I really need to work on my tail's stealth skills.

Eve lifts her sword. "What are you doing on my land?"

"I'm here to meet Eve, the great Steward of the Garden of Eden."

She freezes for a moment before regaining her composure. "I don't know what you're talking about. My name is Ekke."

I cough, but it might sound a little like *bullshit.*

A moment ago, Eve was all sword-wielding sass. Now she drags her horse past me at double-speed. "Excuse me."

Thanks to my recent encounters with the Beast, I'm well

versed in how to handle this particular kind of attitude. I step into her horses path and blocking their retreat. My eyes flare red with demonic light.

"You're Eve," I declare.

"Again, my name is Ekke. I'm a human under the protection of the House of Cuthbert. Not sure where you got the idea that I'm Eve."

"Good question." I whip out some papers from my pocket and shake them dramatically. "According to these documents, there was a woman named Eve who was given this cottage at 1053 AD. And then every hundred years after that—*just like clockwork*—the mistress of this house dies from a fever, only to leave the place to someone with a similar name. Eve to Ewa. Ewa to Eya. It goes on and on until Ekke."

Eve lifts her chin. "I don't see what that proves."

"It shows you need to do some research before trying to impersonate someone. Humans rarely live to 100, let alone take over a castle at 23, live to 123, die from a fever, and then give that same palace to someone else who's name rhymes with theirs. If this is you being tricky, you suck at it."

Eve sighs. "What do you want?"

I eye Eve carefully. She gives in easily, yet there's a steely look in her eyes that says she's waiting to make a counter-strike.

"Glad you asked," I reply. "I'd love to chat about Bedlam. He's been quite the busy immortal boy. How about we talk inside?" Without waiting for an answer, I cross the courtyard and let myself into her cottage.

The sight that greets me is not what I expected.

Bedlam's not the only one who's been busy.

## THE BEAST

*C*rouching in the forest shadows, I keep a keen watch on the cottage of the woman who calls herself Ekke.

In truth, she's Eve. And she wields powerful magic in the form of a signet ring. The documents Cissy found showed where to *find* this steward, but nothing about her personality.

How will Eve react when confronted?

Over in the courtyard, Myla and Eve begin to speak. In short order, it's clear that Eve is not pleased with the conversation. On reflex, I reach for my baculum and grip both bars with my right hand. It's unlikely that Eve would attack, but you can never be certain.

*Wait, am I worrying about Myla?*

That can't be out of any warmth of feeling. My only concern is that this mission succeeds.

*Yes, that's it. Nothing more.*

A rainbow appears on the ground before me. It quickly rises into a full loop. Once more, a scene plays out in the center.

I should look away.

Yet I can't.

Inside the circle, I see another version of me standing on the battle floor of Purgatory's Arena. I'm younger and more scarred but somehow also less weighed down by something I can't name.

That must be him. Myla's Lincoln.

Myla herself steps into view. She's lovely and fierce in a fitted battle suit. My heart soars.

Suddenly, a tinea demon rises half-way up from the ground. These humanoid demons are nearly impossible to kill. To take down these wormy creatures, all four limbs must be sliced at the same time. I inhale a sharp breath; how will Myla survive this?

The other Lincoln ignites his baculum as a pair of short swords while the tinea fully surfaces. For her part, Myla leaps over the demon's head while igniting her own baculum as short swords as well. Myla and her Lincoln move in sync to cut all the demon's limbs at once. The tinea falls over, dead.

My thoughts roll back to all the times I gave Myla orders without seeing her as an equal. And in this vision, she and the other Lincoln act in perfect tandem. Bands of sorrow tighten around my heart.

That can never be me. I have fewer scars on my body, but far more across my soul.

The round rainbow vanishes. I refocus on the cottage, careful for any sign of trouble.

No matter what, I must protect Myla.

# EVE

## MYLA

*I*nside the cottage, there's embroidery everywhere.

Framed on the walls.

Covering chairs.

Forming tablecloths.

Used as rugs.

I guess if you have all of eternity and really like embroidery, then this is what happens.

Eve bursts through the door. "You shouldn't be in here. Don't look at the embroidery."

In reply, I shoot her deadpan stare. "This is me, looking at the embroidery."

Eve sighs once more. "Fine. Look at it. I don't care."

Once again, Eve gives in too easily. Probably because she's not wearing her signet ring yet. Chances are, the chick is waiting to get her gear on and then she'll melt me into a slug.

Hey, it's what I would do if I were her.

I step slowly around the room, scanning the artwork as I go. There are images of the Garden of Eden, both in bloom and when it burned to the ground. One picture even includes a charred-out skeleton that's clearly marked *Adam*. Because that's not creepy or anything. Beside those pictures hang portraits of both the Ark and Ether of Eden. Other frames only hold cute sayings, like *Balance is Life.*

Clearly, Eve has a lot of time on her hands and a remarkable resistance to carpal tunnel syndrome.

One image grabs my attention in particular. It shows an old man with a flowing beard who stands on the deck of a ship. If I had to guess, this is Noah, Steward of the Ark of Eden. A phrase is written under his portrait.

*Cad Lien Polos*

I'm about to ask what the heck that means when something else catches my eye. Another portrait.

Only it looks a lot like Gastonne.

I do a double take. Nope, this is the exact same man I saw under the Sahara and in Antrum. *Gastonne. Bedlam. The Titan of Chaos.* Pick your name, it's all the same freak show.

And there isn't just one portrait of Gastonne, either. Dozens of them cover an entire wall. To mix things up, Eve also captured his snake-skin look as well as the diseased Mister Potato Head thing.

Turning toward Eve, I point to this wall of shame. "What's going on ?"

Eve sighs yet again. "The heart wants what it wants."

"You've *got* to be kidding."

"Being a steward is about balance." She shrugs. "Imagine an eternity of keeping everything *just so.* Wouldn't you find chaos exciting?"

I open my mouth, ready to tell Eve she's nuts. But I stop myself. Who am I to judge? After all, I couldn't exactly handle the structure of living under ghoul rule. The only way I survived my teen tears was by killing demons in the Arena. And as long as she isn't hurting anyone, I suppose Eve's infatuation isn't too terrible.

Then again, I *killed* demons. I didn't *ship* them.

"May I give you some advice?" I ask.

"Can I stop you?"

"Not really. If you're bored, perhaps you can get a new hobby. I really think you've explored everything you can with embroidery."

"But I already have other interests. It's like I told you; I'm obsessed with Bedlam's chaos."

"Gotta challenge you on that one. Bedlam is a killer who encases people alive for all eternity. There's a break between craving excitement and being a sicko. Loving Bedlam crosses that line."

Eve's even features twist with rage. "You *would* say something like that to me. You think *you're* his queen." To accent this point, she gestures to another wall of images. I force myself to look.

What I see is a downright shocker. A jigsaw puzzle of framed pictures covers the wall. Only this time, all of them show me in various stages of getting my ass kicked. In some, I'm running in traffic. Others display me being stabbed, falling off a cliff, and drowning at sea. There's even one of me laid out in my casket.

Eve creeps up behind me. "Imagine loving a man. Having his full heart. And then losing him to some little slut."

"It's a *soul-swapping demigoddess slut* to you."

"He sees you as his Queen of Chaos."

"I'm already married. And I'd like to keep it that way."

I spot another set of Gastonne portraits, this time set onto couch pillows. Like Eve's other images, these show the classic Gastonne glamour pose. Only this time, it looks like she's sliced his face through with a knife.

Unlike everything else in this room, I find these pillows to be totally fucked up... yet mildly encouraging.

I lift a pillow from the chaise. "Hey, what's this now? You say you love Bedlam, but I think you hate him, too." I gesture along the slice with true *game show hostess* energy. "This knife cut is an especially healthy addition to your design. I think you should keep going with that. Work out your rage."

Eve sets her hands over her heart. "With Bedlam, it started off as love. Every word from his mouth was unexpected and beautiful. I was lured in. But he's also truly horrible to me. Mostly because he's so obsessed with you."

"Well, I am pretty awesome."

"Sometimes, he just makes me so angry."

I tap my chin, as if really considering options here. "You know how you can work out that fury?" I throw up my arms in a motion that says, *have I got the idea for you.* "Help me destroy Bedlam!"

"I can't." Eve sighs yet again, and it's officially getting on my nerves. "Don't you see? I'm exhausted."

"False. You look pretty rested to me. Plus, you've got a nice castle-cottage situation going here. A free horse. No real job outside of excessive embroidery. Think. Without the Almighty, the world's about to end. It's a thin line between tired and lazy. Help a girl out."

"Any effort against Bedlam is wasted. No one takes him on." Eve folds her arms over her chest. "I cannot aid you. It's time you left."

A knock sounds on the door. I blink extra hard, as if totally shocked.

In all truth, my acting skills are crap today. But in my defense, I really don't think Eve notices.

"Oh my gosh!" I cry. "Who can that be?" Crossing the room, I quickly whip open the door. "Guess who's here? Your prince! What a surprise." I grin up at the Beast. "Why are you here, oh prince who totally owns this property?"

"I'd like to discuss securing Eve's help with Bedlam."

Eve lifts her chin. "Myla and I already discussed this. The answer is no."

"Change of plans," says the Beast. "I'd like a tour of your garden."

It's on the tip of my tongue to say, *garden? Who knew for certain that Eve had a garden?* But the answer's that the Beast is probably fishing around to see if she really has one.

Eve sniffles, which is a nice change of pace from the constant sighing. "Yes, I will take you there now."

At last.

## THE BEAST

While Eve walks ahead, Myla and I hang back and chat in the embroidery room. I work hard to fight a grin. It feels wonderful to be near Myla again.

"Any sign of the signet ring?" I ask.

"Not yet. Eve and I got stuck on the Gastonne boudoir portraits and Myla kill porn."

My people are rather fond of the middle ages. As a result, I've become an expert in the art of embroidery. Before Bedlam struck me with his curse, I was the final judge on four annual embroidery bees. They're rather enjoyable events.

I scan the walls, seeing the oddest collection of embroidered artwork ever. Indeed, there are multiple portraits of Bedlam, each in a different aspect. Handsome man. Part lizard. Living baked potato. All of which makes sense. Having seen how Gastonne has charmed most of Antrum, I can't pretend to be surprised.

There is also tons of Myla-related stuff as well. Clearly, Eve has an attachment to Bedlam and sees Myla as a rival.

"Check this out," whispers Myla. She leads me to a portrait of

Noah. An odd inscription is embroidered along the bottom of the image.

*Cad Lien Polos*

I make a mental note of this clue. Something to look into when we return to the library.

By now, Eve has already reached her garden. We can't leave her alone too long. There are larger issues at play.

Myla and I find Eve in a green space that's located in the center of her massive cottage. Turns out, the building itself is little more than a shell to encompass this garden.

And what greenery it is. Emerald vines. Arching trees. Blooms so bright and lovely, it makes your breath catch. Eve stands in the center, pretending to inspect a rose bush.

As we all stroll closer, Eve takes care to cover her left hand with her right.

Myla nudges me in the ribs. "See that?"

"I do. Eve got here first and used the time to uncover her signet ring. Now she wears it on her left hand, just as Grace did."

"Yyyyyyup." She pops the 'p' on yup.

My pulse speeds. *This is it. The second signet ring of Eden.*

We close in on Eve. The steward looks up from her roses. "I knew my secret would slip out eventually. The rest of the Garden of Eden burned down. But I saved a little bit and placed it here." She turns to us. "Which is why neither of you can leave my home alive."

Eve closes her eyes and curls up her fingers. The signet ring on her left hand shines with dark blue light. Eve blows across her closed fist. When the steward reopens her hand, blue light and mist pour off her palm and spread across the garden.

Everywhere the colored mist touches, the plants come to life. They all have one purpose.

Kill me and Myla.

I've fought many kinds of demons. And I've studied how to battle hundreds more. But I've never fought a living garden of killer plants.

Needless to say, this will be interesting.

I only hope it won't become deadly.

### MYLA

*F*uuuuuuuuuuuuck.

    All around me, Eve's garden comes to life, and not in a good way.

Trees snap down the center, the hefty trunks splitting into legs. Long branchy arms reach toward me. Flower petals morph into the wings of super large and angry insects that fly right toward my face. Vines twist along the ground like hungry snakes, racing to tangle up my legs.

It's an attempt at chaos, but not an effective one. Bedlam is the true expert on using diversion to really screw with your mind.

I turn the Beast. "Kill the caster..." I leave the rest of the logic out there.

His mouth twists into a snarl. "What are you babbling about?" He ignites his baculum into a longsword and slashes at a nearby vine. The emerald plant rears its snake-like head made of leaves.

I'm still stuck on the nasty *babbling* comment, though. We just had such a nice moment in the embroidery room. The Beast waited and talked to me like a person instead of a mindless rage machine.

"Kill the caster, kill the spell," I explain.

A tree swipes its massive branch arm at the Beast's head. He ducks at the last second. "You want me to finish your sentences for you?"

"Oh, just forget it." I leap up into the attacker tree and quickly scale to the peak. The arbor waves its branch-arms at me, trying to pull me down. It doesn't work. Some things just aren't so easy without opposable thumbs. Plus I have a tail. That makes me a pro at climbing.

Once I reach the treetop, I spot Eve. She's racing toward the far wall of the garden. No doubt, that spot hides some kind of back exit.

The tree gives up fighting me and goes after the Beast again. The prince spears it through with his longsword made from angelfire. I'm glad the arbor didn't get the prince, but now the tree is up in flames and I'm sitting atop it. That's just rude.

The Beast pauses by the base of the tree. Cupping his hand by his mouth, he calls up. "Where is she?"

"I don't know. Hard to tell with all this *smoke*." *Cough, cough.* "Oh, I see her. She's heading for the west wall."

"Got it." The Beast swats away a killer flower insect and rushes off toward Eve.

It takes me a little while to get down, mostly because I have to goad another killer tree to approach so I can jump into its branches and shimmy down its trunk instead.

Once I'm back on the ground, I race for the west wall as well. There I find Eve standing by an opened archway. A look of pure triumph shines on her face. "Have fun in my garden," she taunts.

A gentle whoosh of air moves up my back. That's when I remember my last battle.

*The second tree. It followed me here!*

I look back just in time to see a massive branch come swinging toward my head. At the last possible moment, I leap out of the way.

*Whack!* The branch still hits a target.

*Eve.*

For a long moment, Eve stays in place. You wouldn't know she just got walloped by a tree, unless you catch how she gently sways from foot to foot. Eve's eyes roll up into her head and she falls over.

The moment Eve hits the ground, the garden returns to normal. Trees retake their regular spots. Vines stop hissing. Flowers become blooms again. Even the arbor that was burning returns to normal; you wouldn't know it had ever been touched by flame.

So the garden is all right. But what about Eve?

I kneel at her side and check her pulse. "She's unconscious."

The Beast stalks closer. "Remove her ring. Now."

I pause. "*Please.*"

"What?"

"That's what you say when you want people to do things for you. *Please.*" With my point made, I try yanking the band free from her finger. "It doesn't budge. Grace said that only a great magic spell could remove it."

The Beast narrows his eyes. "Should we try cutting off her finger?"

I wince. "That seems extreme."

My tail disagrees. It jabs forward, the arrowhead end stabbing right at Eve's ring finger.

"Down, boy." I slap the pointed end. "Bad tail."

Still, I can't help but look to see if the finger—*I mean, the ring*—is now loose.

It isn't.

"How strong is your tail?" asks the Beast.

"Imagine if a laser and a bulldozer got together and made a knife."

"So, it's strong."

"Yes. That ring is not coming off her finger. Not without magic, anyway."

And just because I'm that smart, I planned for this turn of events. I pull out another one of my souped-up mirror charms. Within seconds, I've duplicated the ring. A shiny second band now adorns my left hand. Lovely.

Eve moans and rolls onto her side. "Gastonne, tell me a story," she mumbles.

I rise. "Now, what'll we do with her?"

The Beast reaches into his pocket. "I have one last memory wipe charm. Now I shall use it. *Please.*"

*Oh, well.* I could correct him and explain how you use please when you ask someone *else* to do something, but it feels mean. After all, he's trying.

I sigh. "Sounds like a plan."

# THE BEAST

*a*n hour after our adventures with Eve, Myla and I step back into the royal library. Once the door closes behind me, an image appears in my mind.

Myla's Lincoln.

Before, I would see things from the corner of my eye. Now, they're in me. Memories.

A name appears. "Myla-la," I whisper.

"What did you say?"

"Nothing," I state. Obviously, my mind is coming apart. I need to stay focused on what must be done... and that's destroy Bedlam.

Myla tilts her head. "Because I thought you called me a name just now. It's one only a few people know."

"That's not important," I state. "I've written down the riddle from Eve's cottage. There may be a secret there to finding the Arc of Eden. I'll work on decoding it."

Myla pauses for a long moment before speaking. "There are some books here on magical copies of supernatural stuff. Maybe there's some way we can use these duplicates in actual battle."

"Agreed," I state. "Let's get to work."

## MYLA

*H*ours pass; the Beast and I work side by side. I learn more about copying magical objects than I ever thought possible.

And I keep thinking about what the Beast called me.

Myla-la.

The Beast has memories from my Lincoln, I know it. But if the Beast is connected to my husband, then why do we feel like two puzzle pieces that just don't fit?

And I can't ignore the darker possibilities here. I certainly wouldn't put it past Bedlam to implant memories in the Beast in order to torture us both.

All the while, that little voice strikes up in the back of my mind, saying *Bedlam is manipulating you, just as Verus did in the past.*

A weight of sorrow settles on my shoulders. I believe true love can fix anything, even this curse. But it's incredibly rare. Can I really count on it here?

Where does the conspiracy end and true love begin?

## THE BEAST

*M*yla and I work at our respective tasks in the library. Food comes and goes. Servants knock and give up.

In other words, the usual.

The silence between us is absolute, yet comforting. I'm not sure how long it lasts. What I can say is that three trays of food have piled up by the time Myla hops to her feet.

"Ah ha!" she cries. "I got something."

I lean back in my chair and stretch. "What have you found?"

"This book says that if we can locate a big enough power source, then it's possible to activate even a duplicate signet ring." She rounds the table and sets her volume before me. I'm all too aware of how close she stands. It's an effort to focus on the page.

Even so, I manage to scan the words two times. Three. It's almost too good to be true. "This could really happen."

"Do you have any stones loaded with energy?"

"We barely have demon patrol charms. But I can send out messages to the houses. Perhaps one of the nobles is hoarding something. You never know."

"You might not need to." Myla sets the two duplicate rings

onto the tabletop. "Remember how I told you I was the Great Scala?"

I do a double take. "Yes."

"My igni have spoken to me. I can summon them one more time."

I try my best not to be an asshat. "That is… plausible."

"Meaning you don't believe me."

"I'll try." I clear my throat. "Oh, yay. You shall summon igni."

Myla shivers. "Go back to being a jerk. You're a horrible actor."

"Still." I can't help but smile. After so many years of failure, this forward momentum means the world to me. "We'll figure it out, one way or another."

"Yes, I think we will."

Myla and I share a charged gaze. Copies of two signet rings are now in our possession. From here, it's a matter of finding the third ring and then filling them all with power. Can defeating Bedlam be far away?

The tension and silence continue. With each passing moment, it's clear that what we're feeling is more than joy about signet rings. Unless one of us says something soon, this could end with a fight. Or a kiss. It's always a tough call with me and Myla.

*Get back to work, Beast.*

Closing my eyes, I picture my two remaining petals as well as an eternity trapped alive inside glass. That does the trick. Opening my eyes, I refocus on the sheet of parchment before me. "I've made some progress here as well. I think I've figured out the riddle."

"Oooh. Cool!"

And there she goes again. Myla lights everything up with her excitement.

"This is an anagram," I explain. "Rearrange the letters and it says, *call Poseidon.*"

Myla nods. "That's a classic summoning spell for the someone you love who's off at sea. Do you think it's that easy?"

"I do. Remember, these are words that Eve embroidered. Back when she was calling upon the Ark of Eden, I'm sure they were all rather close."

"Like a family, I'd bet."

"Exactly." I push away my papers. "Now we can summon the Ark in the morning."

Myla yawns. "Wow, that's three whole hours away."

"It's late. You should get some rest."

Myla shoots me a thumbs up. "On it."

"Needless to say, I must insist that you stay here in the library. No sneaking off."

"Would I do something like that? Why?"

*Which is not the same thing as saying,* I won't leave.

Now it's my turn to yawn. "Why, indeed? I'll see you in the morning."

Within a few minutes, I'm under my own set of covers at what Myla calls our respective *camping spots*. I anticipate it being hard to relax, but with Myla around, that never seems to be a problem.

Soon I'm deep asleep.

## MYLA

*O*nce the Beast is zonked out, I slip out of the library for a second time.

*Serves him right for trusting me, really.*

Besides, I must see Cissy and describe everything that happened today. I mean, Eve and Bedlam are a THING! How does something like that happen? It's just not the kind of conversation one enjoys sharing with a Beast.

I go through the same trip as last time. Once I make my way to the supply closet, I fish around for another set of transfer charms. This time, it's harder to find stuff. In the end, I find a few purple paperclips between the floorboards. These are super-old transfer charms, but they'll still get the job done.

A minute later, I'm back in Cissy's room. Yay!

But there's no Cissy here. Bummer.

The place looks the same as before: a mega-puffy bed surrounded by bare walls and floors. Which is ridiculous. After all, I've seen Acca's bank account. They can afford a rug; they're just a bunch of cheapskates.

There's one addition to the decor, though. Someone's added another ushebti statue. Just seeing this thing makes nausea crawl up my throat. Like the statue beside it, this new ushebti is human-shaped and glassy. The big difference is that while the first one is yellow, this second ushebti is red.

*Either way, yuck.*

How can Cissy sleep with these things around? Sure, there's no sign on them reading, *frozen person magically stuck inside here.* Still, the vibe from these things is creepy-deepy.

Turning away from the frozen people, I rush to Cissy's desk and scribble out a quick note.

*Dear Cis,*

*All went well with Eve. Thanks so much.*
*Remember to avoid you-know-who.*

*-Myla*

Cissy normally insists on tons of detail, but I'm in a hurry and not a natural writer. These few lines will be plenty, I'm sure.

And with that, my job here is done. It's too bad there's no Cissy to gossip with, but it can wait for another day. That is, assuming Bedlam doesn't destroy creation and all.

Reaching into the pocket of my nightgown, I pull out my last paperclip for the magical ride back to Arx Hall. I'm about to snap it in two when I hear it.

Familiar voices in the hallway.

An odd chill crawls up my back. I'm tempted to just break the charm and go, but I can't help it.

I know who these people are. *Maybe.*

With gentle motions, I pull Cissy's door open just the barest crack. Leaning forward, I peep into the outer hallway.

What I see is a total mind freak.

It's Adair and Gastonne.

And their tongues are waaaaaaaay deep down each other's throats.

I pop my hand over my mouth so I don't screech in shock. *These two are a couple!* Does Adair even know he's also a diseased potato guy? How did this happen?

Gastonne breaks the kiss and looks directly at me. "Ready to give up?"

Adair nips his ear. "Who are you talking to, Bedlam?"

I have to bite my lips together to keep from screaming. Adair knows this is Bedlam? What the WHAT?

"Call me Gastonne."

"Of course, my Titan."

All this while, Gastonne keeps staring at me. If I felt slightly ill before, now I want to hurl on my white nightie.

Even worse, I wouldn't be surprised if Bedlam planned for me to walk in on him and Adair. Because now I must tell the Beast his wife is a cheating cheater. That's no fun for anybody. And it's just one more way that Bedlam's screwing with my head.

"The worst is yet to come," whispers Bedlam.

*Hells bells.* It's like the Titan of Chaos knew my thoughts just then.

*Crap... maybe he can read my mind?*

Whatever's going on, I'm getting out of here, pronto. I press the door shut and if I'm not too quiet about it, I don't really care.

Then I snap that paper clip while focusing on one thought.

*Get me back to the library.*

## 65

## THE BEAST

*M*yla snuck off. Again.

Which is not a surprise. If anything, I was counting on it. I'd implanted a magical tracker in her night shift for just such an occasion.

Rising from my pile of blankets, I march over to a little-used table in the far corner. From there, I pull out a map of Antrum on yellow parchment. A blinking red dot shows me where Myla has run off to.

She's with Cissy.

I tap my chin and consider this. Visiting Cissy places Myla awfully close to both Adair and Gastonne. At one time, I might have worried about Myla's welfare in such an encounter. Not any more.

Slogging over to the main entrance, I pull the door and summon a messenger. Time was, only the most senior members of the great houses could act in this role.

That hasn't been the case in years.

When I snap my fingers, a boy of no more than twelve steps up to the doorway.

"Yes, my Prince?"

"Ask the cook to send up a late meal. Extra coffee, too."

The boy nods and runs off.

While I wait for my snack, I head back to the table and sift through ways to charge duplicate signet rings. For as long at it lasts, I must use my quiet time wisely.

Because once Myla returns, things may get very rowdy indeed.

## 66

## MYLA

*W*ithin seconds, I'm transported back to the royal library. The paperclip charm even placed me in a back corner behind a bookshelf. This way, the prince can't see me appear. Total bonus. I've no desire to talk to the Beast, and not for the regular reasons, namely that he's a grump on wheels.

Now, it's Adair.

Gastonne.

Tongues.

Ugh.

I tiptoe out from the behind the shelves, ready to sneak back into my doggie bed. Once I reach the main room, I find out something crucial.

I'm not the only one rumbling around at this hour.

The Beast is awake.

Oops.

A moment passes where I debate how to play this.

Sorry beyond words? *Not my style.*

Pretend I got lost? *I suck at lying.*

So I end up with the third option. *Act like nothing is wrong.*

Not the best choice, but it's late and I don't feel like thinking anymore. That image of Gastonne and Adair still overwhelms my brain.

I shoot the Beast a standard smile. I don't waste a truly engaging grin on him because—*let's face it*—this probably won't work.

"Hey, there," I call.

The Beast sits at a hefty table that's covered in papers and books. He barely looks up from his parchment as I step closer.

"I told you not to leave," the Beast declares.

"Well, I did leave. And now I have news." I try to think of a good way to drop this particular bomb. There isn't. "I'll just say it. Brace yourself."

Seconds pass.

*Aaaaaaaaaand this is me, not saying a thing.*

Damn. This is tougher than I thought.

The Beast turns over another page on the large leather book before him. "Consider me braced."

"It's like this," I begin.

At this point, part of me knows I'm about to babble and over-share. More of me keeps on talking.

"I can't imagine how you'll feel," I continue. "If this happened with my Lincoln, I'd lose my mind. Although technically, maybe I've done this a little bit. I did kiss you on the cheek that one night. And there were other times where I totally checked you out. But that's different because you're basically my husband's double, so I'm only staring at him, right?" I set my hand on my throat and let out a long breath. "Hoo, I'm glad we cleared that up."

The Beast finally looks up from his book. "I have no idea what you're talking about."

The works just blurt from my mouth. "Adair is cheating on you."

The Beast huffs out a breath. "Obviously."

I do a double-take. *Is the Beast actually hiding his inner torture at this news?*

*Nope.* If anything, the guy looks bored.

I plunk down onto the chair across from his. "Explain."

"Adair has cheated on me from the moment we signed our marriage contract." He waves his hand dismissively. "I'm sure you know the story."

"Story? There is no story. In *my* reality, you never signed those stupid engagement papers. I came in and totally saved your butt."

Looking up from his book, the Beast gives me a deadpan stare. "Saved?"

"Come on, like your life here doesn't suck." All this calmness is getting on my nerves, so I hoist myself into a sitting position on the tabletop. A flare of irritation shines in the Beast's eyes. *Ah, that's so much better.*

The Beast glares at my seating choice. "You know that annoys me."

"In my reality, you're a fan of tables and trunks." I let the thought hang out there.

A slight flush colors the Beast's neck. "Sit wherever."

"Tell me more about this Adair situation."

"There's nothing to tell. After a short acquaintance, I knew Adair and I would never get along. She has her freedom."

"Which means you two have never, uh, you know?"

"Consummated our marriage?" The Beast arches his right brow. "That's a rather personal question."

"Not really. You're my husband from another reality."

"So you say." A long pause follows before the Beast speaks again. "No, Adair and I have never had sex. And don't get any ideas, my Amour. I am not in the market for a lover. Once this is over—*assuming I live past this curse*—then you're on the first Pulpitum out of Antrum."

At these words, my inner wrath demon fires to life. "So when

I'm done being useful, you'll kick me out? Why do you say such mean things?"

"Because they're true."

"Right."

Fresh waves of rage and power zoom through my limbs. White hot anger clouds my mind. My eyes light up bright red as I do what I've wanted to for days.

I leap across the table and tackle the Beast to the floor.

## THE BEAST

*M*y own words ring in my ears.

*Once this is over—assuming I live past this curse—then you're on the first Pulpitum out of Antrum.*

I don't know why I said that.

*Strike that. I do.*

Myla is getting too close again. My desire for her is so overwhelming, I simply must push her away. There's too much at risk to allow romance to cloud my judgement.

Still, that doesn't excuse my awful behavior.

All of which is why I welcome the way Myla's shoulder slams onto my chest and knocks me off my chair. I deserve it. With a thud, I slam back-first onto the floor.

And I make no move to fight back.

That said, I'm not insane. I do brace myself for the onslaught.

In the meantime, the sensation of her straddling my waist is making the situation awkward in the extreme. The sooner she punches me, the better. Otherwise, these flannel pajama bottoms won't hide my true feelings for long.

Suddenly, the library door swings open. A familiar figure stands on the threshold.

Adair.

My wife points right at Myla. "Amour!" she cries. "Whore!"

*Oh, no.*

## 68

## MYLA

*A*dair marches through the room, crying out the words *Amour* and *whore* over and over. I'm surprised she doesn't pop a vocal chord.

Because it will undoubtedly enrage her further, I pause while still straddling the Beast.

"I'm unclear," I state solemnly. "Does this bug you? Like how I'm right here on top of your husband?" I glance down to the Beast. He's fighting back a smile.

Adair stomps up behind me and goes to grab a handful of my hair. "Off!"

Before Adair can actually yank anything away from my skull, my tail pops up to swat her hand away. I look over my shoulder. "Thanks, boy."

In reply, my tail does a little happy dance. Whatever else is going on in this alternate reality, my tail is having the time of its life.

Adair hangs back, just out of tail-striking range. "Get off him!"

I slowly rise. "You've got a hickey on your neck." *Which is true.*

Adair's eyes widen. "My husband gave it to me." *Total lie.*

The Beast slowly rises to his feet. "I don't recall doing any such thing."

"Hmm." I fold my arms over my chest. "Let me guess. You saw me in Cissy's room. That got you curious. Wasn't I supposed to be in the dungeons? Didn't I pull out your hair extensions?"

"You're a demonic menace," snaps Adair.

"So," I continue. "You did some asking around and discovered that I've been camping out in the royal library with the prince."

"Camping?" repeats Adair. "You're sleeping on a pile of blankets like a pet."

I round on the Beast. "I told you the blanket thing was weird."

Adair goes back to her favorite hobby. "Amour! Whore!"

The Beast hisses in a pained breath and clutches his forearm. It's happening again.

Another lost petal.

A fresh vision.

Adair marches over to yank on the Beast's shoulder. "Don't you have anything to say to me?"

I move to stand between Adair and the Beast. "He's busy now, don't you think?"

"Like I care about his curse." Adair goes up on tiptoe, all the better to yell at the Beast over my head. "We had a deal. In public, we act like a loving couple. In private, we do whatever we want. You've humiliated me!"

For a moment, I can only stare at Mrs. Beast in shock. When I speak, my voice has a deadly low tone. "He's in pain."

Adair thumps her chest with her fist. "I'm the one who's really hurting here. Who got their hair pulled out?"

"Extensions," I correct. "And they came out really easily. You need a better stylist."

Adair keeps thumping away at her heart. "Who is suffering because everyone thinks my husband and some demon whore—"

"That's enough! You've hit your quota for saying the W-word today." I point at the door. "Out."

Adair pales. "What?"

This time when I speak, I pull on some of my demonic power. "OUT!" The word resonates through the chamber at ear-splitting volume. My irises glow red.

Adair scurries through the exit. Not gonna lie. It's a satisfying sight. Once she's gone, I look to the Beast.

His eyes are clouded over, as if completely filled with blue mist. When he speaks, it's with a low and dreamy voice.

"The Tumult have entered the Dark Lands. They've overrun the Oligarchy. Bodies everywhere. Walker is dead."

The Beast blinks quickly. His eyes return to normal. "I haven't seen Walker since I was a boy."

Sorrow slices through me. In my mind, I know Walker's not really dead, but my heart still mourns. "He's a good man."

"He fights well, but he couldn't see his attackers." The Beast rubs his neck. "This is terrible."

"What about your mark?"

The Beast raises his arm. One petal left.

"Time is running out," says the Beast. "And I can't find it in me to feel sorrow any more. I must be more broken than I thought."

Gripping his shoulders, I force the Beast to look into my eyes. "Listen to me. We will stop Bedlam. And when we do, it won't just end your curse. It will reverse everything that's happened here. All these people who have died will be fine again, I guarantee it. And you'll even regain other loved ones that you didn't even know you had."

The Beast's gaze meets mine. His face is the very definition of tortured. "Tell me about our son. I want to know about Maxon."

My heart sinks. "Are you sure?"

The Beast nods. "I need something to look forward to, even if it's not real."

My eyes sting with held-in tears. I can't remember the last time I've gone this long without holding my child. "Maxon is four years old. He looks innocent, but he has the heart of a wild man."

"I lied before. I do have visions of him. I've seen him running about with a wooden sword."

"That's Maxon, all right."

A minute passes before the Beast speaks again. "Why did you just send Adair away?"

"Beyond the screaming?"

The Beast nods.

"Because this is what it's like." I move my hand back and forth between us. "Someone bugs one of us, the other steps in."

The Beast opens his mouth, ready to say something else. This has been a time of some pretty huge revelations, so I can't wait to find out what he'll say next.

Sadly, another knock sounds at door. The moment is broken.

"Son, open up." It's a woman's voice, and an unmistakable one at that.

"That would be Octavia," says the Beast.

"You want me to kick her ass, too?"

"No, although I appreciate the sentiment." The Beast steps over to the slowly declining pile of linens, takes out a long Henley, and pulls it on. I'm still in my high-necked sleeping gown, so I'm pretty covered... at least, from a clothing perspective.

Because when it comes to Octavia, who knows what will happen?

## 69

# THE BEAST

*M*other swoops into the chamber. She looks prim and lethal in her black Rixa gown. As always, her silver hair is wound into a neat bun at the nape of her neck.

"Hello, my son. How is your curse?"

I haven't seen Mother in more than four years. The most I've gotten are messages through folks like Nat. Oh, and a never-ending stream of Amours. How very much like Octavia to simply burst into a room after four years, give no explanations, and then ask about my curse.

How I've missed her.

"Things are progressing," I reply. "Any news on Father?"

"He's holding steady for now." Octavia taps my shoulder with her pinky. "If you'll back up two paces, I can enter the library and meet your girl."

"Mother."

There are volumes of things wrong with this situation, but none of them can be discussed in an open doorway in front of servants. I back up. Octavia steps inside.

The door has barely closed when Mother turns to Myla. "Oh, my. You really are a quasi demon."

"That I am." Myla's tail arches over her shoulder to wave at Mother. "You're in luck. My tail likes you."

"Of course, it does." Octavia curtsies. "Pleased to make both of your acquaintance. Let's get down to business." Mother claps her hands. "You're probably wondering why I've visited here, even though it's in direct contradiction of the magical compulsion that I placed on my son."

"I'm not confused," I offer.

"Quiet, son. Mother's scheming."

Myla tries to hide a grin under her hand. She doesn't work too hard at it, though. And I can't help but smile as well. The fact that Mother is here and being her bossy self is a rather wonderful thing.

*I'll stay quiet. For now.*

"Here's the situation," continues Mother. "I want this curse over. Then, my son and husband will both recover." Her mouth thins to an angry line. "This is all that Bedlam's doing. Or rather, Gastonne."

Myla gasps. "You know Gastonne is here?"

"I was the one who invited in the man, demon, titan, whatever you want to call him," says Octavia. "When he's in Antrum, I can spy on him constantly. Only trouble is, he keeps enacting his curses and entrapping thrax in glass statues. Although, I must admit, he does choose the most unsavory characters in Acca, so I don't complain."

Myla nods. "I saw more ushebti in my friend Cissy's room."

"That's Gastonne's work, sure enough," states Octavia. "By the way, your friend Cissy is a talented girl. If the world weren't falling apart, she'd make an excellent diplomat or spy."

"Thanks," says Myla. "Going back to Gastonne. Don't you warn people about him?"

"All the time. Haven't you?"

"Yes," replies Myla.

"Doesn't work, does it?"

"No," replies Myla. "I told my friend Cissy to get rid of the ushebti in her room. She won't because of Gastonne."

I raise my hand. "I've had similar experiences with Gastonne over the years. Everyone adores him, no matter what he does. Or am I still not allowed to talk?"

"Don't be silly," says Octavia. "You're my perfect son and I'm always thrilled to hear your voice."

Myla and I exchange a knowing glance. My mother is such a character.

Octavia strides over to the table. "What are you two working on?" I start to explain about the signet rings, but Mother waves me off. "That was a rhetorical question. I can plainly see what you're up to, but it's all a pile of nonsense. I know what will really fix this situation."

I pinch the bridge of my nose. *Here it comes.*

Octavia gestures toward Myla. "Here's my Beauty..." She turns to me. "And this is my Beast. It's just as I thought. So let's see." She folds her arms over her chest and waits.

I frown. "See what?"

"Wasn't I clear? I want to watch you kiss her. Oh, wait. You're the Beast, so that won't work." She points to Myla. "*You* must kiss *him*. Hurry now. There isn't all the time in the world."

Myla tilts her head. She's definitely thinking this through. After an interminable pause, she shrugs. "Why not? It's worth a try." She turns to me. "Are you game?"

It's a good question. I look between Octavia and Myla. There's no way Mother will leave without seeing us kiss. Plus, if I'm being honest, a kiss from Myla wouldn't be horrible. Receiving it in front of my Mother is less than ideal, but nothing about this situation is what you'd call regular.

I nod. "I'm game."

Myla steps up, places her hands on my chest and closes her eyes. She doesn't need to say a word. I know what she's doing; Myla is picturing HIM.

Her Lincoln.

I close my eyes as well, which makes it all the easier to soak in the delicious sensation of Myla's lips brushing against mine. Invisible cords wind between us. An electric sense of anticipation fills the air. It's a moment that's perfect in its delicate touch.

All of which gets shattered when Mother pipes up again.

"Let's see your arm, my son."

I pull up my sleeve. "Still one petal remaining. I am not cured."

"Well, I can tell you what the problem is," announces Mother. "That was clearly a first kiss. I'm going to leave now and let you practice some more." She taps her cheek. "Perhaps I'll have Lucas send over some love charms."

"Mother, I'm immune."

Myla raises her hand. "I also have magical protections from charms. Lucas gave them to me back in my realty."

"*Your* reality?" Mother turns to me. "She's a little odd, isn't she? No wonder it's taking extra time. Well, no point in my hanging around and stalling things further." Octavia walks to the door, opens it, and pauses. Twisting about, Mother flips her gaze between me and Myla. "I expect the pair of you to fall in love within twenty-four hours. Remember that." She slams the door and takes off.

A long silence follows. This is beyond awkward.

"In a way, she's right about Connor," says Myla. "If we kill Bedlam, he'll be healed too. Everything will return to how it is in my reality."

"Let's hope."

That's what I say, but in my heart I still agree with Mother. All this talk about alternate realities? Myla remains a little unstable. As nice as those fantasies may be, it's far more likely that Bedlam is just toying with all our minds.

Although, if I'm being brutally honest, some small part of me suspects that Myla might be right. The thought is both terrifying and elating. Although considering my curse, it's far more on the frightening side of things. In truth, I have a better chance at ending this curse with magic rings than by chasing true love. I'm simply not built for romance.

Another knock sounds. "My prince."

Since I'm still by the door, I pull on the handle. Nat steps inside. "Greetings."

Myla waves. "Nathaniel!"

Nat frowns. "I've never met you before, Miss."

I pat Nat's shoulder. "I already told Myla all about you. Myla, this is Nat. Nat, Myla."

"I've ordered your supplies," offers Nat.

"Have the servants bring it all in."

I step back, allowing a small army of workers to drag in a pair of field cots. As instructed, they set them up by the far wall of the library. Once everything in place, Nat addresses me once more.

"Are these satisfactory, my Prince?"

"Yes, thank you."

Nat does a double take. "Oh."

"Is there a problem?"

Myla chuckles. "Let me guess. Nat, you're shocked that the Beast said *thank you* like a person. You know, instead of a grump."

*That can't be right.*

I look to Nat. "Is this true?" And if the words come out a little harsh, it's not on purpose.

"Ah, *now* you're back to your regular mood." Nat grins and looks to Myla. "You're a good influence on him, Miss."

"Obviously." Myla mock bows. "I have a gift."

"And you're making progress on the Bedlam situation?" asks Nat.

"Yes," replies Myla. "We just got the—"

Nat holds his hand up, palms forward. "Don't tell me any details. That Gastonne has eyes and ears everywhere. If I don't know anything, then I can't slip up and ruin your plans. This room is the best warded spot in all of Antrum. Just keep your secrets here and not with me."

Myla mimes zipping her mouth. "All right, Nat."

"Good night to you both." Nat heads for the door. There's a bounce in his step that I haven't seen in years.

Once the door closes, Myla turns to me. "He's a good friend."

"Yes, I am fortunate."

Myla steps up to the closest cot and pokes it with her finger. "This is real. I almost thought there'd be a booby trap."

I decide to readjust my lion's pelt on my shoulders. Once. Twice. Three times. It's easier than looking elsewhere.

"You're not meeting my gaze," says Myla. "Could it be that you feel guilty?"

"I'm a Beast. We sometimes feel a twinge of remorse. Never guilt."

"Interesting distinction."

"If we're going after the Ark of Eden tomorrow, then you must sleep now."

"And *that's* the Beast I know." She fake-salutes me. "I'll do whatever the Hell *I* want, Sir."

"How shocking," I deadpan.

The truth is a bit trickier. If Myla ever did as ordered, I'd not only be surprised, I'd also feel sorely disappointed.

It's a most confusing situation, to be sure.

And the sooner it's over with, the better all around.

## 70

## THE BEAST

*A*n hour later, Myla and I step off the Pulpitum platform and onto a deserted beach. Fierce ocean waters crash into the rocky shoreline. Countless stars mark the night sky. A lighthouse blinks in the distance. The air carries a crisp edge that means winter hasn't yet given in to spring.

"I've always enjoyed this human territory," I state. "They call it New Bedford."

"I know the place." Myla steps around and inspects the landscape. "A few years back, they had a problem with demon cod attacking some fishing boats." She shoots me a sad look. "I put down the infestation with, you know."

"I know." She fought off the demons with her Lincoln.

Suddenly, I can picture it in my mind. Myla and Lincoln stand on the foredeck of a fishing ship. It's nighttime, just as it is now. The seas churn. Mist hangs heavily over the scene. A great fish breaks through the water, ready to swallow the vessel whole. Myla turns her baculum into a great hook. She spears the fish's mouth with her weapon, holding it in place. At the same time, Lincoln pulls out a massive syringe and jams the needle into the fish's head. Moments later, it returns to being a regular cod and flops back into the ocean.

I scan the beach, looking for the familiar round rainbow that always comes with these visions.

There is nothing.

Was that a view into someone else's life… or a memory from my own?

The moment the thought hits me, I dismiss it. This is all part of Bedlam's plans to destroy my sanity. In the story of Wadget and Ra, it was Wadget who got turned into a Beast. She wasted her time searching for true love as a cure, but it was all an illusion. The only real solution was to destroy Set, the god of chaos.

Although now I wonder, when it comes to Bedlam, what is the real illusion? Does the *true love cure* distract from killing your enemy… or is it the other way around? And why does any means of ending this curse now feel like I'm starting something worse?

Myla steps closer. "Are you all right?"

"Always." *Which is far from true.*

All of a sudden, it's as if someone tied a rope around my heart and pulled it taut. Sorrow spikes through my chest. All this time, I've only wanted to destroy Bedlam and end this curse.

For the first time, I realize that winning against my curse will mean losing Myla. That thought hurts in ways I could never have imagined.

I shake my head. *What nonsense.* Even if true love is the cure, I already know I'm immune.

Best to finish the task at hand.

Raising my arms, I speak the words for Poseidon's Call.

*Wave and froth,*
*Peak and low,*
*Come forth, my friend,*
*Poseidon's call bestow.*

Pale mist rolls out across the ocean. A low rumble fills the air. The sand vibrates beneath my feet, making my very bones shake. A moment ago, the ocean had been a sheet of low rolling waves. Now the waters turn choppy and fierce.

Then the sea erupts.

A great liquid wall rises up before us. On reflex, I grasp Myla's hand. The massive wave curls over our heads. For a moment, it stays frozen in place. I hold my breath.

The towering liquid wall crashes down.

Great currents of chilly water pull me in a dozen directions at once. The force of the strike sends me reeling.

I lose Myla's hand.

With all my strength, I kick toward the water's surface. I break through and take in a deep gulp of air. Looking about, I find Myla treading water a few yards away. She looks unharmed; that makes me unreasonably happy.

Looking around, I find that the shore has completely vanished. Right now, there's nothing but ocean in every direction.

And there's still no sign of any vessel, let alone a massive Ark.

Vibrations move through the water. I look to Myla. "Something's coming."

"It'll be a doozie." Myla pinches her nose. "I am not getting a headful of seawater this time."

Another massive shape rises from the ocean. This time, it isn't a wave. Instead, a great wooden vessel breaks through the water in a way that reminds me of a submarine. The Ark seems to hover in the air for a moment before slamming onto the choppy waves.

Turns out, I should have plugged my nose like Myla. *Ouch.*

Myla and I now tread water beside what looks like a four-story wooden wall. A long rope ladder rolls down from the upper deck to the ocean. A woman's voice calls out.

"Better climb up already."

I hold the ladder steady. "You go first."

A sneaky look shines in Myla's eyes. "I'm not going to say anything about how you're acting like a gentleman for once in your Beastly life."

"Very charitable of you."

And so, Myla and I begin the long climb onto the Ark of Eden.

## MYLA

*a* s I climb up the rope ladder, a brown-skinned man leans over the wooden railing while gazing down in my direction. He's a young guy with spiky blonde hair and a scar than runs down one side of his face.

"You're fast climbers," calls the man. "How long ago did you get shipwrecked?"

"We were only in the water for a few minutes," I reply. "And it was more that we were beach-wrecked."

The man wipes his nose with the back of his hand. "Captain will want to inspect you once you get on deck. Stand still and stay out of trouble."

"Aye, aye!" *I've always wanted to say that.*

In short order, I hoist myself over the wooden railing and onto the deck proper. It's a long space with a small hut-shaped thing in the center. About twenty people mill around. I notice folks of all ages and skin tones. Everyone seems to have a purpose, whether they're dragging a rope around, scrubbing the deck, or shlepping a bucket. Folks chatter happily while they do their thing.

When the Beast and I visited the Ether, it was more organized and quiet. This place gives off more of a family vibe. Plus, the Beast and I make little impression at all. The Ark must regularly pick up folks who got lost at sea.

A woman steps forward. To say she's unusual is an understatement. Curly ram horns frame her head while her skin is a mix of orange, yellow and red. She carries a tall staff in one hand. Somehow the look totally works on her.

And the best part? She's wearing a signet ring. I smile my face off. *This is it.*

The same man I met before steps into the woman's path, stopping her. "We're almost at the target, Captain."

"Good news, Jeb. How far out?"

"Two leagues."

"Let me know when we reach the gathering point."

Jeb and the Captain go on to speak in low tones. I take quick stock of the situation... Jeb must be some kind of boat assistant guy. The woman with the horns is the Captain. And my thrax armor is soaking wet and riding up my butt crack. I really miss my dragonscale fighting suit. At least I'm not the Beast, though. He's soaked through and still shlepping around that lion's pelt on his shoulders.

*Note to self.* Repair dragonscale fighting suit, STAT. None of my repair charms have worked, but I have found some duct tape.

The Captain finishes up with Jeb before marching over. "I'm Norah, daughter of Noah. This is my Ark."

My thoughts race. What's the right way to greet a combination steward and captain? Salute? Curtsey? I opt to give her a little wave. "Hey, I'm Myla." I gesture to the drippy dude beside me. "This is the prince."

Norah sniffs. "I know who you are. My only worry is whether to toss you both back into the ocean." She focuses on the Beast. "Victoria tells me that Bedlam cursed you."

"It's true," says the Beast. I'd like to report that he's acting less growly than usual, but that would be a lie. I wonder if the body armor is chaffing his ass, too.

Norah grips the top of her staff so tightly, I'm surprised it doesn't snap. "You almost ruined the Ether."

The Beast's mouth thins to an angry line. He doesn't like being confronted. "That wasn't by design."

My tail peeps out behind my leg, points to Norah, and slips back.

Norah refocuses on me. "You're quasi."

"Guilty as charged," I state.

"Your tail is acting strangely," adds Norah.

I glance over my shoulder. My tail still lurks behind my ankle. "It doesn't know what you are." Once the statement leave my lips, I realize it's a little rude. "Not that you don't look fabulous."

"Victoria has featherlings that hop on and off her shoulders," says Norah. "I altered myself in a more permanent way."

My tail pops out again. Norah frowns. "What's it doing now?"

"My guess? My tail wants to know why you made the change."

This whole time, Jeb's been hanging out nearby. He pretends to fiddle with some rope, but I'm pretty sure he's just eavesdropping. When Jeb catches my last statement, he chuckles.

"What's so amusing?" asks Norah.

"Everyone knows why you really made the switch," says Jeb. "Crew kept teasing you 'cuz you're the spitting image of your Da. Don't look like him any more, now do you?"

Norah's mouth twitches. "Go check for the target, Jeb." Her voice cracks with grief. "You're not needed here."

"Yes, Captain." Jeb runs off.

"You lost someone," I say. "Just like Victoria lost Grace."

Norah nods. "Yes. My father, Noah."

At this point, I'm very glad that the Beast is doing nothing beyond making a drippy watermark on the deck. The prince is no master of sensitive moments, that's for sure.

"I'm sorry," I say solemnly.

Norah stares out to sea. "Everyone is."

Jeb steps up. "We're at the gathering point, Captain. Port side."

"Thank you," says Norah. She turns to me and the Beast. "Give me a moment."

Norah steps over to the same spot where the Beast and I hoisted ourselves on deck. She lifts her hand. Just as with the other stewards, her signet ring lights up and sends out a wave of blue smoke from her palm.

This time, the indigo cloud pulls a massive blue whale from the ocean. The animal rises into the air before shrinking down to about ten feet long and landing on deck. From there, she and Jeb decide that the creature has taken in some kind of man-made poison. Like Victoria did with the hawk, Norah heals the whale with her signet ring. When done, the steward uses her mist power once again to reset the whale into the water.

Once she's finished her healing work, Norah returns her focus to me and the Beast.

"I know why you're here," says Norah. "You want to make a copy of my signet ring. I've decided not to help you."

Beside me, the Beast hisses and grasps his lower arm. Norah looks to me. "Is he upset I have refused him?"

"No," I state simply. "It's the curse."

Once again, the Beast's eyes haze over so they look as if they're filled with mist. He speaks in a dreamy voice. "The Tumult have breached the Gates of Heaven. So many bodies. Verus, the Queen of the Angels, is dead."

The words tear into me. Verus can't be dead. My hands ball into fists.

*She's not dead. We'll fix this.*

Little by little, the Beast's eyes return to normal. Norah watches the change carefully. "Show me your marks," she orders.

The Beast cuts open his sleeve to the elbow and shows his bare skin to Norah. The sight makes my heart sink.

"You've only one petal left." Norah makes a tut-tut noise. "Oh, you're in deep."

"Not sure if you heard what I said," explains the Beast. "But the Tumult have breached the Gates of Heaven." He pins Norah with a look that could freeze fire, then adds one final thought.

"We're all in trouble now."

# NORAH

# THE BEAST

*A*fter I speak those final words—*we're all in trouble now*—a strained silence falls over the ship.

Jeb rushes up. "Captain, a storm is coming."

"I know," says Norah. "It's his fault." She nods toward me. "He carries chaos within him."

Jeb rounds on me and Myla. "You must get off this ship."

Norah slams her staff against the deck. "Not yet." She raises her arm and displays the signet ring. "You may make your copy. Then get off my Ark."

"Why are you helping us?" I ask. And if my voice carries a snarl, so be it. I don't like how she changed her mind so quickly. I've had enough experience with Bedlam and his tricks to be wary.

"That's a great question," offers Myla. "I'll just make a copy of the signet ring while Norah here thinks through her answer."

Myla whips out her tiny mirror and catches the ring's reflection. A moment later, a perfect replica of the band appears on Myla's finger. Now she wears all three duplicate rings of Eden. "And we're done."

I should feel like cheering, yet I can't shake the suspicion that something is wrong here. "I'll ask again. Why are you helping us?"

"Because Bedlam will break you eventually," answers Norah. "But not while you're on my Ark."

As if flipping a switch, the weather changes. Dark clouds roll over the sky. Flashes of lightning strike the ocean. Great waves rear up and crash over the deck.

"Leave!" howls Norah.

Scooping Myla into my arms, I leap over the wooden railing. Together, Myla and I tumble through empty space. We never land on the water, though. Instead, both of us touch down onto the same stretch of beach where today's adventure began.

Myla feels so right in my embrace, I can't let her go right away. "How are you doing? Are you hurt?"

"I should ask you those questions." We're so close now, I can feel her breath fan out across my mouth.

I tilt my head, considering whether to answer. I know what Myla refers to here. The next time I lose a petal, I'll become encased alive as another ushebti for Bedlam.

Somehow, I'm able to place Myla back on her feet. The moment we're apart, my body aches to be near her once more. There is so much I wish to tell her now, but none of the words will come. It's all I can do to growl out four words.

"Let's hit the Pulpitum."

So that's what we do.

## MYLA

*a*n hour later, the Beast and I are back in the royal library. I wear all three signet rings on my left hand. This stupendous achievement is something that I now celebrate by singing a Beyonce tune. I adapt the lyrics, obviously.

> *I hate Bedlam so I went and put three rings on it!*
> *I hate Bedlam so I went and put three rings on it!*
> *Oh oh oh, oh oh oh, oh oh. Oh oh oh oh.*

The Beast stares at me like I'm nuts. No doubt, this is due to a trio of things.

One, I changed back into my dragonscale fighting suit. Hey, it may be a little stinky, but it's dry.

Two, I got some duct tape and put it over the tears on my ass.

And three, I am doing the appropriate hand-flips as I sing.

> *Oh oh oh, oh oh oh, oh oh. Oh oh oh oh.*

"How long do you plan to do... whatever this is?" asks the Beast.

"At least an hour," I reply. "Don't tell me you're not a fan of Lady Bey."

"She's not big in Antrum," he deadpans. "Neither is human music in general."

"I've noticed. Still, we must do something to mark the moment." I snap my fingers. "I've got it. We could pretend I'm wearing a yellow dress and dance around like they did in Beauty and the Beast."

"Yellow is the color of Acca. I'd rather you went back to flipping your hand and singing nonsense."

I bob my brows. "You're trying to act all tough, but I've gotten to you so badly, it isn't even funny."

A long pause follows. The Beast stares into my eyes with such intensity, it's as if the rest of the world vanishes. "Yes, Myla," he says, his voice low and husky. "You've changed everything for me."

In this moment, the Beast looks so much like my Lincoln, I can't tell if I want to scream or kiss him.

Who am I kidding? It's kiss him.

There's no conversation. We simply start moving toward each other. My heart thuds so hard, I can feel it beating in my throat.

*Creeeeeeak.*

A groan echoes in from the fireplace. The Beast and I share a long look. There's no need for discussion. We're both thinking the same thing.

The sarcophagus.

Bedlam's old home is now perched before the hearth. A memory appears. When I first entered Bedlam's lair under the Sahara, that same creak sounded when Bedlam left his sarcophagus for the first time.

But this place is warded up to the hilt. *Bedlam can't get in here, can he?*

Moving in unison, the Beast and I steal through the maze of bookshelves. With every step, more nervous energy zings through the air. We slip out the other side of the mini labyrinth, ending up right at the fireplace. And it's still there. The sarcophagus stands upright before the hearth.

It is open.

The Beast kneels while setting his fingertips against the floor. This is a classic thrax hunter move. "There's no one else in here."

I step closer to the sarcophagus itself. "There's no lock on this thing. Guess it was a false alarm."

"Help!"

Screams sound from the outer hallway. The Beast and I rush over to the library's main entrance. There, standing just outside the threshold, is the last person I wanted to see right now.

Gastonne.

I grip my hand behind my back, hoping to hide the fact that I wear copies of all three signet rings. Why didn't I summon my igni right away?

*Oh, yeah.* That's the equivalent of setting off a bomb in an underground bunker.

Gastonne grins, and it's one of those toothpaste commercial smiles. Damn, do I ever hate this guy.

"What do you want?" growls the Beast.

"I can't come inside and see what you're up to," explains Gastonne. "That makes me rather lonely. So I brought along some guests."

Gastonne steps aside. Instantly, it's clear why everyone screams. The Tumult are in Antrum. A pack of them now huddle in the hallway just outside the library door. The creatures step away, revealing what they've *really* been up to.

The Tumult brought three captives along, namely Cissy, Nat, and Octavia.

Bands of grief and rage tighten across my chest. All three prisoners have their hands tied behind their backs. Gags loop around their mouths, preventing anyone from speaking. Still, these three don't need to say a word. The abject terror in their eyes is clear enough.

"Your mother thought your curse was like that of Beauty and the Beast," says Gastonne. "I couldn't bring an angry mob of villagers with me today, but I thought the Tumult might suffice."

"What do you want?" asks the Beast.

"Chaos loves to watch things break," says Gastonne. He raises his left hand. The three signet rings clearly gleam on his fingers. The trio of bands light up with power. Mist careens off Gastonne's palm and rolls toward our loved ones. A heartbeat later, Cissy, Nat, and Octavia are all enveloped in indigo-colored clouds.

When the vapor is gone, things have changed. Cissy, Nat, and Octavia are now encased in mottled glass. They're Ushebti. Their prisons aren't as opaque as the statues in Cissy's room, though.

I can still see their faces.

All three are trapped in a scream.

It's a reflex for the Beast and I to run forward and examine these new ushebti. Perhaps there's some way to set our loved ones free.

I'm not two steps out the door when I realize the mistake. We just left the safety of the library wards.

Another trap.

The Beast and I fell right in.

Gastonne rounds on us both. "Your turn," he cries.

## MYLA

*M*ore blue smoke rolls out from Gastonne's signet rings. Within seconds, the Beast and I are enveloped in another cloud of magic.

*Here it comes. My ushebti eternity.*

How like Bedlam to put me through all that pain and hassle, only to encase me in glass at the end.

Total chaos move.

I brace my body, waiting for the confinement to begin.

That doesn't happen.

Around me, the indigo smoke slowly fades. The next thing I know, I'm back at the Sahara. Although it's nighttime, there's no mistaking where I now stand. A familiar round stone sits nearby —it's the same one Lincoln and I inspected when we first searched for Bedlam, four days and a million years ago.

So I'm not confined to glass for all eternity.

Not yet, anyway.

Even better, the Beast stands beside me.

Hope sparks in my chest. Sure, almost everyone I know and love is vanished, dead or encased in glass. But I'm still moving. So is the Beast. There's a chance to fix this. I'm taking it.

The ground rumbles. A great fissure opens in the earth. Lighting bolts strike nearby. The newly-formed pit expands as something rises to the surface.

It's Bedlam's underground lair.

Moments later, the structure sits perched atop the sand, looking just how I remembered it. There's a stone floor whose periphery is marked with mega statues. Glyphs no longer shine out from stone walls—now they hover in the night air. On the far side of the building, Gastonne stands upon a stage made of stone. He wears a fancy red uniform complete with those loopy rope epaulettes on his shoulders.

Like he's the prince here.

Dickhead.

In this moment, I can't remember hating anyone more than I do Bedlam. And I've spent a lot of quality time loathing Adair and Aldred in particular, not to mention the King of Hell.

Trouble is, most of my opponents are folks that I can study over time. Even as a teenager, I never walked out blind onto the Arena floor. But the little I know about Bedlam has only come to light over the last week. And most of what I've learned just seems like chaos. How do you fight that?

The answer's unclear, but I'm not one to give up easily.

Closing my eyes, I tap into my inner wrath demon power. Energy courses through my mind as my thoughts spin through every thread of knowledge I have about Bedlam. The signet rings... the celebration of chaos... and Eve's obsession. These strands form the beginning of a greater design, yet something is missing.

What does Bedlam want?

I've been so focused on how Bedlam wants to marry me and steal my igni, not to mention how he constantly tortures the Beast. But what if that's a distraction? Perhaps I need to consider the bigger patterns here. And it's not the Beast as an ushebti or me as a blushing bride.

It's the Almighty. And that realization forms the final strand that ties everything else in place.

I refocus on Gastonne. "You've had some great distractions going. I almost didn't figure out who you are."

"And what is your revelation?" asks Gastonne.

"My father's the archangel Xavier."

"He's dead," snaps Gastonne.

"Not for long, so shut up and listen. Xavier always says, *there is no courage without fear. No virtue without temptation. And no balance without chaos.*"

The Beast frowns. When he speaks, his voice is gentle. "I don't follow, Myla."

"The Edens are all about balance," I explain. "We've seen it with our own eyes. The stewards make sure the oceans, skies and land are healthy. But without a little chaos, there's nothing to balance."

I actively ignore how Gastonne keeps creepily grinning in my direction. Instead, I focus on the Beast's mismatched eyes.

"Three cities," I state. "Six stewards. Thousands of Edenites. And out of all those those places and people, only one loved chaos. That made balance possible, but it destroyed so much as well." I force myself to switch my attention back to the evil figure who grins down at me from the stage.

"You're not Gastonne," I state. "Or Bedlam. Or even the snake guy with the frilly gils." I point right at his face. "You are Adam."

Gastonne's grin falters a little. I take that as progress, so I keep right on going.

"Eve's cottage was lousy with images of you as Gastonne. But that ultra-bolshy guy is really Adam. Eve talked about how you entranced her by taking unexpected forms. You cast retrograde magic on yourself, just like Norah did. Only you changed your appearance into a snake man. Such unexpected stuff charmed Eve. She became obsessed with you and pandemonium."

By now Gastonne's grin has melted into a frown. With that, it's official. I'm having the time of my life here.

"Let me guess. You and Eve were just having fun, being your chaotic selves. Burning down the Garden of Eden was supposed to be a laugh. But you got caught in the flames and ruined your pretty Gastonne-ness. Now the *real you* is more foul-looking than most demons."

All the blood seems to drain from Gastonne's handsome face, so I know I'm on a roll.

"After the fire, you decided not to blame yourself, because where's the fun in that? Instead, you vowed to take revenge on the Almighty, the one who placed you in the Garden to begin with. That's why you want to wipe out creation and repopulate the world with your nasty Tumult bat-rat-guys. What do you say to that?"

"You are right." Gastonne bows low. When he rises again, he's turned back into his burned-out Mister Potato Head look. "Madam, I'm Adam."

"Your plan won't work," I retort. "I don't know how, but the Beast and I will kick your ever-loving ass. If you're smart, you'll drop this whole thing now and go hang out with Eve. Or not. I can see how Eve could be a little clingy."

"And is that all you have to say?" asks the potato-like Bedlam.

I look to the Beast. "You got anything to add?"

"Not at all." He shoots me a thumbs-up. "Keep going."

I round on Bedlam once more. "Give up now and you can go back to being Captain Chaos somewhere else. Unless you piss me off, in which case I'll hunt you down again and kill you—" I snap my fingers "—like that. Now, what's your deal? Will you leave... or do we fight it out now?"

In reply, Bedlam raises his arms. The signet rings on his fingers flare with indigo light. Dark smoke streams up from his palms and into the night sky. From there, the magic churns and spreads, forming a sheet of dark clouds that blot out every star.

More mist encircles Bedlam himself. Soon the dark smoke encases him entirely.

Yet when the vapor vanishes, Bedlam is gone.

## THE BEAST

*W*hat a night for revelations.

Myla was right—I'd been so focused on stopping the Tumult and my own curse, I hadn't been asking the right questions about Bedlam.

Gastonne.

Adam.

All of them, really.

I've been trapped in my own kind of chaos for years. For the first time, I feel as if I'm on solid footing. My gaze locks onto the woman at my side. Hope brightens my soul. It may be a long shot, but knowing Bedlam's true identity could be the compass that leads us all out of this disaster.

Images pop into my mind. I picture Nat, Mother, and Cissy as they're trapped in soundless screams. Even now, those three suffer due to Bedlam. And I could be hurting alongside them soon.

Yet I set the thoughts aside. Right now, there's hope and Myla. That's where I must hold tight.

The skies above churn. Lightning flashes within the dark vapor. The unmistakable weight of magic hangs in the air. The clouds shift until a massive face takes shape above us. It's Bedlam. When he speaks, his voice booms like thunder.

"I used my powers against Noah first," calls Cloud Bedlam. "I cursed him. Changed him into someone who's angry as a hurricane. His rose marks ran out and he paid the price. I placed him into his glass ushebti coffin and took his signet ring."

Lighting flashes behind Cloud Bedlam's eyes. I think back to Captain Norah and her Ark. That's how she lost her father. Bedlam must have heaped so much sorrow on Noah's shoulders that he became like me. A Beast. And then he was taken away.

"Next I went after Grace," continues Cloud Bedlam. "For her, I took the curse further. I didn't just change her personality. I transformed her into a true Beast. I twisted her body into the very first featherling. As a result, she failed at the curse, lost all her rose petals and ended up as my second ushebti."

Once more, the ground rumbles beneath my feet. Are more surprises about to rise from the earth? I wouldn't put it past Bedlam.

"Now for my third triumph," cries Cloud Bedlam. "I used my trio of signet rings to scry into the future. There I saw the perfect Great Scala. Between my signet rings and her igni, we could take down the Almighty. So I locked myself in hibernation, building up energy and waiting for my future bride. Once Myla and I are magically bound, then I will wield igni as easily as breathing."

Beside me, Myla rolls her eyes. "Everyone thinks it's super easy to be the Great Scala. Just order them around and they'll do anything! Right."

Cloud Bedlam's voice echoes out again. "A moment ago, you offered me the chance to retreat. Now I'll ask you one last time. Myla Lewis, do you accept our marriage? Call it a magical binding, if you will. Our connection can be sweet or painful. It is your choice. What do you say, Great Scala?"

Myla smacks her lips. "What a loser." She looks to me. "Any thoughts?"

"He wants your igni? Give him everything. Fry the bastard. I know you can do it."

And unlike in the past, I mean those words with everything in my heart.

"Stand back." Myla nods, cracks her knuckles and gets to work.

# THE TITAN OF CHAOS

## 76

## MYLA

*Bedlam, you are so going down. Finally.*
Closing my eyes, I call upon my igni.

*Come to me little ones. I need you.*

Instantly, dozens on tiny lightning bolts appear around my left hand. *Perfect.* I send another mental message.

*Flow through my rings. Bring them to life.*

The igni whirl around my hand so quickly, the motion becomes a blur. Then they channel themselves through the trio of signet rings. Power and pain shoot up my arm.

The rings heat and come to life. Blue mist erupts out from the palm. Pure agony moves down my arm and into my torso. Gritting my teeth past the pain, I angle my arm right toward Bedlam's cloudy face.

*Go get him, guys.*

A torrent of igni materialize, one after the other. They flow through my signet rings, up into the column of dark mist and right into Bedlam's cloudy face.

*Take that.*

The pillar of mist and magic slams into Bedlam. He howls in pain, a noise that's so loud, it's almost more hurtful than what's moving through my body.

Almost, but not quite.

More agony streams down my torso and down my legs. It's as if my bones are being ripped out from my flesh. I crumple onto my knees, yet somehow my arm stays angled toward the sky.

Then I see how I'm doing it. The Beast is at my side, propping my arm against his chest. His handsome face is contorted with pain. Whatever is happening with the signet rings and igni, it's hurting him too.

More mist and power flow into Bedlam. Lightning bursts through the sky in an intricate web, burning out the clouds with each strike. Bedlam howls in pain, this time louder than ever before.

Then he falls silent.

The last of my igni flow through the rings and into the sky. All of the clouds have vanished. The desert is quiet and peaceful once more.

I collapse into the Beast's arms. Every inch of my body feels like a wet noodle. And leaning against the Beast is pleasant in the extreme. "We did it," I whisper.

The Beast kisses the top of my head. "You're amazing."

"That's what I've been trying to tell you."

A low chuckle reverberates down from the skies. Every nerve ending in my body goes on alert.

That couldn't be Bedlam.

A familiar voice booms down. "I thought I'd have to bind myself to you in order to take your igni, yet you deliver them to me without any such machinations. Such is the joy of chaos."

At times like these, there's only one thing to say.

"Fuck fuck fuckity fuck fuck."

## 77

## THE BEAST

*F*rustration roars through every synapse in my brain. Myla and I seemed so close to defeating Bedlam. Not only did her igni appear, but they flowed through the replicated signet rings to become the same indigo energy as the Titan of Chaos himself.

That magic should have destroyed him.

It didn't.

Worry presses in around me, tight as a vise. We didn't kill Bedlam. Instead, he's now more powerful than ever.

Overhead, the storm clouds expand and churn. A great pillar of dark mist lowers from the skies. At first, it looks like a tornado. It's not. The indigo-colored vapor takes the shape of a giant Bedlam. Lightning flashes within his cloud-made body. Semi-transparent versions of the three signet rings gleam on his misty fingers.

My mind becomes a blank slate of shock. This is it. Bedlam's final plan. He'll take on the Almighty.

On reflex, I move closer to Myla, wrapping my arm about her shoulders. She reaches up to grasp my hand. Both of us tremble.

We worked so hard to fight Bedlam. Yet in the end, we only delivered more magic into his control.

Soon everyone will pay the price.

The cloud giant that is Bedlam raises his arms. His voice reverberates across the desert. "Now my fellow Edenites shall witness the end of the Almighty."

Columns of indigo mist and light shine out from Bedlam's signet rings. This is more than the vapor he wielded before. Now there's light within the mix.

Igni.

Giant Bedlam angles his new beam toward the desert floor. A noise unlike anything I've ever heard fills the air—it's the combination of grinding stone and thunder. Sand undulates beneath us, making it hard to stay upright.

Suddenly, the desert floor splits upward in a motion that reminds me of a fist punching through a wall. A moment ago, nothing but golden sand stretched off to our left. Now there's a new addition to the landscape.

It's the last piece of the Garden of Eden.

Next Giant Bedlam points his new beam toward the skies. Instantly, a column of water pours down and with it, the Ark of Eden. The massive vessel lands to our right. Voices carry on the night air. It's the ship's crew, scrambling to get off board.

Giant Bedlam arcs his power beam toward the clouds yet again. This time, the Ether of Eden lowers from the mist to crash onto the desert floor behind us. Sand and debris erupt into the air. Birds take flight from their roosts. Edenites try to climb or soar down from their broken city to reach the relative safety of the Sahara.

As for the desert itself, the place becomes the definition of chaos. Sand whirls about in small tornadoes. The ground still heaves from the force of the Garden rising. Edenites wail with fear and sorrow. Above it all, Giant Bedlam stares down with his lightning-bright eyes.

Myla gives my hand a squeeze. "There must be something we can do," she declares.

I can only stare at her, amazed. My only thought has been to soak in my final moments with Myla. She's still trying to regroup for a counter-attack.

"There they are!" cries Myla. "Victoria and Norah. They still have their rings. I bet they'll help us now." She releases my hand and takes off after the two stewards. I follow.

We find the pair huddled in quiet discussion. Myla steps between them. "Why aren't you attacking? You have the power of your signet rings."

"It's not that easy," says Victoria.

Norah looks up toward Giant Bedlam. "Isn't that right?"

The massive cloud man now transforms into a whirlpool of light and mist that concentrates down toward the desert. One moment, a cloud-giant towers over us all. The next second, the burned-up version of Bedlam stands nearby.

"Quite right, Norah." Bedlam turns to me and Myla. "I have their loved ones trapped as ushebti. They'll do what I say. Right now, they may not use their signet rings."

The ground splits once more. A pair of statues rise up to flank either side of Bedlam. Ushebti. These two are more rough than the others, more like mottled pillars of glass. It's only when you look carefully inside that you can see a human form within.

Bedlam gestures to the ushebti. "One of these is your father," he says to Norah. "And the other is your wife," he adds to Victoria. "If you think this is the worst thing I can do to them, you are mistaken."

Victoria and Norah say nothing. Their faces are the very definition of misery.

"You must fight," I state. The two stewards don't even look in my direction, let alone reply.

Bedlam raises his hands. Fresh beams of indigo light slice up into the night sky, forming a column. Where the power hits the heavens, a great seam tears through the darkness. It's cut through the very firmament of life. A swath of white light shines out from behind the new rupture.

"Hello, Almighty," whispers Bedlam.

Having a cloud enemy is one thing. But the version of Bedlam who stands before me is flesh and blood. I pull out my baculum, igniting them as a long sword. Myla arcs her tail. We move to strike Bedlam in tandem.

But before either of us can connect a blow, it happens.

Pain shoots up my arm. I crumple to my knees. Myla crouches beside me.

"What is it, Beast?" she asks. Yet the way Myla poses the question, her voice is filled with sorrow. She already knows the answer.

I slice through my body armor, just as I have done so many times before. One final petal shows on my skin.

It is fading.

Indigo mist surrounds me. Pressure forms around my body, sealing me in from every direction. I try to suck in air, yet can't breathe. I wait to die, but that's impossible now.

Bedlam's voice echoes in my ears. "Welcome to my ushebti collection. I've always wanted a Beast."

## MYLA

*J* kneel beside the mottled lump of glass that now encases the Beast. I brush my fingers across the rough surface. He's inside, both alive and dead.

Every time I think I've found a way to end chaos, it's resulted in failure.

My igni only made him stronger.

The other stewards won't even consider fighting back.

And now, I've failed the Beast as well.

What else is left?

A new figure steps through the pandemonium of screams and sand.

It's Eve.

She pauses beside me. "Adam and I have been in league this whole time, you know."

I roll my eyes. "Of all the surprises from today, that is not even on the top ten."

"Bedlam has your power now," adds Eve. "You're of no more use to him. Once he destroys the Almighty, I'll make sure he kills you next."

"Thanks for sharing."

"You never should have tried to take what's mine."

I shake my head. "You're so focused on Adam, you're not seeing the true threat here." Eve stares at me as if I'm speaking nonsense. Guess I have to spell it out for her.

"Once the Almighty is gone, we're all doomed."

Eve stomps off in a huff while Bedlam sends more power into the skies, tearing an ever-greater rupture in the firmament. A heavy sense of sorrow fills the air, as if all creation knows death approaches.

It's happening.

Bedlam is killing the Almighty.

My soul wilts. All along, I've thought this reality was only temporary. But in this moment? Maybe it's real.

My Lincoln.

Parents.

Maxon.

Walker.

Verus.

Igni.

And now, the Beast.

All gone. Forever.

# THE BEAST

*N*o breath.
No life.
No death.

Every attempt to move is locked and sealed away. Impossible. All is stillness and yet, there's also the internal chaos of pain and loss.

Through the rough glass, I can just make out the figure of Myla kneeling beside me.

"Oh, Beast," she whispers. "I'm so sorry."

I want to tell her she should have no regrets. I have plenty for both of us. Only my greatest remorse isn't that I'm encased alive.

No, I'm sorry I didn't fully savor the precious time Myla and I had to share.

That changes now.

Before, I saw visions of Myla through magic. Perhaps now I can leverage the same power in a new way. Through the pain, I focus all my thoughts and energy toward sending a simple message.

*Know this, Myla Lewis...*

*I love you.*

## MYLA

*T*ime takes on an odd cadence. As I kneel beside the Beast's glass prison, it's as if each moment becomes forever and nothing, all at once. I try to see through the opaque glass. There's a dark form inside, nothing more. Then a familiar voice rings through my heart.

*Know this, Myla Lewis...*
*I love you.*

It's the Beast. Something connects us again, as it has so many times before.

I glance up from the ushebti glass to scan the Hellscape around me. Bedlam pumps more of my igni into the skies, creating a far deeper break in the firmament than ever before. When it began, the gash in the heavens had shone as a thin slice of white in the night sky.

Now that tear changes.

Little by little, the rupture becomes blood red.

Creation is dying.

I contemplate the chaos around me. It reaches much farther

back than Bedlam. There were those roadsigns on Purgatory's highways. Whispers of an Angelic Conspiracy. Cutting words about manipulation. And questions that undercut true love. I got caught up in the vortex of chaos, allowing turmoil to blind me from more than just Bedlam's true identity.

I burrow within, seeking perspective and guidance. Deep inside my soul, new energies align. Spirits link. Memories appear. Minutes ago, I'd pulled together threads of Bedlam's history into a greater picture. Now I see a fresh vista of my own. I don't know if any of us will survive this, but I won't die without sharing my new vision.

I lean in close to the glass. "There's something you need to know. With all the chaos, I lost sight of what's important. Now I can see clearly again. Back when I fell into this reality, Bedlam tried to erase my memory. For days, I thought igni preserved my history. I was wrong. What saved me was how I tapped into my soul's connection with my Angelbound love. A round rainbow appeared. And that loop pulled in my igni power."

My voice trembles. "It sounds crazy, right? Rainbows and love. Both are so beautiful that it's hard to trust in what they really mean. But what if the bravest thing we can do is believe in true love?"

I take in a long breath. "So that's what I'll try to do right now —be brave and share what I know. When it comes to how you and I feel about each other, the truth is this: the reality that we inhabit doesn't ultimately matter. There's a part of us, a center, that does not change. And it draws like souls together. In other words, you've always had my heart."

Leaning in, I press a gentle kiss against the glass. "My Beast Lincoln."

As I shift to sit upright again, I catch my reflection in the glass. Back in my reality, my eyes are angel blue. In this place, my irises are brown.

Not now.

My eyes now gleam with every color on the spectrum.

A round rainbow.

New power moves through me. Where once the ushebti casing was mottled and hazy, now everything is clear. I can see the Beast's eyes.

All hues of the rainbow shine in his irises, too.

# I LOVE YOU

# LINCOLN

*y Beast Lincoln.*

  Myla's words ricochet through my soul. Deep within me, powers connect. Energies align. What I must do next becomes perfectly clear.

I reach for Myla.

In this moment, I want nothing more than to feel her warm skin under my fingertips. Before the ushebti glass prevented any movement. Now when I shift my arm, the surface cracks.

Focusing my strength, I push myself harder. This time, the glass breaks around my arm if it were nothing more than a thin layer of ice.

I flex my legs and press myself up to stand. More glass shatters around me. Wind caresses my skin and tussles my hair. I'm vaguely aware of standing still within the pandemonium of the desert.

Yet all I can focus on are the memories flood through me. The first moment I saw Myla, she fought Doxy demons in a lake. My heart was hers at the very sight of how she laughed while in the midst of battle. So many adventures appear in my mind, from the

House of Acca to the King of Hell. I see the moment she rescued me from Earth while pregnant with Maxon.

And our boy.

I recall Maxon's fierce grin as he practices battle poses. The way he reaches for me while saying, *Daddy read!* A thousand giggles and tantrums all weave together into my history with my son.

And other recollections get added into the mix as well. Being the Beast. Forgetting my true name and nature. The curse. Bedlam. A vengeance against the Almighty.

The torrent of the past dies down. Now all I can focus on is her.

I cup her face in my hands and smile. "Myla la."

She shares my grin. "Mine."

## MYLA

*H*e's back. My Lincoln.

Powers deep within me stir. Magic awakens once again and comes alive. A great loop of a rainbow forms before me and Lincoln. It hovers in the air before us.

An image appears inside the center of this loop. It shows me and Lincoln setting our joined hands within the full and round rainbow.

So that's what we do.

Lincoln and I stand face to face. I look down at my left hand. The trio of signet bands still glimmer on my fingers. Reaching over, I lace my left hand with Lincoln's right. His skin is warm and calloused in just the right ways for a warrior. The zing of his touch makes me smile.

All around us, the world falls apart. The desert is a cacophony of screams, small tornados and torn-up ground. Bedlam stands, arms raised as he shoots a beam of indigo light and magic into the clouds, creating an ever greater tear in the night sky. Beyond the break, there's nothing but red. Heavy tendrils of crimson drip down from the breach.

No one notices me and Lincoln at all.

Moving in unison, my husband and I raise our arms until our joined hands sit right within the center of the hovering loop.

My signet bands flare with light and life. The great round rainbow contracts until it encircles our wrists. Power races up my arm. On reflex, I press myself closer to Lincoln. The energy runs around my torso, charging up every cell in my body. My very bones vibrate with power. The energy zings through me until it feels as if I'll explode from the inside out.

I look to Lincoln. "You too?"

He nods. "It feels like a lion, pulling back before making the leap."

Sure enough, the power changes direction, shooting down our arms and out through the rings. A single beam of white light emanates from our joined hands.

My eyes widen. An understanding appears. *A rainbow is refracted white light.*

"Bedlam or sky?" asks Lincoln. It feels beyond wonderful to have this kind of synchronicity with someone again. Lincoln only said three words—Bedlam or sky—but I know what he's really asking. *Should we focus our joint energy at healing the rift in the heavens or taking down the Titan of Chaos?*

"Let's kill Bedlam."

In a single swoop of our arms, Lincoln and I point our joined power beam right into Bedlam.

Now the Titan of Chaos notices us and how.

Bedlam screeches with pain and tumbles onto his knees. The pale beam sears into his skin, causing it crumble.

Eve leaps forward, surrounded by hundreds of Tumult. She stands between our beam and Bedlam himself. "I have an army, you fools. I won't let you—"

*Poof!* Eve transforms from flesh and blood into a figure made of indigo-colored dust. Her body collapses onto the desert floor.

*Can't say I'm sorry to see her go.*

One by one the Tumult around her burst into dust as well.

*Not really weeping that they're gone either.*

As a side bonus, the moment Eve explodes, so does the glass encasing Noah and Grace. the two stewards step out from the pile of broken glass. They both look stunned but other than that, perfectly fine.

Some part of me wants to rush over and confirm this is true, but Lincoln and I still have work to do here.

Namely, kill Bedlam.

Keeping our arms level, we keep the beam searing into Bedlam. As every second passes, more of Bedlam's body literally folds in on himself. In less than a minute, Titan of Chaos is nothing more than a speck of indigo light that hovers above the desert floor.

*BOOM!* The spot of blue light explodes into a shower of indigo dust. The night breeze carries the remnants of the Titan of Chaos, making strange and curling patterns in the air.

Above us, the great tear in the sky becomes impossibly bright. I wince against the intensity, feeling the heat burn into my skin. Little by little, the brightness fades. It might be my imagination, but I can almost hear music as the last of the tear heals up. When I look back up to the sky, its returned to being a perfect sheet of nighttime and stars.

Turns out, the Almighty is a quick healer. Good to know.

Another beam of light captures my attention. This time, it's the brightness from the three duplicated signet rings. For a moment, the white light burns more brightly then ever before. Then it vanishes. Afterward, the signet rings turn brittle as charcoal. Ruined. All three break off and tumble in pieces to the ground.

A final flare of brightness appears. It's the loop of multicolored light that surrounds our joined wrists. Like the pale beam, it also brightens for a moment before disappearing entirely.

The desert turns impossibly quiet. No Edenians seem to move.

Lincoln shoots me a sly smile. "Mother was right."

I can't help but return the grin. "How so?"

"In the end, my curse really was Beauty and the Beast. All we needed was to fall in love."

And he's absolutely right. So I go up on tiptoe and kiss him for all I'm worth.

# LINCOLN

*M*yla's mouth collides with mine. I pull her to me, loving the feel of her soft curves against the hard planes of my body. Our tongues tease and explore. Myla wraps her legs around my waist. All is right in the universe.

Myla nuzzles into my neck. "What happened to you?"

"I went to another world."

Myla leans back to meet my gaze straight on. "Sounds like an adventure."

"It was. I'll tell you about it sometime." I press my forehead to hers. "I spent every minute trying to find you. Every so often, I could sense this other part of me. The Beast. When that would happen, my counterpart here would get a vision of you or Maxon. We were both different and the same person, all at once. I don't know how to explain it, but I hold his memories now."

"Wow. Whenever you're ready to tell the full story, I can't wait to hear it. My doppelgänger ruined my muscle tone a little, but other than that? I don't sense her within me at all."

"How fortunate." I brush another kiss across her lips. "What's wrong?

Myla frowns. "Things aren't back to normal."

"What do you mean?" I gesture across the desert. "Norah and Noah are reunited. So are Grace and Victoria. They've already begun wielding their magic to rebuild the Ether and Ark of Eden."

"It's not that," says Myla. "It's my ass."

"Believe me, nothing is wrong with that."

"It's like this. My dragonscale fighting suit got ruined in this reality. There were big tears everywhere, but especially on my butt. I used duct tape to fix the worst of it."

"I noticed. You make duct tape look good."

"Well, we've destroyed Bedlam. Everything should be back to normal. Like my parents and your parents, not to mention Maxon, Walker, Cissy and Verus. But it's not. My fighting suit is still trashed."

I nod slowly as this news sinks in. "We need to get back, which means we need more magic." I cup Myla's face in my hands. "You must summon your igni. Bedlam always said igni were more powerful than anything he could wield. We need to see if they can fix this."

"Right."

Myla closes her eyes. Her mouth forms silent words. This is what always happens when Myla calls on her Scala power.

For a moment, nothing happens. With every passing second, my pulse turns more fierce. Soon, I can hear my heart thud against my rib cage.

This simply must happen.

Suddenly, millions of tiny lightning bolts appear. Tiny and bright forms swirl and dance like so many birds. Childlike singing fills the air.

The igni have returned.

They all rush toward Myla. Her small form becomes swamped as countless lightning bolts wheedle their way inside her body. I saw this once before, back when the old Scala died and transferred his power to Myla.

Myla screams in pain. I scoop her into my arms, close my eyes, and whisper one word, over and over.

"Please."

## MYLA

*Ow, ow, ow.*

I lean into Lincoln while million little lightning bolts of pain zoom into me at once.

Why does this part always have to hurt like a mutha? Can't I get a superpower upgrade so this feels like a massage or something?

Fresh agony singes every inch of my skin. I'd like to say I grit my teeth like a boss. That's not what happens. I scream my guts out.

All of a sudden, the pain vanishes. I open my eyes to find myself standing in front of my house in Purgatory. The lawn is loaded with tons of useless crap. I wear my dragonscale fighting suit and—YAY—the thing doesn't have any tears. Lincoln sports body armor and his lion's pelt.

We share a long look and then whoop with joy.

Octavia steps out the front door. "What are you two doing out here?"

"Mother!" Lincoln wraps her in a huge hug. "I love you so much."

"I'm aware, my boy." She gives him the side eye. "What has gotten into you?"

"Can't a man love his mother?"

"Not when guests are due." She looks between us for a long moment. "Is this how you plan to look? Folks arrive any minute for a simple yard sale and the two of you look ready to slaughter demons. And this—" here Octavia pinches at the lion's pelt on Lincoln's shoulders "—belongs in a zoo."

Lincoln shoots me a side eye. "That's mother's way of saying she loves me too."

"Obviously," says Octavia. This time, she actually cracks a grin.

"This is how we're dressing today," I state. "You know us. We're always more comfortable in battle gear."

*Which is true.*

But also? The truth is something Octavia is not ready to hear.

Plus, the guests are now arriving. At this point, I'm greeting everyone no matter how I look.

It turns into a blast of a day. Not only does Octavia run everything—*who knew she loved both formal balls and yard sales?*—but Connor joins us and actually socializes instead of sulking. I consider that major parental growth.

Walker joins us and I get a little misty. The same thing happens when Verus does one of her fly-by visits. Even Nat makes a quick appearance. Octavia tries to drive hard bargains, but if someone has an interest, I let them take stuff for free.

I sell the fountain to the parents of Maxon's friend, Uther, because they assure me they're experts at demolition. I say that as long as that thing gets blown sky high, I'm a happy lady.

Cissy joins with Zeke. It's great to see her back in her Senatorial robes. Camilla and Xavier hang out in the kitchen where they spend much of the day recalling the best battles from yesterday's Drizzle Festival. Turns out, all of Xavier's warriors won their matches. *Go, Dad!*

Lincoln and I make our rounds and say hello to everyone we thought might be wiped out of creation. Then Maxon decides that he loves what he calls, *the Mommy Unicorn ride*. We spent hours where Lincoln and I pretend to be demons while Maxon runs at us with his mighty steed and new favorite wooden sword.

And when everyone's gone, we all watch Beauty and the Beast together. It could be weird, but it's not.

All day long, I've been saving up for my big moment. It happens after Maxon is asleep. I guide Lincoln into our bedroom.

"Remember back at the Pulpitum when we were leaving the Sahara?" I ask.

"You mean where you asked to go double-or-nothing on our bet?"

I chuckle. *Why did I even pose that as a question?* Lincoln's the kind of guy who never forgets stuff like that.

"Yes, that's the one. I'm ready to pose my trivia question to you now."

"Are you sure? It's been a rather active week. Perhaps you want to think about it."

"Nope. I know exactly what I'll ask."

Lincoln laces his fingers with mine. We swing our arms back and forth between us. It's wonderful. "Let's hear it."

I shoot him a sly grin. "What's the best use for duct tape?"

Lincoln pulls me against him. When he next speaks, his voice is all low and growly in my ear. "Let's head to the bedroom and discuss that question in more detail, eh?"

So we spend the night making each other a little sore and a lot happy.

And the best part?

When we wake up the next morning, Lincoln and I are still holding hands.

∾

*The adventure continues with CLOCKWORK IGNI, Book 9 in the Angelbound Origins series. Be sure to order today!*

# DESCRIPTION: CLOCKWORK IGNI

"*I* absolutely love Myla Lewis as a character! She's beautiful, witty, smart, and she has a license to kill." - *Angelic Reviews*

Along with my hottie husband, Lincoln, I rule the underground realm of Antrum. Being queen is hella fun… until the Forbidden Tombs.

Antrum is all caves and—considering how I'm no spelunker—let's just say I don't roam around much. So when I learn about some sealed-off caverns that no one can enter, it doesn't even register. All I hear is *blah blah blah* Forbidden Tombs *blah blah blah* massive bronze pyramids *blah blah blah* creepy ticking sounds. I'm warned to stay away at all costs. Not a problem.

Then the Forbidden Tombs burst through the ground in my home realm of Purgatory. Bronze pyramids smash through abandoned buildings and highways, making rush hour a nightmare. Even worse, the metal structures attract tiny lightning bolts called igni, which are my very special supernatural buddies. Within minutes, every last igni gets stolen away.

Now. I'm. Pissed.

Whoever hides inside those pyramids? Time to dust off your mummies and shine up your sarcophagi. Because Lincoln and I are breaking in and kicking ass.

*Order CLOCKWORK IGNI, Book 9 in the Angelbound Origins series!*

# ALSO BY CHRISTINA BAUER

# CLOCKWORK IGNI

## ANGELBOUND ORIGINS BOOK 9

The story continues in CLOCKWORK IGNI, Book 9!

LINCOLN

Enjoy Lincoln's perspective with the Angelbound LINCOLN series! Read on for a sample chapter…

OFFSPRING

The next generation takes on Heaven, Hell, and everything in between with MAXON!

ANGELBOUND

Reread ANGELBOUND, the kick-ass paranormal romance that started it all!

FAIRY TALES OF THE MAGICORUM

A modern fairy tale that *USA Today* calls a 'must-read!' Check out
WOLVES AND ROSES!

# PIXIELAND DIARIES

PIXIELAND DIARIES tells the story of sassy pixie Calla and 'her' elf prince, Dare.

BEHOLDER

Medieval mages ... Slow-burn love ... And heart-pounding action! Check out the BEHOLDER series!

*B*efore me looms a dissolus demon. Think about a waist-high glob of mayo—only both alive and deadly—and that's the general idea.

No face.

No limbs.

Just mega-bacteria with attitude.

For hours, I hunted this creature through the forests of Purgatory. Why? I'm both part angel and a demon hunter. *One of the thrax.* Killing monsters is what my people do. Now I've cornered this slime ball (as in a ball literally made of slime) against the back wall of the royal stables.

All that remains is the kill.

This won't be easy.

Little by little, I pin the dissolus against the wall with my body. The white goo of the demon's exterior smears across the legs of my Kevlar armor. The creature's round form pulses, heartbeat style. Reaching forward, I slip my hands through the monster's outer layer, careful to keep my palms tipped at precisely forty degrees. Unless I use that exact angle combined with slow speed, the demon's interior will transform from ugly slop into deadly acid.

Then I'll be dissolved in seconds. Painfully.

Sweat beads down my spine as I search inside the monster. My goal is to find the creature's nucleus—the equivalent of its heart—which is solid, transparent and egg-shaped. I shift my arms inside the demon's gooey interior. Slurping sounds ricochet through the air. Across the stables, a horse whinnies. Adrenaline spikes through my system. There's a time limit here. If I don't grab the nucleus fast enough, then the demon's insides will turn acidic anyway.

Again, death. Not a fan.

It's an effort, but I somehow keep my motions slow and steady. All thoughts collapse into a single goal: Grasp the nucleus.

A familiar voice breaks up the quiet. "Interesting monster, eh?"

*Seriously?*

That's Aldred, the Earl of Acca and an extraordinary scumbag. At this point, he and I are the only people in the stables, if you don't count the demon. Aldred's a portly fellow, middle aged with thinning hair and long jowls. His clan, the House of Acca, is a perennial pain in my royal backside. While I spent hours hunting the dissolus, Aldred followed behind at a safe distance. All the while, he released a steady stream of chatter.

"I said," Aldred really drags out the word *said*. "Interesting monster, right?"

"*Interesting* isn't the word I'd use," I reply.

"What can I say?" Aldred steps beside me, scanning the scene. "I'm an earl, not a walking thesaurus."

For a moment, I see myself in Aldred's eyes. I'm Lincoln Vidar Osric Aquilus, High Prince of the Thrax. My family rules the land of Antrum, which is hidden far below Earth's surface. The rest of the After-Realms consist of the angels in Heaven, demons of Hell, quasi-demons in Purgatory, and the ghouls of the Dark Lands. At eighteen, I'm tall and broad-shouldered with brown hair and mismatched irises. I also happen to be leaning over a possessed blob of white goo the size of an engorged Hippity Hop. Being a demon hunter is rarely glamorous. Neither is being royal, for that matter.

"This is taking too long," declares Aldred. With mincing steps, the earl creeps up beside me.

"Stay back," I warn. "That's for your own safety."

"No, I shall kick it for you."

"Absolutely not," I counter. "You'll end up losing your leg, and that's if you're lucky."

Aldred holds his hands palms forward, in the universal motion for, *it's not my fault.* "No need to get testy."

Frustration sends my thoughts reeling. How did I end up here anyway? The answer flickers through my mind like images on a carousel. On orders from Verus, the Queen of the Angels, my family and I are temporarily residing in Purgatory, along with all our court. Since my people enjoy a medieval lifestyle, we've constructed cabins in Purgatory's Alighieri Woods. This morning, a dissolus broke free from our royal menagerie. Cue me chasing the monster through the forest while the earl follows behind.

Which brings me to the present moment and imminent death.

At last, my fingers brush against the creature's hard nucleus. *Yes!* Normally I give demons a chance to retreat before killing them. However, dissolus have the mental powers of paramecium. To them, attacking is nothing personal—it's just what they do.

Time to end this.

Tightening my grip on the nucleus, I yank with all my strength. The clear sphere breaks free from the gelatinous demon. For a moment, the dissolus quivers in place. Then— SPLASH—it collapses into a puddle of translucent sludge. The scent of rotten eggs fills the air. In my right hand, the nucleus transforms into a bright white orb before vanishing altogether.

The gooey entrails covering the floor also disappear. Easy cleanup; that's one benefit of this demon type.

I exhale a long breath. "And *that's* how to kill a dissolus."

"Glad I was here to help," declares Aldred. "We make a great team." He moves to stand directly in the main aisle of the stables. In other words, blocking my departure. I've seen this action from Aldred before.

"Is there a particular topic you wish to discuss?" I ask.

"As a matter of fact, yes. Now that we've spent the morning together, I thought we could talk, man to man."

I tilt my head. "Go on."

*Here it comes. Another discussion about my marriage contract.*

For weeks, Aldred has been pestering me to sign a betrothal contract with his daughter, Lady Adair. At one time, I might have been interested. Now, not so much. The local residents of Purgatory are quasi-demons, and one of those ladies happens to be an excellent warrior named Myla Lewis. As of this moment, it's been eight days, six hours, and thirty-two minutes since I last saw Myla. At the time, she was fighting off Doxy demons in a nearby lake. Her battle technique displayed the perfect combination of beauty, intellect and lethal power.

*Ah, Myla.*

Long story short, I'm no longer interested in signing a marriage contract. Instead, my time's been consumed with researching a certain Miss Lewis. To that end, I've learned she's fighting in Purgatory's Arena tomorrow morning. I plan to sneak into an access corridor and watch her battle from a distance. The very idea makes my heart soar.

Aldred clears his throat, breaking up my thoughts. "Did you hear what I said?" he asks.

"No," I reply. Evidently, the earl was blabbing away while I contemplated Myla. Even so, I doubt I missed anything. There's only one topic of interest to Aldred these days.

*My marriage.*

"Please repeat your statement," I say.

Aldred makes a great show of scanning the stables. "I've news for you about Minister Devak." He narrows his eyes to conspiratorial slits. "Great information."

This is what humans call a *red flag*. Why the concern? I've been working on what I call an anti-Acca treaty. By uniting the armies of Kamal, Horus and Striga, I'll have enough warriors to make Aldred kowtow on any number of topics, including my marriage to Adair. Of all those houses, my negotiations with Minister Devak—and therefore the House of Kamal—are the farthest along.

"And?" I prompt.

"Devak's been asking around." Aldred lowers his voice. "About quasi warriors."

A chill rolls up my limbs. Can Devak be interested in Myla for some reason? When I next speak, it's an effort to keep my voice calm. "What is Devak's precise concern?"

"Wouldn't *you* like to know." Aldred smirks.

At this point, that smug grin of Aldred's tells me two things. First, the earl knows exactly what Devak is up to, and second, Aldred wants something in exchange for the information.

I stifle the urge to roll my eyes. "Name your price, Aldred."

The earl exhales a long-suffering sigh. "I might confide everything, but it's sensitive information … the kind you share with *family*, you know?"

*Meaning: ink my betrothal contract and I'll tell all.*

I chuckle. Aldred always overreaches in negotiations. However, what he lacks in finesse he more than makes up for in persistence. "I am *not* finalizing a contract merely to discover Devak's plans."

"Please; I never expected you to sign this very second," lies Aldred. No doubt, the man keeps the document in the folds of his tunic along with a quill, just in case. "But perhaps you can commit to spending more time with my sweet Adair? If so, then I might feel like sharing."

Aldred thinks he's being sneaky, but I already made this decision last night. "Mother is organizing a garden party at the Ryder mansion. My plan is to request Adair's company for the event." After all, I've said all of five sentences to the girl. We may be compatible. It's a long shot considering my blooming obsession with Myla Lewis, but there it is.

Aldred rubs his palms together. "Excellent, I'll tell Lady Adair today."

"Your turn," I state. "What about Devak's interest in quasi warriors?"

Aldred bobs his thick eyebrows. "No doubt, you're aware how the court itches to hunt local demons."

My eyes widen with shock. "No, I wasn't." A memory flashes through my mind.

*I'm fifteen and late for monitoring a demon patrol in the Canadian Arctic. As I exit the transfer platform, a woman's screams echo through the cold air. I race out of the ice station and onto a sheet of white tundra under a grey sky. Freezing winds batter my body. Before me, a dozen Acca warriors tear apart a Vantys—a harmless she-demon who's equal parts human and reptile. Aldred stands behind them, pumping his fist in the air. Fresh sprays of blood darken the snow. I race over, my young voice bellowing.*

*"Stop!"*

*But the Vantys is already dead. And Aldred's men have placed her head on a pike.*

*"This is disgraceful," I announce. "We are thrax, not a mindless mob."*

. . .

Blinking hard, I try to wipe out that recollection. However, the image of a severed head stays seared in my mind. Thrax should act as ethical warriors, yet Aldred transformed them into something else. There's no avoiding the truth. With the wrong encouragement, my people can do terrible things.

And now, their baser instincts may be focused on Myla. I shudder. I'd been actively avoiding thoughts of any future with Myla. Contemplating her in the present was just too enjoyable. But now? I must consider the risk my people pose to her, myself included.

"You know us thrax," continues Aldred. "We're always seeking a new challenge."

Protective energy runs up my spine. I round on the earl. "The Queen of the Angels herself, the oracle Verus, sent us here to interact with the quasi population, not hunt them down."

"Bah." Aldred waves his hand dismissively. "It's only a matter of time before some quasi marches into our camp, looking for trouble. After all, they're semi-demonic. It's in their blood. And once those quasis come after us, then we'll have to protect ourselves. It's only right."

Images of Myla appear in my mind. She did indeed sneak into our compound, but only because she was on the trail of a mutual enemy, the Doxy demons. A weight of worry settles into my stomach. What if someone other than me saw her? Aldred is correct; my people would kill first and ask questions later.

"You still haven't shared specifics on Devak and quasis," I point out. "What did he say, exactly?"

"Devak's asking about Purgatory's Arena."

My heart sinks. *That means he's focusing on warriors like Myla.* "What's his interest?"

"My guess? Arena warriors are the best fighters. Here's the thing. Maybe you and I can team up." Aldred grins, showing off his mouth of yellow teeth. "Together, we could claim the first official quasi kill."

At those words, anger zings through my nervous system. "Let me make one thing absolutely clear." I prowl toward Aldred, my voice deep as thunder. "Hunting the local population is off the table, whether they are Arena warriors or not. If you or anyone else speaks of this again, I'll have you shipped back to Antrum and tossed into the dungeons." For every final word I speak, I tap Aldred on the center of his chest. "Do you understand?"

"All right." The earl forces another laugh. "No need to get sensitive."

I glare at Aldred with a look that says, *I'm done here*. "The dungeons, Aldred. I mean it."

Without waiting for a reply, I storm past the earl and out of the stables. Hunting quasis? *Outrageous!*

Suddenly, I wish my parents weren't away on a demon hunting excursion. I'd like nothing better than to open a formal inquest, find out who's threatening quasis, and then fill our dungeons to overflowing. But starting an inquest is serious business. For the process to have teeth, my parents must sign off. And they won't return for at least four days.

*Ah, well.* Better to wait and do this correctly, much as I hate that fact.

All the way back to my cabin, my thoughts race through everything I've just learned: that Aldred is still pressing my marriage to Adair … the fact that my own people might be targeting quasi warriors … and how the entire situation could place Myla in danger. It all adds up to one terrible conclusion.

If I'm not careful, Myla might end up dead. That's not an option, so I take a silent oath.

*With all my mind and body, I vow to protect the woman who already holds my heart.*

—*End Of Sample*—

*Order LINCOLN, Book 2 in the Lincoln series today!*

# APPENDIX

## IF YOU ENJOYED THIS BOOK...

...Please consider leaving a review, even if it's just a line or two. Every bit truly helps, especially for those of us who don't *write by the numbers,* if you know what I mean.

Plus I have it on good authority that every time you review an indie author, somewhere an angel gets a mocha latte. For reals.

And angels need their caffeine, too.

# ACKNOWLEDGMENTS

If you're reading my freaking acknowledgements, chances are, I should thank you for something. So, for the record: you are awesome, dear reader.

That said, huge and heartfelt thanks must go out to my husband and son for their rock-solid support. Being an author means a lot of early mornings, late nights, long weekends, and never-ending patience. You two are the best guys in the universe, period.

After that, I must thank the extensive network of reviewers, friends and colleagues who helped me build my writing chops in general. Gracias.

Finally, deep affection goes out to my late, much loved, and dearly missed Aunt Sandy and Uncle Henry. You saw the writer in me, always. Thank you, first and last.

# ABOUT CHRISTINA BAUER

Christina Bauer thinks that fantasy books are like bacon: they just make life better. All of which is why she writes romance novels that feature demons, dragons, wizards, witches, elves, elementals, and a bunch of random stuff that she brainstorms while riding the Boston T. Oh, and she includes lots of humor and kick-ass chicks, too. Christina lives in Newton, MA with her husband, son, and semi-insane golden retriever, Ruby.

**Stalk Christina on Social Media**

Blog:
http://monsterhousebooks.com/blog/category/christina

Facebook:
https://www.facebook.com/authorBauer/

Instagram:
https://www.instagram.com/christina_cb_bauer/

Twitter:
@CB_Bauer

VLOG:
https://tinyurl.com/Vlogbauer

Web site:
www.bauersbooks.com

# AUTHOR'S NOTE

Dear Readers,

Welcome to the end of the book! Here are some of the most common questions I've received about QUASI REDUX. I figure if others wonder about these things, then maybe you will, too!

Also: HUGE thanks to all the awesome bloggers who have interviewed me over the years. You can see links to the hosts for all my tours at www.monsterhousebooks.com!

-CB

**How did you begin writing?**

I began writing poems when I was six years old. My inspiration was my Aunt Sandy, who was both a hippie and a full time writer. I still want to be just like her.

**How did you come up with the title of QUASI REDUX?**

Quasi is a type of demon from my series, so that's why I picked it. Also, I'm obsessed with finding good words that have X in them. Redux has been on my hit list for a while.

**Who is your favorite character from your book and why?**

Every character is a part of me, both the good and so-called bad. In terms of being fun to write, I have to go with the main character from this book, Myla. She's a part of me that's irreverent and full of energy!

**What gave you the inspiration for the Angelbound Origins series?**

I grew up Roman Catholic and always asked the nuns fun questions such as, *what's it like in Purgatory?* Needless to say, I didn't get all the answers I wanted. When I got to be an adult, I figured I'd 'fill in the blanks' and Angelbound was born.

**Why did you choose this specific genre?**

I'm big on myths, and there's a reason the stories that really resonate are set with young adults. It's about reinventing yourself, not being a certain age. Changing lives for the better through storytelling--that's what motivates me to write. Long story short, I write for everyone but the age set is Young Adult (YA).

**What is your favorite part of the creative writing process?**

There's a time--usually late in the writing process on a book—where the words just flow and it's like I'm taking dictation. It's such a rush!

**Tell me about your book covers and the inspiration behind them.**

For the Angelbound series, I wanted a badass sexy chick on the cover with a tail. I feel like I've really cornered that market.

**How has Myla's character evolved since Angelbound?**

Myla's grown up in a lot of ways. For instance, she's learned to work with other people, deal with losing her son and much more. That said, in other aspects, she's still the same person. People sometimes critique my work by saying that no grown woman would act like Myla. I'm like, I'm exactly like her in a lot of ways... and I'm 50... and it's a blast!

**What was the hardest part of writing Quasi Redux?**

There was so much I had to cut. I could have done a whole book on Myla meeting her mother and what happened to Camilla without her daughter. In the end, I had to focus on Myla and Lincoln. It's really their love story reborn.

**Was there a moment that you said, "I give up"?**

Often! I also have a time with every book where I think, *this is it. I've jumped the shark.*

**What's next?**

The next story after QUASI REDUX is called CLOCKWORK IGNI. It's a mash-up of steampunk and Ancient Egypt where Myla's igni go berserk on her. After that, I have outlined LADY REAPER, where Myla meets the Grim Reaper, who happens to be both a female and super evil. After-after that, I've one called ANGRY GODS, where Myla goes up against the deities of ancient Greece and Rome. So no sign of stopping Myla's stories yet!

**What hobbies do you enjoy when you're not writing?**

Reading, listening to lectures, and watching AMERICAN GREED.